Paul Doherty was born in Middlesbrough. He studied History at Liverpool and Oxford Universities and obtained a doctorate at Oxford for his thesis on Edward II and Queen Isabella. He is now headmaster of a school in north-east London and lives with his wife and family near Epping Forest.

Paul Doherty is the author of the Hugh Corbett medieval mysteries, The Sorrowful Mysteries of Brother Athelstan, THE SOUL SLAYER, THE ROSE DEMON and THE HAUNTING, all of which have been highly praised.

'Vitality in the cityscape . . . angst in the mystery; it's Peters minus the herbs but plus a few crates of sack'   *Oxford Times*

'The book is a pleasure to read and written in an uncompromising prose, the plot developed with intriguing twists and turns. Doherty's deep understanding of the period and the nitty-gritty of historical detail are to the fore without intruding on the rhythm on the plot. Superb entertainment'
Historical Novels Review

'The maestro of medieval mystery . . . packed with salty dialogue, the smells and superstitions of the fourteenth century, not to mention the political intrigues'   *Books* magazine

'Paul Doherty has a lively sense of history . . . evocative and lyrical descriptions'   *New Statesman*

'As always the author invokes the medieval period in all its muck as well as glory, filling the pages with pungent smells and description. The author brings years of research to his writing; his mastery of the period as well as a disciplined writing schedule have led to a rapidly increasing body of work and a growing reputation'   *Mystery News*

Ghostly Murders

The Priest's Tale of mystery and murder
as he goes on pilgrimage from London
to Canterbury

Paul Doherty

headline

First published in 1997
by HEADLINE BOOK PUBLISHING

First published in paperback in 1997
by HEADLINE BOOK PUBLISHING

Reprinted in this edition in 2002
by HEADLINE BOOK PUBLISHING

10 9 8 7 6 5 4 3

ISBN 0 7472 5437 0

Printed and bound in Great Britain by
Clays Ltd, St Ives plc

HEADLINE BOOK PUBLISHING
A division of Hodder Headline
338 Euston Road
London NW1 3BH

www.headline.co.uk
www.hodderheadline.com

For Richard, Nijolé and Thomas (O'Brien)

The Prologue

The pilgrims were lost. They had passed St Thomas' well on the ancient route to Canterbury but, late in the afternoon, a sudden mist had come swirling in over the flat Kent countryside. At first this had caused laughter and a little merriment as the Summoner took advantage of the confusion to clutch the generous thigh of the Wife of Bath. The Man of Law and the Prioress hung back in the confusion and, when Mine Host turned round, he was sure the lawyer and the nun were kissing each other, albeit chastely.

'By Satan's cock!' he growled to the Knight. 'We must not become separated.'

The Knight shifted in the saddle, easing his sword out of his scabbard. He did not like such mists. They awoke nightmares in his soul from when he had campaigned in Anatolia: they'd be crossing the floor of some heavily wooded valley when the devil's fog boiled up. He would ride ahead of his troops listening for any strange sounds: the clink of steel, or the creaking of harness. The only signs that the ghostly silence was to be broken by blood-curdling screams just before the Turckopoles, on their nimble horses, burst like demons out of the swirling mists.

'We must keep together,' the Knight declared. 'Yeoman!' He turned to his bodyguard. 'Sound the horn!' The Knight stood up in his stirrups. 'Listen now!' His voice boomed through the mist. 'Follow the sounds of the horn!'

The Yeoman rode up to the head of the column.

'Oh, pray we don't get lost!' Mine Host moaned. He raised his voice. 'Let's pray,' he said, 'to St Thomas à Becket whose blessed bones we go to venerate at Canterbury!'

The Miller gave a loud fart in answer, making the Carpenter snigger and giggle. Nevertheless, the pilgrims grouped closer. The Summoner moved his fat, little horse behind that of the Franklin. He was not just interested in the Franklin's costly silk purse, white as the morning milk. Oh no, the Summoner smiled to himself: he, like some others, was increasingly fascinated by this motley group of pilgrims making their way to Canterbury in the year of Our Lord 1389. All seemed to be acquainted with each other and he definitely knew the Franklin. They had met many years ago on a blood-soaked island. He was sure of it, as he was that the Franklin had had a hand in his father's death. He would have liked to have talked to his colleague the Pardoner but he was now suspicious for the Summoner had recently discovered that the Franklin and the Pardoner were close friends. Indeed, this cunning man, with his bag full of relics and the bones of saints slung on a string round his neck, was certainly not what he claimed to be.

Behind the Summoner, the Friar, nervous of the cloying mist, plucked at the harp slung over his saddle horn. As he played, the Friar glanced furtively at the Monk, riding alongside him. The Friar closed his eyes and strummed at the harp strings, calling up a little ditty he had learnt, anything to drive away the fears. He did not like the Monk sitting so arrogantly on his brown-berry palfrey: that smooth, fat face, those dark, soulless eyes and that smile, wolfish, the eye-teeth hanging down like jagged daggers. Who was the

Monk? Why was the Knight so wary of him? And the latter's son? The young, golden-haired Squire, he always kept an eye on the Monk, hand on the pommel of his sword, as if he expected the Monk to launch a sudden assault upon his father the Knight. Was the Monk, the Friar wondered, one of those Strigoi mentioned by the Knight in his tale? Did the Monk belong to the Undead? Those damned souls who wandered the face of the earth, finding their sustenance in human blood?

The Yeoman issued another loud blast on his hunting horn. The sound was not comforting; it pierced the mist like the wail of a lost soul.

'The mist is getting thicker!' the Reeve exclaimed.

And so it was, billowing like clouds around them.

'Where does it come from?' the Merchant asked.

'It's the devil's fog!' the Pardoner screeched.

'It's a sea mist,' the Sea Captain interrupted. He held up his hand. 'Kent is flat, smooth as a piece of well-shorn wood bounded by the sea and, after rain or when the wind shifts to the east, the mist boils in like steam from a cauldron.'

'I wish I was with my cauldron now,' the Cook moaned. 'Stirring some sweet pottage.'

The Reeve looked away in disgust as the Cook pulled up his hose and scratched the ulcer on his shin.

'I could make a lovely blancmange,' the Cook continued.

The Reeve hawked, spat and spurred on.

Another wail from the hunting horn.

'Stop!' the Yeoman shouted. 'No further, look!'

Mine Host, joined by the Knight and the cheery-faced, merry-eyed customs collector Sir Geoffrey Chaucer, rode to the front of the column.

'What's the matter?' the Knight asked.

'Listen!' the Yeoman replied.

3

The Knight did. 'I can hear nothing. Nothing at all.'

'Exactly!' the Yeoman declared. 'There should be bird song, even the crows and rooks will not be silenced by a mist. What is more, the path has petered out.'

The Knight looked down: the beaten trackway had vanished. He dismounted and walked tentatively forward. Immediately he felt as if the earth was giving way beneath him: his high-heeled hunting boots became stuck in the cloying mud.

'It's a marsh!' he yelled.

Already the mud was creeping up his leg. Chaucer took off his broad leather belt, threw one end at the Knight and, turning his horse round, moved backwards, scattering the pilgrims as he dragged the Knight out of the mire.

'Thank you.'

Sir Godfrey ran his fingers through his iron-grey hair. Even then, despite his narrow escape from the marsh, he glanced quickly around making sure where the Monk was: his enemy just sat upon his horse, face hidden deep in the cowl of his cloak. Nevertheless, Sir Godfrey glimpsed the sinister smile: those eyes gleaming at him, lips bared like a dog. I'll kill him, Sir Godfrey thought. God be my witness, he is a Strigoi. When we reach Canterbury, perhaps before we go to the shrine, I'll challenge him.

'Where to now, Sir Godfrey?' Mine Host shouted.

The Knight, helped by his son, remounted. He raised himself high in the stirrups.

'We cannot go on,' he declared, 'whilst to move sideways could invite disaster.'

'Oh, my goodness, look!' The Miller pointed where the mists swirled over the marsh. 'Look, there's a light!'

All the pilgrims turned, their hearts beating a little faster, mouths dry. At first they thought the Miller had been drinking. The Carpenter was about to tell him to go and play his bagpipes when the mist swirled again and he glimpsed the pinpricks of light, like torches shimmering through the mist. The Carpenter was about to go forward but the Poor Priest, that gentle-eyed man, caught him by the shoulder.

'Don't be foolish!' he said. 'They are not human lights.'

His words only increased the pilgrims' fears.

'What are they?' The Wife of Bath turned, fingers fluttering to her generous lips.

'Corpse candles!'

The Ploughman, the Poor Priest's brother, clutching the bridle of his brother's skinny horse, stared anxiously up at the Priest.

'Corpse candles?' the Miller asked. 'Bugger that!' He drew his rusty sword.

'They are called corpse candles,' the Poor Priest explained. 'According to some, they are gases from the marsh which ignite like fire-flies above a pond. Others claim they are the Devil's lights, candles lit in hell and brought by the fiends to lure poor souls to their deaths.'

'Oh, Lord save us!' The Wife of Bath pushed down her broad-brimmed hat more firmly on her head. Her cheeks were no longer red but pale. She forced a gap-toothed smile at the Knight. 'Oh, Sir Godfrey, save us!'

The Knight gently dug his heels into his horse. The pilgrims parted though none of them wished to be forced off the trackway.

'Follow me,' the Knight ordered. 'Ride in single file. Mine Host, Sir Geoffrey, keep to the back. Yeoman, at my signal, blow your horn!'

None of the pilgrims protested, only too willing to follow the Knight out of danger. They must have journeyed for at least an hour when the Miller gave a whoop of joy followed by a blast on his bagpipes.

'Look!' he yelled. 'The mist is lifting!'

And so it was. As if, according to the Pardoner, the blessed Thomas himself had come and brought back the sun. The mist disappeared but, as they came to the foot of a small hill, the Knight let his reins drop. He scratched his head and stared back over the wild Kent countryside.

'We are away from the marsh,' he declared. 'But, Pilgrims all, I beg your pardon, we are lost.' He pointed to the sun, still hidden by a haze, now drooping like a molten light into the west. 'It will soon be sunset. When darkness falls the mists might return.' He stared round and shrugged. 'I'm sorry but we'll have to camp out in the open. We have provisions, we have wine, fresh meat as well as pastries bought at Singlewell . . .'

'We can go there.' The Squire who had ridden to the brow of the hill was pointing down the other side.

The others joined him. The ruins lay at the bottom of the hill: a derelict church, a parson's house, further along the overgrown high street were the shabby remains of a tavern with decaying houses on either side.

'A ruined village,' the Poor Priest breathed. He pointed to the birds clustered on the old roofs. 'No sign of any habitation,' he added.

'What happened there?' the Prioress spoke up. 'Qu'est-ce que?' she added in her Stratford-Le-Bow French.

'The plague, my lady,' the Poor Priest answered.

The Prioress glanced at him in surprise. 'I did not know you understood French.' She pouted.

'Madam, you didn't ask.'

His brother came up beside him. 'It brings back memories, Brother.'

'Yes, yes, it does,' the Poor Priest murmured.

'Well, we can't stand here talking,' Mine Host declared, now reassuming leadership of the group once the mist had lifted. 'Sir Godfrey is right: soon it will be dark and I don't fancy roaming the wilds of Kent and blundering into another marsh.'

They slowly descended the overgrown path into the derelict village. From the top of the hill, bathed in sunlight and surrounded by green fields, the village had appeared comely, even welcoming. Now, as they made their way along the desolate high street, the pilgrims were not so sure. The sun became hidden behind a cloud and a light breeze whipped up the dust and rattled the drooping shutters or creaked a battered door. They gathered in the centre of the village near the well, its surrounding wall crumbling. On the other side of it a gallows, driven into the earth, had slid sideways so it looked like some accusing finger pointing at the sky. A piece of rotting rope hung from its rusting hook; this danced in the evening wind as if some ghostly corpse still hung there.

'What did happen here?' the Prioress repeated. 'Why is it desolate?'

'Over thirty years ago,' the Poor Priest replied, 'the Black Death visited!'

His words stilled all clamour, even the horses seemed cowed by the mention of the ghastly pestilence which had swept across England, killing two out of three in every town.

'It's true.' The Knight spoke up. 'You can find such villages the length and breadth of the kingdom. Ghostly houses, empty taverns, rotting churches. The people just died; those who survived, fled.' He looked around. 'Somewhere here must lie the communal burial pit.'

7

'Is it safe to stay here?' the Reeve squeaked, his bulbous eyes full of fear. He stared across through the empty doorway of the old tavern as if the Plague lurked there, watching them all, ready to strike.

'Of course it is.' The Physician spoke up, hitching his furred robes around his shoulder. 'The Death has gone: the constellation and stars have dispersed the malignant humours. Moreover, I have, in my fardel, a powerful potion against its return. It only costs—'

'Yes, yes,' the Knight interrupted. 'The village is empty because the people died. Such places are avoided even by outlaws, so we'll be safe here tonight.' He pointed towards the ruined steeple of the church. 'We'll stay there, collect some wood, build a fire and make comfortable beds. It will be cleaner and better than staying in any tavern. Come on.'

They rode on down. The pilgrims were still subdued: the desolate village had an eerie, macabre atmosphere. A banging door or a bird bursting out of some open window would make them jump, then they'd laugh to cover their nervousness.

'Perhaps the ghosts still live here?' the Poor Priest muttered out of the corner of his mouth. 'They may resent our presence.'

'Then, Brother, we will say our prayers,' the Ploughman replied. 'We have nothing to fear. We have atoned for our sins.'

They reached the church, crossed the overgrown cemetery and went in through the shabby corpse door. The nave of the church was in fairly good repair: a few holes in the roof, some rubble on the floor but otherwise a comfortable enough place to spend the night. The horses were unsaddled and taken to a nearby house. The Miller and the Reeve offered to collect grass and ensure each animal had its portion of oats. The Knight ordered the Yeoman and the Squire to collect brushwood for fires. The Prioress, of course, had to have a corner all to herself, though she didn't object to her handsome, sallow-faced priest joining her there for discussions. The Poor Priest and his brother walked off through the crumbling rood screen and into the sanctuary. They wanted to convince themselves that no blasphemy could occur but the altar had gone: only a hook in the ceiling showed where the pyx, containing the Body of Christ, had once hung.

Whilst the rest busied themselves, the Poor Priest and his brother, usually so eager to help, wandered around the church looking at the faded wall paintings, scenes from the life of Christ or those of the prophets. The one above the main door showed St Michael driving Satan and his angels, monkey-faced imps, into the roaring fires of hell. The Poor Priest shivered.

'It brings back memories, Brother.' He breathed in deeply. 'A desolate village, a ruined church. It reminds me of Scawsby.'

'No, Brother,' the Ploughman reassured him. 'The Spectantes . . .'

'Speak in English,' his brother interrupted. 'Lest someone overhears us.' He grinned. 'Hedge priests and ploughmen are not supposed to understand Latin!'

'Whatever,' the Ploughman replied. 'The Watchers are not here!'

'Come on! Come on!' the Miller shouted.

They walked back to the centre of the nave. The Reeve had lit a fire and the flames caught the dry branches and leapt boisterously, providing warmth and light. The pilgrims gathered round. The Yeoman returned with a pheasant and two rabbits. The Cook took these and, in the twinkling of an eye, had gutted and prepared them for roasting. He packed the soft flesh with herbs and placed them on makeshift spits above the flames. Soon the nave was filled with the savoury smell of roasting flesh. The Pardoner and Summoner brought across the supplies, pannikins of wine and a small hogs-head of ale whilst each pilgrim brought a cup from their own small saddlebags. The meat was shared out on makeshift platters with bread, cheese and a little dry bacon. Wine warmed their bellies and everyone relaxed, chattering merrily, telling each other that the nave was as good as any tavern or hostelry. Nevertheless, as the evening wore on, the fire began to die: the pilgrims began to be aware of the shadows dancing against the walls, of the pressing loneliness outside, broken now and again by the mournful hooting of an owl, the yip yip of a fox and, on one occasion, the shrill scream of some animal in its death throes.

'The mist is returning,' the Manciple called out.

They stared through the glassless window at the wispy tendrils seeping into the church.

'Build the fire up,' the Knight ordered. 'Keep it vigorous and merry. We'll sleep around it. No harm will befall us, I am sure. The sun will rise bright and strong and we'll find our path again.'

The Miller lifted himself up and gave a huge fart.

'I'm not sleeping near you,' the Prioress protested bitterly. She fingered her silver brooch bearing the words AMOR VINCIT OMNIA which hung round her neck. She caressed her little lap dog which she always kept warm in the folds of her robes. 'You are disgusting!' she continued.

The Miller, who had drunk deeply, just burped.

'Like some nuns I know!' he muttered.

'What was that?' Dame Eglantine the Prioress snapped, angry that this oaf would not move away.

'Just like some nuns I know.' The Miller staggered to his feet, his bagpipes in his hand, the fire lighting up his craggy face and broad, spade-like beard. 'I'll tell you a story about nuns. There's a house in London just overlooking the Steelyard. My aunt, who was a very old nun and blunt in speech, was sent there. The little ladies,' he added maliciously, glancing at the Prioress, 'didn't like her rough tongue and coarse language, so they protested to Mother Superior. She told them that if they were in a room when my aunt used such language they were to leave immediately.'

'Oh, stop this!' the Prioress interrupted.

'No, go on!' the Reeve shouted. 'Let's hear the story.'

'Well, one day,' the Miller continued, bubbling with laughter. 'The King's fleet came up the Thames and anchored within bowshot of the convent. My old aunt came in: "Satan's bollocks!" she cried, peering out of the window. "The King's ships have berthed and his lusty men will soon be ashore!" At this the young nuns fled the room.' The Miller began to laugh. '"Come back, you noddlepates!" my aunt shouted. "There's no need to rush! The sailors are hot and lusty but they'll be here for at least a week!"'

The Miller and Reeve began to crow with laughter. Dame Eglantine got up and walked to the other side of the fire. The rest of the pilgrims began to tell similar funny stories. The Poor Priest, his belly now full, his mind still absorbed in the past, got up and walked to the corpse door and stared out into the night. The mist hung like smoke over the overgrown cemetery. The Poor Priest walked outside. The sky was hidden. Only the twisted trees and bushes could be seen, like bodies writhing in pain. The Priest closed his eyes. Just

like Scawsby, he thought, yet everything had begun so well
. . . He heard a sound deep in the mist, as if someone was
walking across the graveyard towards him.

'Who is there?' he called out.

No answer. The sound now came from his left. The Priest
whirled round. The mist shifted. His heart skipped a beat.
He was sure he had seen a cowled figure there and a pair
of eyes, like red coals, glowing in the darkness. A breeze,
cold and sharp, caught at the Priest's face. He was about to
step back when he heard the whisper.

'Spectamus te! Semper spectabimus te! We are watching
you! We shall always be watching you!'

The Priest went back into the church, almost colliding
with his brother.

'It's time,' the Priest muttered.

'Time for what?'

'Time I exorcised the ghosts.'

The Priest shook off his brother's hand and walked
towards the fire. The pilgrims looked up expectantly. The
Priest was usually as timid and quiet as a mouse, now he
walked, shoulders back, head held up. His face had lost
that soft, easy smile. He was gaunt and pale, fixed-gazed
and thin-lipped.

'Mine Host. This is a sombre place!'

'It is indeed, Father,' Mine Host replied curiously.

'And a tale should be told?'

'Why, of course,' the taverner replied. 'I doubt if anyone will really sleep tonight. Now, remember.' He held
a finger up. 'Whatever the weather, wherever we are,
we all promised to tell two tales. One during the day
and one at night. The latter must always be one of mis-
chief: of dark things in hidden places. Tonight is to be no
exception!'

'Oh, I like to be frightened.' The Wife of Bath spoke up. 'And what a place for it?'

She stared round and her smile faded. Perhaps it wasn't. The church looked more forbidding: the flames lit up the lurid paintings on the walls. The Wife of Bath swallowed hard and moved closer to the clerk sitting next to her.

'I'll tell you a tale,' the Poor Priest began. 'But I must warn you. It will chill the heart and curdle the blood. It's about a village called Scawsby here in Kent.' His eyes took on a faraway look. He glanced over the heads of the pilgrims. 'A tale of ghosts, of sorcery, of the Spectantes.'

'The who?' the Summoner shouted.

'The Watchers,' the Priest replied. 'Oh, don't worry, you'll meet them soon. However, before I begin, I must give you a prologue about events which happened many years ago. About a small Templar force under Sir William Chasny. He, too, was crossing the wilds of Kent on a dark, wintry night. He, too, became lost. He, too, saw the corpse candles. What happened next is the beginning of a tragedy which cost the lives and souls of many.'

'The Templars?' the Knight interrupted. 'Scawsby?'

'Yes, I have heard about that,' the Man of Law added. 'Legends about a great treasure trove?'

'Who are the Templars?' the Cook asked.

'They were a religious order,' the Knight replied. 'Warrior monks, sworn to defend the Holy Sepulchre. In 1307, yes that's the year, Philip of France accused them of witchcraft, sodomy.' He lowered his voice. 'And other terrible crimes.'

'The Order was spread all across Europe,' the Friar added. 'It was even greater than my own. They owned vast treasures and were said to possess magical powers.'

'Is your story about these?' the Wife of Bath asked.

13

'The Templars are the source of my story,' the Poor Priest replied. 'They play a role.'

'And this treasure?' the Pardoner asked. 'What are the legends? Do you know about that, Sir Godfrey?'

'From the little I know.' The Knight scratched his chin and stretched his hand out towards the fire. 'The English crown was reluctant to believe the stories against the Templars. For a while they were given a respite. Now, if you have been to London, you will have seen the Templar church?'

Many of the pilgrims nodded and said they had.

'It lies between Fleet Street and the Thames,' Sir Geoffrey Chaucer explained. 'Near Whitefriars.'

'Well,' Sir Godfrey continued. 'The Templars stored their wealth there. It was really a treasure house as well as a church. Eventually the English king had to obey the orders of the Pope so a group of Templars gathered up their treasure and left London, travelling south across the Thames and into Kent. They were led by one of their most holy and redoubtable fighters, Sir William Chasny.'

'And what happened to them?' the Cook asked.

'I don't know,' Sir Godfrey replied. 'They just disappeared. Some people claim they slipped in disguise out of the kingdom. Others that they were spirited away by angels.'

'But you, Sir Godfrey?' the Franklin asked.

'Oh, different kings and princes have searched for that treasure but no one has ever found it. There are many legends. One that they were attacked and massacred: that the treasure lies somewhere in the wilds of Kent.' He laughed harshly. 'Perhaps even here.'

The Yeoman, who had left the fire and been walking round the church half listening to the conversation, now came back.

'Sir Godfrey?'

'What is it, man?'

'You talk of the Templars?'

'Yes.'

'How did they dress?'

'Oh, like any knight except for their surcoats, white with a great six-sided cross upon it. Sometimes they wore the same cross on the shoulder of their tunics.'

The Yeoman pursed his lips. 'I think you should see this.'

'See what?' the Squire asked.

'I'd just like Sir Godfrey to see it,' the Yeoman replied.

The pilgrims stirred. The crop-headed, weather-beaten face of the Yeoman was always a source of strength: dressed in his lincoln green, with his jaunty dirk pushed into his belt, his long bow and quiver on his back, the pilgrims regarded the Yeoman as their fighting man. Now he was pale and agitated.

'There's something on the wall in the sanctuary,' he declared. 'Something you should all see.' He pointed to the darkness outside. 'And I do not wish to alarm you but I'm certain, sir, I heard a sound . . .'

Sir Godfrey clambered to his feet. He took a burning brand from the fire and told his squire to do likewise. They all followed the Yeoman up into the sanctuary, turning left into a small enclave which led into the dark, crumbling sacristy. The air was dank and cold. The pilgrims shivered and looked longingly over their shoulders at the merry fire they had left.

'Well, what is it?' the Poor Priest asked.

The Yeoman held up the brand against the wall. The Priest's heart skipped a beat. The Ploughman groaned, his fingers going to his lips. There, on each side of the wall

15

leading into the sacristy, were the Templar crosses. The red paint was beginning to fade, the plaster on which they were painted crumbling and wet. Nevertheless, the insignia could be clearly seen.

'This must have been a Templar manor?' the Man of Law spoke up. 'Probably the church and the village were once owned by the Order. When the Templars disappeared, their possessions were sold to the highest bidder.'

'It's true,' the Priest exclaimed.

He crouched down, asking Sir Godfrey to lower the torch. He pointed at the fading picture beneath the cross, two knights, swords drawn, making obeisance to the crucifix above them.

'And these sounds outside?' Sir Godfrey asked.

Everyone scampered back into the nave. The pilgrims gathered round the fire. Mine Host said he would stay and look after the ladies. Sir Godfrey, sword drawn and accompanied by his son, the Yeoman and Sir Geoffrey Chaucer, who had also drawn sword and dagger, went out into the darkness. The Poor Priest took a brand from the fire and, accompanied by his brother, followed them. They clustered just outside the door, ears straining as the mist swirled about them.

'Silent as the grave,' the Squire murmured. 'Not even an owl hoot.'

'That's what concerns me,' the Knight replied. 'Surely there should be?'

'I'll go,' the Squire offered.

'No you won't.' The Poor Priest pushed his way forward. 'I and my brother will go.'

'But there's nothing there,' Sir Godfrey declared.

As if in answer they heard a twig snap and a clinking, as if mailed men stood in the darkness watching them. Before

16

anyone could stop him, the Poor Priest had darted forward. They watched him go, the firebrand a pinprick of light in the swirling mist. The Ploughman would have followed but Sir Godfrey held him back.

'No,' he whispered.

The Poor Priest, now resolute, crept forward, moving slowly now, fearful lest he trip over a crumbling gravestone: the ground was also uneven, small dips and mounds to catch the unwary. He lifted the firebrand.

'Who is there?' he called.

No answer.

'Are you watching me?' he whispered. 'I have made atonement and I will make atonement.'

Certain that there was no one there, he sighed and made to go back to the church.

'Spectamus te!' The voice seemed to come from the blackness. 'We are watching you!'

The Priest spun round.

'We are watching you!' The words now seemed to come from his left.

Was that a shadow or a man standing? he wondered. The Poor Priest walked slowly back to his companions outside the corpse door.

'There's no one there.' Nevertheless he glanced anxiously at his brother.

They all walked back in to join the rest of the pilgrims. Mine Host filled the wine cups. Now they were all attention, the Poor Priest stood up and began to tell his tale.

The Poor Priest's Tale

PART I

Prologue

The Weald of Kent, near Scawsby, February 1308

Sir William Chasny, knight commander in the Order of the Templars, reined in and looked back through the driving snow at his companions: nine brother knights and two serjeants-at-arms from the Templar headquarters in London. They all huddled on their horses, great war cloaks protecting the icy, gleaming mail beneath. Cowls were pulled as far across their heads as possible, anything to protect their faces from the biting wind and driving snow.

'Sir William.' One of the knights pushed his horse forward. 'We must camp. The horses are beaten and, if we go on, some of the men will collapse.' He lowered his voice. 'And there's the treasure, surely . . .'

Sir William, his face burnt almost black by the fierce sun of North Africa, lifted his hand for silence. He stared along the line of men and horses. He studied the sumpter ponies waiting so patiently and the little palfrey with its precious burden. Sir William glanced up at the sky. No stars. The clouds were full of snow yet to fall. He looked round. The land was harsh: not a tree to sit under, not a barn or a cottage, or even a shepherd's bothie, where his men could shelter to build a fire and warm themselves.

'We must go on a little more,' he declared.

The man made to protest. Sir William leaned across and grasped his wrist. 'We must go on,' he repeated. 'Brother, we are no longer Knights Templar. We are fugitives. In France all our companions are either dead or lie in dungeons awaiting execution. Our Grand Master is the prisoner of Philip IV. Edward II has followed suit. Warrants have been issued for our arrest and the seizure of our treasure.' Sir William pointed down to the palfrey. 'If we are taken, that is lost. If we go on, we might find shelter, some food, some heat. Tomorrow, God willing, we may reach port and go—'

'And go where?' his companion asked bitterly. 'Where can a Templar go, Sir William? Heaven is closed, Hell awaits. A year ago we were the most puissant Order in Christendom. Now, look at us, felons in our own country! We can be cut down by any peasant with a hoe or scythe.'

'People are good,' Sir William replied. 'People here are good, they will take pity.' He smiled, brushing the snowflakes from his moustache and beard. 'Well, as long as they don't know about the treasure we carry.' He raised himself in the stirrups and shouted down the line of men. The wind snatched at his words. 'We go on!' he yelled. 'Soon, I know, we'll be in Scawsby. We can shelter there. Food and wine for our bellies and a roaring fire to burn away the cold.' He turned his horse and led his men on.

Nevertheless, Sir William was worried. Earlier in the day, before the snow had begun to fall in earnest, they had passed through a small hamlet and stopped at an ale-house for some greasy food and watered wine. The villagers had been suspicious. One man in particular, a tinker who said he was going on to Scawsby, had studied them, narrow-eyed. Sir William and his companions had not worn their Templar cloaks with the tell-tale cross. However, the rat-faced trader seemed able to read their thoughts: one of the serjeants had found him out in the stable looking at their horses. Sir William pulled his cowl over his face. Head down, reins loose in his hands, he let his horse plod on.

The man had not, thankfully, been up to the hayloft. He'd run away but where to? Had he gone further along the road to warn others? After all, the fall of the Templars was now well known and every sheriff, constable, bailiff, harbour master and port reeve had been warned to stop and arrest any Templars and seize their goods. Sir William closed his eyes, praying for his brothers now awaiting the scaffold in prisons in London, Paris, Rome and Cologne. For what? For charges that weren't worth the parchment they were written on? Nothing more than the ruses of cunning and avaricious princes to seize Templar wealth and lands. Sir William was determined that the holy and precious treasure from the Templar church in London would not fall into the greedy hands of such despicable men. He and his companions, hands extended over the sacrament in a secret chapel beneath the church in London, had sworn great oaths.

'We will guard this treasure,' they had intoned. 'By day and night. With body, mind and soul. May God, His Angels, Saints and all the Heavenly Court witness that we shall do all in our power to protect this sacred gift of the Temple!'

They had slipped out of London two days later and made their way south, hoping they'd find someone to help them. A merchant; a fisherman, anyone who'd transport them across the seas to the Chasny ancestral home in France. But would they find such a person, or just more treachery? Sir William recalled the words of the psalm.

'Out of the depths have I cried to thee, oh Lord, Lord hear my voice. Let thine ears be attentive to the voice of my supplication.'

'A light!' someone shouted. 'Look, Sir William, a light!'

The commander lifted his head and searched the blackness: he glimpsed the pinprick of light. Then another. His men were already turning their horses. Sir William did likewise, thanking God his prayers had been heard. They left the trackway, a protective line of jingling harness and clopping hooves around the still figure on the palfrey. The lights became more distinct. Despite the iron discipline of the Temple, Sir William could not have stopped his men if he had wanted to. They were tired, dispirited, starving and freezing. One of the serjeants spurred on almost to a charge. The snow was not too thick and the ground was iron-hard, easy to cross. Sir William could see that the lights were now torches. His heart leapt with joy. If they could rest tonight, if they could eat and sleep by a warm fire. He recalled the maps in the Templar library showing the trackways and paths of Kent. Too late, he remembered the warning given to him about the marshes and the strange lights which also shimmered above them. What had the old archivist called them? Corpse candles! Were these them?

'Be careful!' he shouted.

But his men rode on.

'They are torches!' a knight shouted. 'There are men!'

The thunder of hooves grew. The sumpter ponies, despite their weariness, picked up their legs as if they, too, could smell sweet oats and soft, warm straw. Sir William heard a scream from the blackness. The serjeant who had ridden ahead was now struggling.

'It's a marsh!' he shouted. 'Oh, Christ, help me!'

Sir William tried to rein in, but his own horse was also

mired in the mud. The night air was now rent by shrieks and cries of his men. The neigh of horses, the braying of the sumpter ponies. Sir William slipped from the saddle. The icy cold mud crept up his leg but he kept his nerve. He drew his sword and poked at the ground around him, soft, oozing with mud, but then he struck hard earth. He waded towards this. A small path, a trackway through the marshes. Gasping for breath, Sir William dragged himself towards it and began to shout at his men.

'Towards me!' he screamed. 'Towards me! Bring the palfrey!'

Some of his men reached him but Sir William's heart sank. Only six or seven and the rest? The Virgin and her precious treasure? He could still hear those awful screams and shrieks from the darkness. The snow was falling thicker now. Heavy flakes, as if heaven itself was weeping at what was happening. Chasny knew he was going to die. This was where it would end. For a few seconds he recalled his childhood, playing in golden fields outside a small village in the vale of York. His parents, hand in hand, laughing as they searched for him. His admission to the Templar Order, his novitiate. He had spent his life fighting for the faith. Now he was to be treacherously killed in this God-forsaken marsh. Sir William stretched his sword towards the sky.

'Avenge me, God!' he cried. 'Avenge me!'

His men were now grouped around him, swords out, staring at the torches which surrounded them.

'We have been trapped,' one of the knights whispered. 'They have led us into a marsh.'

'There must be paths!' Sir William exclaimed. 'Just like the one we are standing on.' He grasped his sword tighter. 'The Virgin, the Veronica?'

'God knows, Sir William,' the Templar commander groaned.

'Well, we can't stand here all night,' one of his companions whispered.

'Murderers!' Sir William screamed. 'Traitors! Close with us now! Sword to sword! Dagger to dagger!'

An arrow whipped out of the darkness and took him full in the shoulder. Chasny dropped to one knee. More arrows fell, his companions began to die. Some silently as the deadly shafts took them in the neck or the chest. Others were knocked off the narrow pathway into the marsh and died screaming as they were buried alive. Sir William dragged himself to his feet but his legs felt like lead, his whole body devoid of strength. He crouched back down and, being a priest as well as a soldier, began to recite the words of absolution for himself and his companions.

'Absolve, Domine, nos a peccatis nostris.'

He heard sounds along the path and looked up. The assassins were closing in. He stayed still as a stone, head slightly to one side. Out of the corner of his eye he watched the shapes slip through the darkness. He smiled in satisfaction as he recognised the tinker he had seen earlier in the day.

'Come on!' a villain shouted, lifting him gently. 'They are all dead!'

'But the sumpter ponies are in the marsh. They have the treasure!'

'The marsh can be dragged: it's not so deep!'

The tinker drew closer. Sir William lunged with all his might and drove his sword straight into the man's midriff.

'Deus vult!' Sir William shouted the cry of the Crusaders. 'Deus vult! God wills it!' He withdrew his sword and the man toppled into the marsh.

Sir William felt new strength course through his body.

'Before heaven and earth!' he shouted, his voice booming through the wind. 'I curse you all before the Lord and His Angels! I summon you before His court to answer for your crimes. I curse you with all the power my Order has given me! We shall return! Do you hear me? We shall return! We shall be watching you! We shall always be watching you!'

He was still shouting when the arrows shot out of the darkness, piercing his body. Still the old knight shouted his curses, in English, in Latin, in French.

'We shall be watching you! We shall always be watching you!'

At last they saw him tumble, fall to his knees on the path. Head bowed, he keeled to the ground. They ran forward. One man drew his dagger and tentatively turned Sir William's body over. He heaved a sigh of relief but then jumped as the Templar's dagger took him full in the belly with hot searing pain. Locked together in death, the knight and his assailant, faces only a few inches apart, stared in their dying agonies at each other.

'Remember!' Sir William whispered. 'We shall return! We shall be watching you!'

Chapter 1

Scawsby – 1382

The three riders reined in at the top of the hill and looked down at the village nestling in the shallow valley below. A bright February morning, the sun was surprisingly strong, quickly burning off the mist.

'A pleasant sight.' Edmund Trumpington leaned across and grasped his brother's hand. 'Philip, I am so pleased I am with you. This will be my first parish.'

Philip pushed back the cowl of his cloak and smiled. His brother was only two months ordained. Just before Christmas, the Bishop of Rochester had finished the Rite of Ordination by anointing Edmund's head, lips and hands. Edmund, like himself, was now a priest with the power to preach the gospel, celebrate Mass and shrive the faithful. Philip had been ordained three years previously and served in parishes at Gravesend and Maidstone. Now he and Edmund had been given the parish of St Oswald's in Scawsby. The bishop believed that the two brothers serving together would be of benefit to the faithful.

'Always remember.' The bishop had smiled. 'That quotation from the Book of Proverbs: "Brothers united are as a fortress."'

Philip had visited Scawsby on a number of occasions,

getting to know his parishioners, walking the village. Above all, he had studied the church which, local tradition averred, had been old when the Conqueror and his Normans had swept into Kent.

'You priests should be pleased, it's a good living,' the third rider teased.

Philip looked over his shoulder at his close friend Stephen Merkle. He had known the blond-haired, fresh-faced young man ever since they had shared the same hall at Cambridge. He, Philip and Edmund were now the closest friends, inseparable in all things. Merkle was a brilliant mathematician, a master of Geometry. He'd already gained his qualifications as a master mason and been employed in the king's service at the great abbey of Westminster and, more recently, St Bartholomew's Priory in Smithfield.

The three friends always kept in touch by letter. When Philip had decided that the church at Scawsby was too old and should be pulled down and rebuilt elsewhere, Stephen had volunteered to be the architect. He had ridden straight to Maidstone, almost confronting Philip in the parlour of the priest's house.

'I was born near Scawsby,' Stephen declared. 'I will build you a church. One that will last for centuries, in the most beautiful style. Not these old Norman blocks and square entrances. You'll have spanning arches, a rose window, transepts lined with bays. A soaring roof, a sanctuary which can be viewed from any corner of the church.'

Stephen had gone on and on, until Philip had held his hands up. 'Concedo.' He laughed. 'Stephen, you can come, though the fees will be low.'

Stephen had drawn his brows together. 'Philip, what does it profit a man if he gain the whole world?'

'Stephen, Stephen,' Philip replied. 'I am a priest and

you are a master mason. I expect to be poor. You expect to be rich. You have a fine house in London. I know from the gossips that you are always searching for gold and silver.'

Stephen had waved his hand placatingly.

'I'll come to Scawsby,' he declared. 'I'll accept whatever you pay.' He had clapped his hands like a child. 'Philip, Philip, I'll confess – every mason dreams of building his own church, that's the path to fame and fortune!'

Philip had accepted: perhaps his friend would think again but Stephen had been most excited about the project. He, too, had visited the village, staying overnight in the old priest's house, studying the church and searching for a new site. He eventually wrote to Philip how he had found a suitable location at the other end of the village, amongst the old Saxon ruins at High Mount.

Philip now studied Stephen closely. The mason was gazing down at the village, a rapt expression on his face. The vicar felt a twinge of unease. Stephen seemed absorbed by the village and his plan to build a new church. Oh, he could understand Stephen's enthusiasm, but the young mason had even neglected his work in London to carry out the most extensive surveys. Moreover, in the last few weeks before they left for Scawsby, Stephen had changed slightly, growing more subdued, even secretive.

'Do you like the village?' Philip asked abruptly. 'Stephen, for the love of Heaven, are you asleep?'

The young mason shook himself from his reverie.

'Of course I like the village,' he replied. 'It's a fine place, Philip. Wealthy as well. Look.' He pointed down to the high street which ran up to the church: on either side stood the cottages and houses of the peasants. 'They are prosperous,' Stephen continued. 'Some of them are built of stone. Look at the tavern, Philip. It has a tiled roof with the most beautiful gardens at the rear.'

Philip could only agree. Even from where they sat on the brim of the hill, he could almost feel the richness of the soil, the open meadows all waiting for spring. A cheerful, bustling place. Wood smoke rose from many houses, the sound of children laughing carried faintly on the breeze. Narrowing his eyes, Philip could make out the herds of sheep and cattle grazing in the meadows. Elsewhere the men were busy with their oxen, laying down manure, enriching the soil so the harvest would be plentiful.

'Scawsby's a prosperous place,' the bishop had declared. 'You'll like it, Philip.'

'How did you find Lord Montalt?' Philip asked, gathering up the reins of his horse.

'He is an old warhorse,' Stephen replied. 'But a good seigneur, kind to his tenants. He, too, thinks the church should be moved to High Mount.'

'Yet there's a serpent in our paradise, isn't there?' Edmund declared, pushing his horse forward. 'Have you ever found out what it is, Brother?'

'No, I haven't.'

Suddenly the morning didn't seem so bright. The death of the previous incumbent was a matter neither Philip nor Edmund had referred to. Father Anthony had been a kindly, middle-aged man, a gentle scholar. No one had yet explained why, one night at the end of November, he had gone out and hanged himself from a yew tree in the cemetery. Even the bishop did not know. The aged prelate had simply shaken his head and muttered about the nonsense of ancient legends and left it at that.

'I am cold,' Philip declared. 'Roheisia, the widow woman

who looks after the priest's house, said she'd have the place ready. It's time we went down.'

They rode down the hill into the woods following the trackway as it wound along into the village. The trees, black and gaunt after a severe winter, blocked out the sunlight. A fox ran across their path, a rabbit in its mouth. Crows circled, calling raucously, fearful of the hawk hovering so close to their nests. The three men rode in silence. Stephen, as if resenting the brooding quietness of the trees, hummed a song they all knew. Philip was about to join in when he glimpsed movement amongst the trees. Philip held his hand up. He turned his horse and stared into the darkness of the wood.

'What is it, Philip?' Edmund asked.

'Horsemen,' his brother replied. 'Perhaps a trick of the light, but I'm sure I saw men, cowled and hooded.'

'Horsemen!' Stephen exclaimed. 'Philip, are you sure?' Merkle's face was pale.

'What's the matter?' Philip asked. 'You look frightened.'

'It's nothing.' Stephen shook his head. 'No, no, I'll be honest, Philip. When we entered the forest I, too, thought I saw horsemen, a line of knights, as if they were moving alongside us.'

Stephen glanced furtively at Philip. The priest looked even more severe than usual. Unlike Edmund, with his boyish good looks, plump cheeks and laughing eyes, Philip always carried himself with authority. Keen-eyed and thin-lipped, Philip, when angry, had the look of a hawk with his sharp nose and those eyes which never seemed to miss anything.

'Come on, Stephen,' Philip urged. 'This has happened before, hasn't it? You don't frighten easily.'

Stephen stared into the trees.

'Yes, it's happened before,' he replied slowly. 'Oh, the village is good, pleasant and welcoming. However, here in the woods, or out on the heathland, you have this impression of someone watching you, of being followed.'

'His Lordship the Bishop,' Philip declared, 'talked about legends. Have you heard about these, Stephen?'

'Oh, every village and hamlet in Kent has its ancient lore,' Stephen retorted crossly. 'Scawsby's no different.' He urged his horse on. 'Come on, Philip. I'm cold and I'm hungry. Every wood has a life of its own. It's only shadows moving amongst the trees.'

All three were relieved to be out of the trees and on to the road leading into Scawsby. Men in the fields on either side stopped to shout their welcome and raise their hands. Some of the children, armed with slingshot to drive away the marauding crows, came running up, their dirty faces brightening with pleasure.

'It's Father Pip!' one of them shouted, waving his hand. 'It's Father Pip!'

'They can't get their tongues round my name,' the vicar whispered. 'So Pip I've become and Pip I'll remain. God knows what they'll make of Edmund and Stephen!'

They all reined in as the men left their ploughs and walked on to the trackway. The villagers were pleased to see their new priest. It was sad for a man to be buried without a requiem Mass or for babies waiting to be baptised. The young lovers, who wanted to become handfast at the church door, also had to wait until the priest consulted the Blood Book to pronounce they were not within the forbidden degrees: only then could wedding arrangements go forward. The sick would now have a visitor to bring the viaticum, hear their confessions and shrive them. The great Holy Days would be blessed and, once again, the Mass would celebrate the beginning of the day and the end of the week. Accordingly, Philip and Edmund were welcomed as if they were Princes of the court. The children danced around. The men, unwilling to shake the priests' hands with their mud-flaked fingers, just shuffled their feet and grinned in pleasure.

'It's good to be here,' Philip declared. 'My brother Edmund and I will become members of all your families. My good friend Stephen Merkle is a master mason. He has come to advise us on our new church.'

The villagers were not so pleased at this. Smiles disappeared, replaced by glowering glances in Merkle's direction.

'St Oswald's good enough.' A burly farmer stepped forward. He pushed back his leather hood, his great red face scored and chapped by years of wind and rain. 'My name's Falmer,' he declared. 'I was baptised in St Oswald's. My father, and his father's father lie buried in God's acre.'

'The new church,' Philip replied tactfully, 'will be built in their memory. However, now is not the time to discuss the matter, there will be meetings enough.' He raised his hand in benediction.

The labourers clapped, stood aside and the horsemen continued on into Scawsby.

Despite the protests about the new church, the rest of the village were welcoming enough. Philip felt immediately at home. A prosperous, hard-working place; some of the peasants owned their own land and had used the profits to build stone houses with red tiled roofs. In front and behind these were large garden plots for vegetables and flowers. Some even had their own stables, piggeries, hen coops and dove cotes for pigeons. All these supplied the necessary manure for the great open fields around. A busy, bustling place: dogs and pigs roamed the streets; chickens pecked at the hard-packed earth; women sat in doorways weaving or, just inside, busily baked bread or brewed their own ales. The sweet smell from these kitchens hung heavily on the air. Philip stopped time and again to introduce himself. He caught Stephen blushing as some girl or young woman caught the man's eye and gazed boldly at the stranger. Strong, handsome people who fed well on the riches of the earth. Philip knew that many of these peasants were now free of any seigneurial dues and, like others in East Anglia or the rich vales of the Cotswolds, were becoming landlords in their own right. It took him at least an hour before they could leave the huge taproom of the Silver Swan tavern which stood in the centre of the village. They rode on, past the well, the gibbet and the stocks, down the trackway and through the lych-gate into the cemetery.

St Oswald's was a low, squat building, built of grey ragstone with a dark slate roof. The church was built like a barn, one long huddle of bricks. The front formed into an apex, the carved tympanum above the heavy oaken doors long faded by the weather. A square tower had been built alongside, its top crenellated. There were only three narrow windows in the tower and, despite the length of the church, its windows were really no more than mere arrow slits. All three walked round the church stepping over crumbling crosses and decaying headstones. Stephen, carefully examining the outside, pointed to the crumbling buttresses, the decayed sills beneath the window, the cracks in the eaves.

'There will be rottenness in the wood inside,' he declared.

Philip stared round the broad, gloomy cemetery which bounded the church on every side.

'This will be a problem,' he announced. 'The parishioners will be deeply upset to lose their cemetery.'

'What does Canon Law say?' Edmund asked.

'The Church's ruling,' Philip replied, 'is that corpses buried within living memory may be exhumed, or indeed, the remains of any can be duly removed to a new cemetery. There must be thousands of corpses buried there.' He added, 'This will be a most difficult obstacle to overcome: persuading our parishioners, not only that their old church should be pulled down, but the cemetery should be grassed over and eventually forgotten.'

'Why not build a new church here?' Edmund asked.

'Because we are at the foot of a hill,' Stephen explained. 'The ground becomes water-logged. Centuries ago they probably raised the church here because it was the easiest land to build on. High Mount is different. There are some ruins but they can be cleared. It would make an excellent place. The land is owned by Montalt, the land around it could become a cemetery.'

Philip stared round the cemetery. A cloud now covered the sun and the graveyard looked dank and grim; the yew trees twisted and gnarled, their branches snaking out like skeletal fingers.

'Father Anthony hanged himself from that one.' Stephen pointed to a yew tree which stood in the centre of the graveyard, between the church and the priest's house.

Philip walked over. 'How did he do it?' he asked. 'I mean, the lowest branch is high off the ground?'

'According to what I have learnt,' Stephen replied, 'he used a ladder. He went up, tied the rope round a branch, the other end round his neck, then jumped.'

Philip said a prayer for the repose of the man's soul but the question hammered inside his mind. Why should a gentle, scholarly, old priest go out on a winter's night and hang himself in his own graveyard?

'Let's go inside,' Stephen offered. 'It's getting cold and my belly's grumbling.'

Philip agreed. They walked back to the church porch. Stephen opened the door; he and Edmund went inside. Philip paused and stared around. Was there someone else here? Someone in the graveyard watching him? He gasped. Beneath the yew tree, the very one from which Father Anthony had hanged himself, stood a cloaked and hooded figure. Philip could make out the face, tanned and weather-beaten: grey beard and moustache, he had the air of a fighting man. The eyes seemed almost larger than the face, black and hard as pebbles. Philip blinked and rubbed his eyes. When he looked again, there was nothing there.

'Are you all right?' Edmund came back. 'Philip, what's the matter?'

'Nothing at all. Let's see the inside of this church.'

They walked into the vestibule: the air was dank and smelt of mildew. On the left was a door leading to the tower; to the right a small, narrow room dusty and full of cobwebs where broken benches and other items had been stored. The nave was long, the pillars on either side were round and squat. Because of the poor light, the transepts on either side were dark and gloomy. Philip gazed up at the hammer-beam roof.

'That's new!' Stephen explained. 'Probably no more than sixty years old. New beams were put in to reinforce the roof. It must have been a costly enterprise. What I can't understand,' the master mason continued, 'is they also started to replace the slates on the roof but discontinued it? I mean, what's the use of putting new beams up if the water is allowed to drip through and rot them?'

Philip walked up the nave, where his foot caught on a loose paving-stone. He stared down.

'That's another reason,' Stephen continued. 'The church is built over wells and, in places, the floor is beginning to subside.'

Philip walked on more carefully. He stopped before a great stone coffin built just in front of the entrance to the rood screen which divided the nave from the sanctuary. The tomb was a long, rectangular shape. On top lay an effigy of a knight, mailed legs crossed, hand grasping the hilt of his sword. There was a Latin inscription on the side of the tomb. Philip crouched down and translated the faded Latin: 'Died in the year of Our Lord 1311.'

'The present lord's grandfather!' Stephen explained.

Philip's attention was then held by the strange markings above the inscription. He had never seen the like before, a pair of eyes and, beneath, a faded Latin tag. Philip peered closer and translated it.

'We are watching you!' he whispered. 'We are always watching you!'

Chapter 2

Philip moved round the tomb. On the side facing the sanctuary was another inscription. It caught his eyes because it was not professionally done but gouged into the pillar by a chisel and a hammer.

SUB ALTO MONTE,
PRETIOSA COPIA
FILI DAVID
RESIDET ET SEMPER RESIDET
DOMINE, MISERERE NOBIS
WALTER ROMANEL 1312

Philip called Edmund across and read him the inscription. Edmund went into the sanctuary. He struck a tinder, lit a candle and brought it back; the crude lettering flared into light.

'"Under the high mountain,"' he translated, '"the precious load of David's son resides and will always reside. Oh Lord, have mercy on us. Walter Romanel 1312."'

'Romanel!' Philip got to his feet. 'Wasn't he—?'

'He was a priest here,' Stephen interjected. 'He went mad and had to be taken to St Bartholomew's hospital in London.'

'This is a strange place,' Philip declared.

He went up and studied the Lady Chapel to the left of
the sanctuary. The statue of the Virgin was like the one
at Walsingham. Mary, a crown on her head, the robes of
a queen round her shoulders, embraced the infant Jesus on
her lap. Philip took his own tinder out and lit a taper. The
damp Lady Chapel had faded paintings on either wall: Philip
felt repelled by the air of neglect. He then walked round
the transepts; these were no better, being dark and shabby.
Some crude paintings covered the walls but the plaster was
beginning to crumble, lying like snowflakes on the uneven
flagstones. The parish coffin, which stood on an open-sided
cart, also looked as if it had seen better days.

'I can't understand it,' Edmund declared. 'St Oswald's is
a wealthy parish yet I have seen better churches in some of
the poorest villages in Kent.'

'Now that's one thing I do know,' Philip replied. 'His
Lordship the Bishop was rather reluctant to discuss the
matter but I have seen the list of vicars who have served
here over the years. Their names should be painted on a
board in the church but I can understand why they are not.
Very few of them remained here for more than a few years.
Father Anthony, who served here for at least twelve, was
an exception.' Philip smiled. He had always considered the
Bishop of Rochester a cunning old fox: now Philip realised
why, at such a tender age, he, who had only been ordained
recently, had been given such a benefice.

'Look at the pillars,' Edmund declared.

Philip did so. He noticed how, just above head height
on each pillar, a pair of eyes had been painted. This
had been crudely done, yet all the eyes looked towards
the sanctuary. Moreover, each pillar bore the same faded
inscription: SPECTAMUS TE, SEMPER SPECTAMUS TE.

'"We are watching you,"' he translated. '"We are always

watching you." What does this mean, Edmund? Who is watching? Why?' He looked round the church. 'Stephen, where are you?'

His words echoed, bouncing off the wall. Philip had the impression that someone was mimicking him, chanting the words back. He was concerned about this cold, damp place, very aware of a watching malevolence. Philip hurried into the sanctuary. He had seen this before and matters had not improved. A bare, empty place with an altar, sedilia, lavarium and lectern. The cloth across the altar was of good quality whilst the silver pyx, hanging from one of the beams, shimmered in the light of the red sanctuary lamp.

'Stephen!' he shouted. 'Stephen, where are you?'

'I am down here, Philip. Don't worry!'

Philip closed his eyes. 'Of course,' he murmured. 'I had forgotten . . .'

In the far corner of the sanctuary, almost hidden in the shadows, was a small door leading down to the crypt. Stephen had taken the candle and gone down. Philip followed. If the church was gloomy, the crypt was dismal. Some light seeped through from a grating in the ceiling into this bare, empty place. Low-roofed, bare walled, the crypt was devoid of anything except supporting pillars. The central one was at least two yards wide and the same across: Stephen was studying it carefully.

'If we could weaken this, Philip.' He looked up at the plastered roof. 'The entire church would crumble.'

'And how can we do that?'

'Oh, quite easily,' the master mason replied with a smile. 'I've talked to soldiers, master gunners from the wars in France. They did the same to French castles. You dig a mine beneath the pillar, place the gunpowder and fire the fuse. The entire church would collapse inwards.'

'I'd love to do that,' Philip replied. 'Stephen, have you ever visited such an eerie, depressing place? What shall we do with it?'

Stephen stood back, still more concerned with the pillar.

'Oh, don't worry, Philip,' he replied. 'We'll get permission from Lord Richard to build a new church. You are a fine preacher: the parishioners will accept what you say. We'll level this church and build another on High Mount. One that will be the talk of Kent.' He grasped Philip's hand. 'Just think of it, Philip.' He turned and put his other hand on Edmund's shoulder. 'A jewel of a chapel: soaring roof, light transepts. Painters will come from Canterbury. They'll work for free, just to have their scenes on the walls of our church!'

'Stephen, do you know much about the history of this place?' Edmund asked abruptly.

The master mason took the candle off a wall ledge and sat down with his back to a pillar.

'Just a little.' He smiled shyly. 'The parish is a wealthy one. You know that. You probably also know that vicars who come here do not stay long. Now that is not extraordinary. I can think of similar parishes where the same has occurred. Father Anthony was writing a history, doing his own research. Apparently it all began with Romanel.'

'The vicar who did the carving on Montalt's tomb?'

'The same. He was apparently a man of ill repute. Scawsby is not far from the coast and, in the chaos of Edward II's reign, Romanel and some of the villagers did their fair share of smuggling.'

'Oh come, Stephen!'

Philip sat down beside him, trying to control his shivers as he stared into the shadows which filled the place. The candles they had brought down only intensified the eerie atmosphere: every time they moved, dark shapes danced all around them.

'I know. I know,' Stephen declared. 'What is wrong with a little smuggling? There's not a Kentish man over the age of sixteen who has not been involved with some smuggling, my own father included. However, Romanel was different. He wanted wealth so he also dabbled in the black arts.'

'A warlock?' Edmund asked.

'Warlock, wizard, sorcerer, gibbet-master. Whatever.'

'And where did he practise his rites?'

Stephen began to laugh, low and mocking. 'According to local law and Father Anthony, here.'

'You mean in the church?'

'No, Philip, I mean here in the crypt. The usual, noddle-pated nonsense. Animal sacrifices . . .'

Philip sprang to his feet. He did not like this place. Closing his eyes, he quietly cursed his own arrogance. I should have asked, he thought, I should have made my own enquiries. He felt Stephen's hand on his shoulder.

'Come on, Philip: that was years ago. Romanel died mad. The church has been blessed and re-consecrated.' His smile faded. 'Though I should show you this.'

He stepped across and held his candle up against one of the pillars which supported the floor just near the staircase. Philip expected to see the eyes as he had on the tomb but, as Stephen held the candle up, he glimpsed what he thought was a damp patch which marked part of the pillar. As he studied it more closely, he realised it was like a shadow caught on the pillar forming the figure of a knight. Walking closer Philip could make out the chainmail coif, the moustached face, the cloak falling in folds, the breastplate, greaves, even spurs on the heels: it reminded him of the vision in the graveyard.

'What is it?' he whispered.

'I don't know,' Stephen replied. 'Father Anthony mentioned it in his notes. I have also talked to others. Some say it is a painting of a knight which has faded. Others are more mysterious, they say it's the imprint of a ghost.'

Philip grasped the candle and studied the pillar closely. For the first time ever he felt frightened. He had seen faded wall paintings before but this was different. He thrust the candle back into Stephen's hand.

'I tell you this.' He glanced at the master mason and his brother. 'Soon it will be spring. Before another winter comes to Scawsby, I'll have this church levelled and a new one almost built.'

They left the crypt and went out of the church into the cemetery. The day was dying, the light was beginning to fade. Tendrils of mist curled round the yew trees. Philip glimpsed the welcoming light from the priest's house.

'I am looking forward to a good meal,' he declared. 'Roheisia has a reputation for being a good cook and I want words with our clerk Adam Waldis.'

'He's a furtive little man,' Stephen declared. 'Scurries round like a mouse, always muttering to himself but he's a closed book. Try and talk to him about the parish, or Father Anthony's death and he'll just look at you like some frightened rabbit then run away.'

Laughing and talking they walked to the back of the church. Philip was interested in inspecting the wall most open to the elements. As they did so, he caught a movement amongst the trees. He stopped, heart in mouth.

'Philip, what's the matter?'

At first the priest didn't want to reply, to be accused of having a fanciful imagination. Then he saw the movement again, a stooped figure crossing from behind a grave stone to the trees clustered at the east end of the cemetery.

'Who is that?' Edmund asked.

Philip laughed and relaxed. He was not having visions; his good humour, however, soon turned to anger. Was this the figure who had been watching him when he had first entered the church? He strode across the grass.

'Stop!' he shouted.

The figure turned: an old woman, a veritable crone, her two hands clenched on an ash stick. She gazed fearfully as the priest approached. Philip felt confused. On the one hand, he was curious and relieved that the figure he had seen was flesh and blood. On the other he was rather repelled because the old woman was ugly. She had a long, thin face, broken nose, eyes constantly blinking, whilst her tongue kept licking her bloodless lips. She seemed furtive, frightened, dressed in a shabby, black gown frayed at the hem, cuffs and round the neckline. A grey, woollen cloak hung across bony shoulders, her white hair, thinning and sparse, was gathered and tied at the back. Philip paused. Was this really the figure he had glimpsed earlier?

'Please stay!' he called out. Philip stooped and extended one hand. 'I am Father Philip Trumpington, the new vicar.'

The woman's sea-grey eyes held his: no longer nervous, Philip believed the woman was quietly mocking him.

'I've just arrived here,' Philip declared.

The grey eyes moved: Edmund she dismissed with one glance but her eyes narrowed as she recognised Stephen.

'I've seen one of you before.' Her voice was low, surprisingly strong. She drew herself up as if the quiet scurrying was a pretence, protection against any threat. 'I have seen the fair-haired one. You are a mason, aren't you?'

'Yes, Mother.'

'I'm not a mother or a woman,' she replied. 'I am the coffin keeper. I am not of the female kind.' She continued

44

dryly, 'My breasts are shrivelled, my juices long dried up. People know me as the coffin, or corpse woman.'

'The what?' Philip exclaimed.

'The coffin woman,' she repeated. 'You know about coffins, priest, the dead go in them.' She gestured with her head towards the grave stones. 'We all think we are so important but, in the end, one way or the other, the earth claims us.' She sighed in exasperation and drew closer. 'No, I am not a mysterious, old woman,' she continued, her eyes bright with excitement as if she relished the repartee. She grasped Philip's hand; her fingers felt warm. 'Father, this is an eerie, sometimes evil place. No, I do not wish to frighten you; you must not believe the village lore, I am no witch.' She smiled up at him. 'I was born Edith Romanel. Oh yes,' she caught the surprise in Philip's face. 'I am a vicar's by-blow. An eye for the ladies had Parson Romanel. A father to his people in more ways than one.'

Philip now joined in her laughter.

'And do you know what happens to the illegitimate children of priests?' she continued. 'They are cast out to fend for themselves. My father went witless, mad as a March hare. The new priest arrived and I am thrown out.' She waved her hand. 'Behind the trees there's an old cottage near the graveyard wall. I live there. I pick up twigs. I clean the cemetery. When someone dies, someone poor, with no one to wash the corpse or prepare it for burial . . .'

'The coffin woman does it.' Philip finished her sentence.

'Yes, Father, the coffin woman does it. And in return I am paid a shilling every quarter and, if the priest is good, some food and other sustenance.'

'You talk well, coffin woman.'

'I was twelve when my father went mad,' she replied. 'He taught me my horn book. I could count past fifty by the time I was ten. When the other priests came I served as their housekeeper. I am not a peasant.' She drew herself up. 'I am not what I appear to be. So, what do you say, priest? Will you keep me as the coffin woman?'

'Of course.'

'I hope you do,' the coffin woman replied, stepping back. 'You have a kindly face, despite your sharp eyes. You have a zeal for souls, haven't you, Father?' She shrugged. 'But, there again, others have come and then they leave.'

'Why?' Philip asked.

The woman half turned. 'I don't know,' she murmured. 'I am supposed to. One priest said that to me. Just because you've got grey hair and a wizened face they think you're a wise woman. But, as God is my witness, I don't know. Indeed, if I told you my suspicions, the things I have seen, then I'd no longer be a wise woman but witless, mad as my father.' She smiled slyly. 'And what would happen to me then?'

'So you know things?' Philip insisted.

'No more than other people, Father,' she quipped. 'You know what I am talking about, Father: the ones before you, no priest wants to stay here long. Oh, it's not the village, there are no dark secrets there.' She glanced up at the church tower. 'It's here,' she added wearily. 'This is where it all happens.'

'What happens?' Stephen asked.

'Why, sir.' She glared at them. 'Whatever you want, whatever you see. Priests come here, they hear the stories. Some even wonder where my father's old treasure is!'

'Treasure?' Edmund asked.

'Stories,' the woman taunted. 'My father was,' she smiled, 'well, he was as madcap as a March hare, dabbling in this and dabbling in that. When I was a child, money came into the villagc, Heaven knows where from? Like you, he wanted to change the church. Oh yes, I have heard the rumours. But then he went mad.'

'Why?' Philip asked.

She sighed. 'Some people said he was born mad, others that it was the demons: all I can remember is my father waking up screaming or, now and again, in church, when celebrating Mass, he would stop and shout: "They are watching me! They are always watching me!"'

'And did he ever tell you who?' Philip asked.

'As God is my witness, Father, never. No one ever knew. Or, there again, it could have been the disappearances. Go down into the village and ask. They'll tell you the same story. Some of them just disappeared when Romanel was vicar. All sorts of professions: one was a miller, another a ploughman, a tanner, a shepherd, a journeyman. All gone.' She clapped her hands. 'Like the mists which swirl in here.' She blew her cheeks out. 'Anyway, I have spoken enough!' She lifted her head, sniffing the air like a dog. 'Roheisia has a meal ready for you, beef I think. Highly salted but covered in spices. She and her mad son Crispin. Well, he's witless, but he'll look after your horses.' And, turning on her heel, she scuttled into the trees.

They went back and collected their horses. They led them out of the cemetery and further along the road following the wall around. The priest's house was a grand, imposing affair built of the same stone as the church: three storeys high with a slate roof and a chimney stack built along one side. Most of the windows were shuttered but those on the ground floor were filled with mullioned glass. The main door was approached up some steps. Whilst Stephen held the horses, Philip and Edmund went up and knocked on the door. Roheisia opened it. A red-faced, smiling woman, plump as a ripe pear, her grey hair caught up under a white veil. She was dressed in a long, dark-blue smock, slightly threadbare, covered in flour which also stained her fingers and wrists. She waved excitedly.

'Father Edmund, Father Philip, you shouldn't knock. It's your house! Come in! Come in!' She looked over at Stephen holding the horses. 'Take those round the back,' she called.

'I'll get them myself, Mother.'

A young man, vacant-eyed, with a smiling, simpleton's face under a shock of greasy hair, came running down the passageway. He almost knocked his mother aside, hastening down the steps, clapping his hands.

'He's harmless,' Roheisia added. 'He just loves horses. He'll take care of yours.'

Philip watched the boy gather the reins and take the horses round the side of the house where he knew, from recent visits, stood the small stables, garden and outhouses.

Roheisia led them into the house, chattering excitedly about how all the rest of their baggage had arrived, safely brought by a carter from Maidstone. She explained how she'd moved it all upstairs though she didn't know where to put it. And were they hungry? And had they seen the church? And was it true they wished to build a new one? Roheisia chattered on as she led them through the house. Philip and Stephen had seen it before. It was pleasant and spacious enough: a parlour, a small refectory adjoining the kitchen, scullery and buttery. The rooms were clean, the plaster freshly painted, crucifixes and small, painted triptychs hung there. The rushes on the floor were green and newly cut: pots of herbs stood in the corners. The rest of the furniture had also been cleaned and washed whilst the kitchen was full of the sweet smells of freshly baked bread and roasted meat.

'It's very clean,' Philip remarked.

'Oh yes,' Roheisia declared. 'I keep a good house for the Fathers.' She paused, her hand on the balustrade, and looked round at them. 'You will stay, won't you?'

'Of course,' Philip replied.

'Other priests come and go.'

'So I noticed,' Philip replied. 'And you've been house-keeper to them all?'

'For the last twenty years, yes.'

'So why did they leave?'

The old lady turned, gathering up the hem of her gown, and climbed the wooden, spiral staircase. When she reached the top she sat on a stool, mopping her face and smiled up at them.

'It's a steep climb. There are three chambers along this gallery. There are also rooms above and garrets under the eaves but they are rarely used.'

'Why did the other priests leave?' Philip asked.

'Well, some were old and became sick. Scawsby can be a lonely place. Others became frightened and withdrawn. They didn't say much. They learnt about Romanel, the priest who went insane and was taken off to London. Perhaps they brooded too much?'

'And Father Anthony?'

'Yes, he stayed longer. He liked the church and was interested in its history, particularly the legends.'

'So why did he kill himself?'

'Father, I don't know.' She got to her feet. 'It happened very quickly. He and the parish clerk Adam Waldis, they were often closeted together whispering about this or that. They'd often go out to High Mount where the ruins of the Saxon priory lie. Towards the end, Father Anthony changed, he hardly slept: always looking out of the window. One morning I came in here. The house was empty, I couldn't find Father Anthony. Waldis lives in the village. There was this terrible hammering on the door. You've met the coffin woman?'

'Aye,' Philip replied. 'I have.'

'Oh, she's harmless,' Roheisia declared. 'Does a work of charity she does. Anyway, she found poor Father Anthony hanging like a felon from the gallows. Crispin my son cut him down.'

'Where was he buried?'

'In the churchyard. Lord Richard Montalt said he shouldn't be buried at the crossroads like a suicide. He said Father Anthony had probably lost his wits and didn't know what he was doing.' She sighed and got to her feet. 'They haven't even erected a grave stone yet. Anyway, your chambers are here. You have Father Anthony's, that's the largest.' She opened a door and ushered Philip in.

The chamber was large: it contained a small four-poster bed, two chests, an aumbry, shelves on the wall beneath the black, stark crucifix and a large writing desk under the window.

'Father Anthony left all his books and papers. No one has claimed them. Lord Richard said the next priest could have them.'

She showed Edmund and Stephen their chambers. Roheisia apologised for the lack of rushes on the floor and said she'd see to it the following day.

'All the baggage is in your room, sir.' She nodded at Stephen. 'I am afraid I don't know what belongs to whom. Now I'll go back to the kitchen, you'll be hungry.'

She went slowly back along the gallery, then turned at the top of the stairs, hand to her mouth.

'Oh Lord save us!' she gasped. 'Father Philip, I am sorry,

but Lord Richard has invited you to supper this evening, you and your companions.'

'And will you look after the house?' Philip asked.

'Oh Lord no.' Roheisia smiled with her mouth but her eyes took on a stubborn look. 'I have my own cottage in the village. When it gets dark, Crispin and I will be leaving but we'll be back at dawn.'

'Why?' Philip asked, walking towards her. 'Why don't you like to stay here?'

'Why, sir, I have my own house,' she flustered.

'And nothing else?' Philip asked. 'No other reason?'

'Oh, the house is fine, Father. Well, I have no concerns but it's the graveyard at night. I don't like to be near it. Ask the coffin woman.' Roheisia chewed the corner of her lip. 'In summer, when the sun sets and the bees and the butterflies fly, it's God's acre. However, in winter, when the mists seep in, I don't like it and I never shall.'

'Come, Roheisia.' Philip smiled. 'Surely you will tell me the legends?'

She lifted her hand. 'Father, if your clerk Adam has not returned, and he will do, because he can smell food from a mile away, then I'll tell you what I know. Now, unless you want your bread black and beef burnt . . .'

Roheisia almost ran down the stairs. Philip glanced at his companions.

'Well, let's unpack. It looks as if we are going to be entertained as well as fed.'

Adam Waldis, clerk to the parish of St Oswald's, stood in the ruins of the ancient Anglo-Saxon priory. Its buildings were only a shell: its walls crumbling, the small sanctuary, nave, dormitories and outhouses lay open to the sky and the elements. Waldis walked up to where the high altar had once stood. His heel caught in a cracked paving-stone and he looked down. He could make out the crumbling lettering over the brothers who had been buried there. He crouched down and wiped away the dust and spelt out the name 'Aylric Abbot'.

Waldis heard a sound and looked up but only a bird, nesting high in the wall, had perched on one of the window-ledges, sending down a small hail of pebbles and plaster. Adam got up, brushed his knees and stared up at the sky: darkness was falling and already the sea mist was making its presence felt, blotting out the setting sun. Adam closed his eyes. He'd been here many times, especially with his good friend Father Anthony until the priest had become distant, strange. Ever since, yes that night, Adam walked up into the sanctuary and gazed down at the loose tombstone. Father Anthony had moved this. Now Adam did. Pushing it aside he stared into the shallow grave below. The grave was a mystery to Adam. According to the ancient lettering, this had been one 'Alcuin Prior' and yet, Adam knelt by the grave, if that was the case, Alcuin appeared to have died a very violent death. Waldis picked up the whitening skull and turned it over. Someone had beaten Alcuin to death, shattering the bone at the back of the head. What was more interesting, there were no artefacts in the grave, no cross or rosary beads, nothing; as if the good monks had stripped Alcuin of every item of clothing and not even provided him with a shroud. Adam started as he heard the jingle of harness.

'Who's there?' he called.

The old ruin was filling with mist. Adam replaced the paving-stones, crossing himself against any ill-fortune. He went back into the nave, collected his cloak and staff and walked out of the old priory. He looked down the hill.

Despite the mist, he could still make out the lights of the village, the men coming home from the fields. Adam closed his eyes: the new priest would have arrived. He would certainly question Adam about Father Anthony but what could he say? Adam certainly did not want to share his secrets with anyone. He knew great treasure was buried somewhere in the vicinity of Scawsby and Adam intended to find it. He gripped his staff and, with one backward glance at the priory, took the path which wound down the hill through the woods towards the village.

Adam remembered what Father Anthony had told him, about a great treasure being taken across Kent by the Templars. How the king's men had caught up with them and killed each and every one of them but not before the Templars had taken refuge and hidden their gold. At the bottom of the hill, Adam paused and glanced back up towards the ruins. Father Anthony was sure the treasure was buried there. Indeed, hadn't Father Anthony discovered the remains of those poor Templar soldiers? The clerk narrowed his eyes but then jumped: the shifting mist parted. Adam was sure he glimpsed horsemen, cloaked and hooded, just clustered at the top of the hill. Adam controlled his shiver. He had heard the rumours: the French were at sea and, if the stories could be believed, were landing raiding parties along the Kent and Essex coasts. The French were striking inland, pillaging, raping, burning. Adam hastened on. The woods closed in about him. A chilling wind caught his hood and tugged at it like some mischievous imp. Adam stared into the trees on either side. The mist was wrapping itself around branch and trunk, creeping over the undergrowth. Now and again, crows raucously protested and the silence would also be shattered by the snap of twig as some fox, stoat or weasel hunted for its last meal before dusk. Ahead of him the mist was forming into a curtain, closing off the road.

'Spectamus te, semper spectamus te! We are watching you, we are always watching you!'

Adam froze, eyes starting out of his head. He glanced around. He was sure someone had whispered, someone behind him. Adam whirled round. There was nothing. He walked on, heart beating, mouth dry. He recalled Father Anthony. Hadn't the old priest complained about that? About whispers? About people watching him? Waldis heard the jingle of harness now quite distinct in the trees to his right. Adam broke into a run dropping his staff. If he could only reach the village, he'd throw himself into the taproom and let a bowl of wine wash away his fears. Adam sobbed as horsemen loomed out of the mist. Five, six, more, all blocking the road. He heard the clop of hooves behind him and turned. The horsemen were cloaked, their faces hidden deep in their cowls. Adam turned and fled; leaving the path, he entered the wood. He knew this would be safe. Horsemen couldn't ride so fast and he'd escape. He glanced to his left and right. The horsemen were moving through the trees with no difficulty at all. Adam kept on running, lungs fit to burst, heart thudding like a drum. He should have known his way. As a boy he'd played in these woods, he and Roheisia. He swerved, not caring whether he was going backwards or forwards, forgetting everything he had learnt. All he wanted to do was put as much distance between himself and these mysterious horsemen. He crossed another glade. The ground beneath him gave way. Horrorstruck, Waldis realised he had blundered into one of the woodland marshes. He tried to climb out but he was sinking fast. The line of horsemen grouped around him. Waldis stretched out his hands.

'Help me! For the love of God, help me!'

He sank into the marsh, spluttering and gasping. The horsemen remained impassive, as the parish clerk of St Oswald's choked slowly to death on the mud and slime of the marsh.

Chapter 3

Rockingham Manor house was a stately, luxurious building. About half a mile from the church, it nestled amongst the low-lying hills with woods behind. Within its walls were small orchards, gardens, stables and outhouses. A small village in itself, all serving the great manor house, built four storeys high with a grey and red brick base. The other storeys were of black beam and yellow plaster whilst the thatched roof had long been replaced with gleaming sheets of red and black slate. A testimony to its owner's wealth, the manor window frames were of gleaming wood and the glass was thick-leaded, stained and coloured so the windows caught the light. The house looked like a church, an impression helped by the imposing front door which Philip and his companions now approached along the white, pebble-dashed pathway. They had followed this from the manor gate, past the gardens and trees across a large lawn, with ornamental bowers and stew ponds, into the front of the house. Philip was surprised by how busy the manor was: horsemen coming and going, bailiffs and other officials gathered in the hallway. There were even men-at-arms carrying the gaudy pennants of the sheriff of Kent; these were now splattered with mud whilst the men looked tired and weary.

'It's the damn French!' Lord Montalt explained when they met him in the parlour.

He ushered them to chairs in front of a fire which roared merrily beneath the great mantelpiece.

'Bloody French!' Montalt repeated: he shook their hands, half listening to the introductions.

'I heard rumours,' Philip declared, taking his seat. He fought to hide his smile from this bluff, old soldier who was more concerned with fighting his ancient enemy than he was in welcoming his visitors.

Montalt went and stared out of the window.

'It will be dark soon,' he murmured, his white moustache seeming to bristle. He ran his hand over his hair which fell in iron-grey curls to the nape of his neck. Montalt was dressed simply in a lincoln-green tunic and hose, the woollen leggings pushed into short, leather boots. He kept hitching his great war belt strapped round his waist, tapping on the pommel of his sword. He turned and glanced at Philip, icy-blue eyes almost popping out of his head.

'We are in a bad state, priest. The old king's dead, the Black Prince is dead. King Richard is only a boy. We have been driven out of France and now the French want to follow us home.'

'Father, for goodness' sake, sit down!'

Philip turned as a young man entered the room. He had a long, thin, friendly face, clean-shaven and weather-beaten, under an unruly mop of brown hair. He was dressed very similarly to his father but Philip's attention was taken by the young woman who rested on his arm. The priest had a clear view of his vow of celibacy. He prayed, he fasted, he wanted to do God's work and knew he could never marry. However, the young woman was strikingly beautiful. She was dressed simply in a blue gown fringed at the neck and collar with white linen, her raven-black hair hidden under a white wimple. Her face, oval-shaped with a creamy complexion, was perfectly proportioned: her nose was small, her mouth full and merry whilst the eyes were sea-grey and full of life.

'This is my son Henry.' Lord Richard waved the young couple forward. 'And Isolda, daughter of one of my old war comrades, Henry's betrothed.' His smile disappeared. 'The French have landed on the Kentish coast,' Lord Richard continued abruptly. 'They are burning villages, the sheriff has called out the posse.'

The old manor lord walked back to the window, peering out, as if he dared the French to jump up from behind a bush. Henry and Isolda, fighting hard to control their laughter, introduced themselves to Philip and his two companions.

'He's an old war horse,' Henry whispered. 'He fought at Poitiers. So, for God's sake, don't mention that name to him, otherwise you won't get away before Easter.'

Philip smiled back. He found he couldn't stop looking at Lady Isolda. She was so beautiful, so good natured, with none of the simpering coyness or petty flirtatiousness he found in some attractive women. She began to imitate Lord Richard: Stephen put his face in his hands, Edmund just laughed.

'I know what you are doing, young lady.' Lord Richard came and sat down in the central chair, drumming his fingers on the arm-rest. 'I wish the bloody French would come here, to Rockingham or Scawsby!' He shook a fist. 'I'd show them cold steel. Like I did at Poitiers.' He looked at his three visitors. 'I was there, you know, on the right flank!'

'But, Father,' Henry intervened quickly. 'Our visitors have come to introduce themselves. They are our guests, they may have questions to ask.'

'Yes, yes, quite.' Sir Richard bawled at a servant to bring wine and sweetmeats. 'And speak we shall. But look, sirs.'

Lord Richard grabbed the tray of sweetmeats from the servant and began to arrange them on the table. 'This is the English line at Poitiers.' He popped one sweetmeat into his mouth. 'That's the Genoese, I've taken care of them. Now, I was over here on the right . . .'

Lord Richard, despite the protests of his son, launched into a detailed and elaborate description of the battle of Poitiers and how he had fought under the Black Prince. Henry raised his eyes heavenwards. Isolda folded her hands on her lap and sat as if fascinated. Every so often Lord Richard would break off to call her a minx. Outside darkness fell, servants came in to light torches as Lord Richard drew his account to a close, sipping at his wine cup, mournfully shaking his head. He then broke free of his reminiscences and apologised profusely for being so excited when his guests arrived. For a while he chatted to Edmund and Stephen. Philip, still fascinated by the Lady Isolda, soon realised she and Henry were deeply in love.

'So, what do you think?' Lord Richard turned to him.

'About the parish, my lord?'

'No, man, about the French! Do you think they'll ride inland?'

Philip made a face and shook his head. 'I am a priest, not a soldier, Lord Richard, but, yes, it's possible. The Kentish coast is flat, only round Scawsby do you get hills and valleys. If they seize horses and ride inland they would create havoc: they'd not necessarily return to the place where they landed but, perhaps, meet their ships further north.'

'Good man! Good man!' Sir Richard tapped his arm. 'We'll make a soldier of you yet.' He breathed out noisily. 'I've sent out scouts.'

Somewhere in the house a bell sounded.

'But, come, my seneschal declares the food is ready.'

Supper was taken in the great hall of the manor, finely furnished with the loot of war and the profits of the wool trade. Dark oaken panelling covered the walls; above these, hung gaily coloured banners depicting the Montalt arms as well as those they had married into. Lord Richard took his guests to a prepared table on the dais, a lavishly furnished alcove at the end of the hall. The heads of foxes, stags, deer, boar and other hunting trophies decorated the walls. The table was well furnished, dominated by a great silver salt cellar carved in the shape of a castle. The meal was exquisite, Lord Richard being a generous host: brawn soup, meat pastries, a haunch of venison and gaming birds stuffed with herbs. The wine flowed: Lord Richard did not return to the wars of France but sat quietly letting the others discuss local affairs and the gossip from London.

At first Philip thought the old man had either drunk too much or was still worried about the French. However, Lord Richard soon proved he was as cunning and as quick as a fox. At the end of the meal, he deftly arranged for Henry and Isolda to take Edmund and Stephen around the manor.

'Show them the scroll room,' he bellowed. 'Where my ancestors had their library. It's a fine place. You'll like it, Edmund, you too, Stephen. If you see anything you like, borrow it.'

However, as soon as the group had left the hall, his smile faded. He glanced at Philip now sitting on his right, pushed his chair away and turned to face the priest squarely.

'Talking of books, Father Philip. You know the old adage: never judge one by its cover? I may appear a bluff, old warrior, concerned about the French. I chattered like a buffoon because I did not want to alarm my son and my prospective daughter-in-law.' He smiled thinly. 'She is as

60

beautiful as she looks. A good woman, sharp-witted and blessed with common sense.'

'So, why did you chatter, my lord? Why didn't you want to worry them?'

'You are sharp too,' Lord Richard replied. 'I can see that. You've been down to the parish church.' He picked at his teeth. 'Dismal, isn't it? I can see why you want to build a new one.' Lord Richard paused. 'And you've talked to Roheisia: I mean about Father Anthony?'

'She told me a little: the priest was old, a scholar. He was deeply interested, if not fascinated, by the history of the village . . .'

'Ah yes, history. And the legends?'

'In the end she told me very little,' Philip replied.

'Well, let me tell you the truth.' Lord Montalt eased himself back in his chair. 'At least the truth as I have been told it in the history of my family. In the winter of 1308, the English king at the time, Edward II, issued an order that all Templars in his kingdom were to be arrested. He was forced to do this at the behest of his father-in-law Philip IV king of France. You know something about that?'

Philip nodded.

'Well, according to legend, a group of Templars fled from their church in London. A good baker's dozen they say, twelve or thirteen. They took with them the treasure of their Order: gold, silver, precious cups and plate. Now my ancestor at the time was, well to put it bluntly, a pirate and a smuggler; a man who feared neither God nor man. He was also a close friend of the local priest, Walter Romanel. Now, so tradition says, my ancestor discovered this treasure was crossing the wilds of Kent, not far from Scawsby: he and Vicar Romanel made a plot. Have you ridden round the district yet?'

Philip shook his head.

'In winter, the land can be treacherous, pathways can suddenly end, trackways lead into marsh. All the time there's the mist, boiling like the devil's stream, sweeping in so quickly that, even if you are born in these parts, you can soon get lost. Now, to cut a long story short, Romanel and my ancestor, God forgive him, organised a party of ruffians from the village. They played the old smugglers' trick, lighting torches, guiding the unwary off the trackways into the marsh.'

'But armed knights, warriors . . . ?'

'On a battlefield perhaps, Father Philip. However, stuck in a marsh with the mists swirling about, they would be easy victims, quickly brought down by a volley of arrows.' Lord Richard paused. 'God knows what happened,' he whispered. 'But the legend says these ruffians seized the treasure and brought it back. I think they began to use it. My grandfather bought more land, refurbished this house. Vicar Romanel began work on the church, he had the same ideas as you.'

'I am sorry,' Philip intervened. 'But how do you know all this?'

'Word of mouth from father to son. I mean, no one is going to be stupid enough to write down an account. You must remember that the king at the time, Edward II, was furious that he had lost such a great treasure. Royal commissioners came into Scawsby but they went away empty-handed.' Lord Richard drank from his wine cup, cradling the bowl between his fingers. 'The years passed. The villains must have thought, and I call them villains, that they would escape unscathed. However, according to the legend, Romanel began to talk of the Spectantes, the Watchers, and the whispering that can be heard in the graveyard and round the house. You have seen the inscriptions?'

'Aye, Lord Richard. The same phrase occurs time and time again: "WE ARE WATCHING YOU, WE ARE ALWAYS WATCHING YOU." There's also the eyes painted on the pillars. Anyway, what happened to your grandfather?'

'Something similar to Romanel. Lord George, my forebear, used to wake at night screaming and yelling. He talked of mailed horsemen out in the courtyard. One morning his bed was found empty. He was discovered in the orchard, lying there in his night shirt, dead of an apoplexy. Others say that, by the look of horror on his face, he had stared into the depths of Hell. Sometime later Romanel went mad. He was taken to St Bartholomew's in London where he died in a cell, screaming that they were still watching him.' Lord Richard put his wine cup down. 'Do you believe in ghosts, Father?'

'The Church teaches us about the Powers of darkness, Lord Richard.'

'But are these from Hell?' the manor lord replied. 'Let us say it is true that my grandfather and Vicar Romanel slaughtered innocent men, who were also priests and warriors of Christendom and did so to seize the Templar treasure.' Lord Richard waved a hand. 'Now these murderers came from Scawsby so the village should be cursed. But you've seen the place? The prosperous houses, the fertile fields; people are born, live, marry and die. They are happy, provided the bloody French don't return!'

'So, you are saying the place is not cursed?'

'I don't know. The church certainly is. Oh, I know why the priests don't stay. They can sense a presence. I suspect Father Anthony, as well as our ne'er-do-well clerk, Waldis, were looking for the gold. I wouldn't touch it for all the angels in heaven though I suspect it's buried in the old priory out at High Mount. It's the one place my grandfather and Romanel never approached, they stayed away from there as if it was cursed.' The old knight pulled his chair closer. 'Anyway, I've been thinking. Perhaps curses work in a different way. My grandfather was married to a beautiful, young heiress. She gave birth to my father and died within weeks. My own mother died the same way, as did my wife . . .'

Philip gripped his wine cup tighter. The hall didn't seem so merry now. The roaring fire lost some of its warmth.

'Can't you see, Father?' The old knight's eyes brimmed with tears. 'Are you going to tell me it's a coincidence that three times in successive generations in the Montalt line, a young wife dies immediately she gives birth? Can't you see what that portends for the future? Henry is handfast to Isolda.' His voice trembled. 'Is she going to be punished, Father? Is she going to die for a sin my grandfather committed?' The old man's head slumped. 'Now you know why,' he mumbled, 'I act the old war horse. I don't want to talk about these legends and curses in the presence of Henry or Isolda.' He raised his face. 'What can I do, Father?'

'How long have you known this?' Philip asked.

'Only recently. Only when I began to reflect. I also did a scrutiny of the villagers. Do you know, Father, in many ways Scawsby is a most fortunate place? Even the great plague hardly touched it whilst famine and murrain are strangers. We are well away from both highways and other towns so Scawsby survives. However, I went through the parish registers: there's a pattern I have described. A young man marries, his young wife gives birth and then dies. Father, I know women die in childbirth yet I wonder, I really do, if there is a curse on Scawsby. Not on the village, but on those particular families who were involved in that treacherous attack on the Templars and the theft of their gold.'

Philip stared round the hall. In his training as a priest he had attended the schools in Cambridge and, when studying Theology, Philip had taken more than a passing interest in Demonology, the involvement of Satan and his angels in the fall of man. Philip did not believe in the silly stories or old wives' tales. He took the cynical view that Satan and his legions worked in more subtle ways. Moreover, in this situation, who and where was the evil? The good Templars who had been plundered and destroyed, or the men who had carried out such a bloodthirsty assault? What if this was God's justice at work rather than any diabolical game?

'Isolda can't die,' Montalt grated. 'I am not an old man fuddled in my wits, Father; and, before you offer, I spoke to some of the other priests years ago: you can bless this house, Henry and Isolda until the crack of doom, it won't do any good.'

Philip leaned his arms on the table. 'If I go to the bishop,' he began slowly, 'he wouldn't believe it. Lord Richard, isn't there any clue? Any key to all this mystery?'

'Come, I'll show you.'

He almost dragged Philip by the arm and led him out of the hall. In the distance Philip could hear Stephen and the rest laughing and talking. Montalt lit a lantern and took the priest into the kitchen. He opened a small door at the far end.

'This leads to the cellars,' he declared. 'When Grandfather lost his wits, he used to hide here. He'd spend his day in a small chamber built in a cellar.'

He led Philip down the steps. The walls on either side were white-washed, the tunnel thin and narrow as a needle. Montalt opened the lantern and lit the sconce torches fixed high in the wall. Wheezing with exertion and muttering under his breath, the old soldier took his guest further down the passageway. He opened a door and they entered a mean, narrow cell. It had no windows and, when the torches were lit, all Philip saw was an old table, a chair and a battered chest. Cobwebs hung like drapes in the corners. Lord Richard took Philip across.

'Look at this, Father.'

Montalt held the torch up. Philip made out the scratches which were carved there. His blood ran cold. Whoever had drawn these was a tortured soul: they had been hacked into the plaster with a knife. 'George Montalt' was scrawled a number of times, as if the long-dead knight had been trying to remember his own name, as if he was clinging to the last vestiges of sanity. The other markings were disjointed: 'Spectantes, the Watchers', 'Jesus miserere', 'May Jesus have mercy on me.' Then the name 'Veronica' carved a number of times.

'Who was she?' Philip asked.

'I don't know,' Lord Richard replied. 'There's never been a woman in our family called Veronica. The only one I know is the saint who wiped Jesus' face as he made his way to Calvary.'

'These numbers?' Philip asked. 'Six and fourteen, quite distinct?'

Again Lord Richard shook his head. Philip grasped the lantern and studied the rest of the wall. His apprehension deepened as he made out the eyes, similar to the ones painted on the pillars of the church, and that phrase which now beat like a drum throughout this whole mystery: 'SPECTAMUS TE, SEMPER SPECTAMUS TE.'

'Does it mean anything to you, Father?'

Philip shook his head. 'Nothing at all. Lord Richard,

66

what was this treasure the Templars were supposed to be carrying?'

'Father, I can only guess, as can you: precious plates, gems, cups, a veritable king's fortune. If the old wives' tales are to be believed.'

'Now, here's a strange thing,' Philip declared, handing the lantern back. 'I know a little about the Templars. They were fighters, monks and priests. The allegations against them were spurious: they were accused of worshipping a disembodied head, practising sodomy and magical rituals. In truth, it was all a pack of lies put together by the Pope and others as an excuse to destroy the Order.'

Philip sat down on a chair as he tried to recall what he had read in the chronicles at Cambridge.

'Yes, that's right,' he continued. 'Their Grand Master at the time, Jacques de Molay, was burnt in front of Notre Dame. He publicly cursed the architects of his downfall: King Philip of France and Pope Clement V. As the fires were lit around him, de Molay summoned Philip and Clement to appear before God's tribunal within a year and a day of his own death.'

'And that happened?' Lord Richard asked.

'Oh yes. Both Clement and Philip died. A dreadful judgement must have befallen them.'

'But what has this got to do with the problem at Scawsby?'

Philip rubbed his face. He was tired after the wine. His mind was rather fuddled but he knew, deep in his heart, that if he wished to serve the people of Scawsby, he had to confront this silent, lurking menace.

'Lord Richard, I don't boast. I am a scholar as well as a priest. Aristotle teaches us that there must be a logic to everything.'

'But there's no logic to curses, to ghosts?'

'No.' Philip shook his head. 'That's what's missing from this, the logic of it all. Let us accept that the legend is fact: we have a group of Templars, guarding their treasure, fleeing through the wilds of Kent. They are ambushed and killed, their treasure is taken off them. Now the Templars' souls go before God. Oh yes, they died terrible deaths. They were murdered but, Lord Richard, not a day passes without good men being murdered. Moreover, the Templars died the way they wanted to, struggling to protect their Order, fighting against evil.'

'So, why the curse? Why did Romanel and Grandfather George go witless?'

Philip grasped the old man's hand and squeezed it. He had taken an immediate and very deep liking to this old manor lord, this bluff soldier who could face the French but was terrified that his beautiful daughter-in-law might die before her time.

'See this as a puzzle, Lord Richard,' Philip insisted. 'As I have said, every day good men and women, even children, are murdered for gold. Yet the kingdom is not full of ghosts striving for vengeance. No, on the night these Templars died, something else happened. What it was I don't know but it is something which must be put right.'

Lord Richard looked at this sharp-featured priest. He cupped Philip's face in his great hands. 'I'm glad you came here, Father,' he said softly. 'You believe me. You know there is something here which has to be confronted. I believe you are right.' He moved the lantern and put it on the table. 'Look at the table top.'

The priest did so. There were fresh carvings, the same word time and time again. REPARATION! REPARATION! REPARATION!

'Did he make reparation?' Philip asked.

'Oh yes,' Lord Richard replied. 'In the year before he died Grandfather drew up his will: there's nothing extraordinary in it except he left a rich bequest to the Hospitallers, another crusading order, to help them in their fight against the infidel. He also paid good silver to the priests throughout Kent to sing Masses for the souls of those he had wronged. He gave money to the poor . . .'

'But,' Philip intervened, 'apparently that was not enough. Is there anything else, Lord Richard?'

The old knight shook his head. 'Philip, you know as much as I do,' he replied. 'You see, my grandfather or old Romanel never wrote anything down. How could they? The king's commissioners came to Scawsby looking for the Templars' treasure. They went away empty-handed but can you imagine what would have happened if Grandfather and Romanel had been convicted of this offence? The Templars were a condemned order. All their property belonged to the Crown. Grandfather George would have faced charges of murder, robbery and treason. He would not only have lost his life but the Montalts would have forfeited everything to the Crown. Grandfather had to remain silent.'

'Lord Richard! Lord Richard!' Isolda called from the top of the cellar. 'For goodness' sake, what are you doing down there?'

'Showing our visitor my fine wines.' The old knight winked at Philip. 'We are coming up now.' He grasped Philip's shoulder. 'Solve this mystery,' he whispered. 'Save us all, Father, and I'll build as many churches as you want!'

Philip, Edmund and Stephen left a short while later. Darkness had fallen. They refused Lord Richard's offer to stay overnight but gratefully accepted his offer of two servants to go before them carrying torches. The night was cold but the sky was cloud-free and they soon found themselves back at the priest's house. Philip gave each of the torch-bearers a coin. They then led the horses to the back, put them in the stables and entered the house by the small postern door at the rear. Roheisia and her son had long gone. The fire in the kitchen had been banked down but the place was clean and swept, the table laid out for the morning meal.

'We'll not say a dawn Mass,' Philip declared. 'Let's wait till the men come in from the fields at mid-morning.' He tapped his brother on the shoulder. 'We'll concelebrate together.'

Philip sat down on a stool in front of the fire. Edmund murmured that he was tired. Philip just nodded. He was listening to the house, watching for any sign, any sound, but the place was silent, save for a creaking of timbers and the noise of Edmund dragging himself up the stairs, opening and closing the chamber door above. Stephen came and sat beside him.

'Do you think Lord Richard will support the new church?' the master mason asked.

'I think so. But, as you know, Stephen, there's a mystery here.'

'Legends,' the master mason scoffed. 'Old wives' tales. We come from the schools of Cambridge. Oh, I am not being a heretic. I believe in God, his angels and the kingdom of heaven but I have heard the stories about Templar treasure, there's nothing to it. What I am interested in is bricks and mortar, plans to build a new church. By all means look after your parishioners, humour Lord Richard but we should strike whilst the iron's hot. Tomorrow, Philip, let's go out to High Mount.'

'Are you sure you want to be here, Stephen?'

Stephen rubbed his hands together. 'Philip, you are my friend. Oh, I have worked as a master mason at Westminster, at Smithfield, in Cripplegate, but to build your own church!' Stephen got to his feet. 'That's the fulfilment of a dream.' He walked to the door, then came back. 'But a man has to live, Philip. Who will pay for the church?'

'I understand the parish has revenues,' Philip replied. 'But Lord Richard is a generous lord: the stone can be cut locally and Scawsby is not short of labourers.'

'Then it's time we began. Good night, Philip.'

Stephen clapped his friend on the shoulder and went up to his chamber. For a while Philip just sat staring into the dying embers of the fire. It had been an eventful day but he kept remembering two faces: the agony in Lord Richard's, and Isolda's merry-eyed looks. He got up and walked to the front door. He paused with his hand on the latch and went out, bracing himself against the night air. Philip walked through the small side gate and into the cemetery. It was bitterly cold: the branches of the yew trees moved slowly in the night wind. The silence was deathly. Philip stared around. In the faint moonlight he could make out the crosses and headstones towering against the dark mass of the church. He was about to turn away when he heard the first whisper, like a breeze carrying the words of someone far away. Philip paused, clenching his hands. He'd heard the words, 'Spectamus, We are watching', but was that his imagination? He glared towards the church as if the building was responsible for these fears, these nightmares. He was about to turn away when he saw the glow of light from a window: someone was inside the nave, moving about with a torch or lantern. Philip thought of calling for Edmund or Stephen but, feeling slightly ridiculous, he walked across to the church, took the key from his pouch and opened the

71

corpse door at the side. Philip fought against the sense of dread, of dark foreboding. Once inside he could see no light, no torch, no lantern. Narrowing his eyes, he could make out the pillars, the dark mass of the rood screen and the great oblong shape of the Montalt tomb. Richard took a few steps forward: the sound was like someone clapping. He stared through the rood screen, glimpsed the red sanctuary light and took comfort from it. He remembered the opening verse of Vespers: 'Oh God, come to my aid. Lord make haste to help me!' He repeated the words as he walked towards the sanctuary but froze as he heard a voice whisper back: 'I will go unto the altar of god, the God who gives joy to my youth.' Philip spun round, his hand going to the small dagger he kept in the sheath of his belt.

'Who's there?' he shouted. 'This is God's house! In the name of the Lord Jesus . . . !'

'Spectamus te! Semper spectamus te!'

'Aye!' Philip screamed back. 'And I am watching you! I, Philip, priest of this church!'

Something was moving at the bottom of the church. Philip drew his knife and ran towards the main door but there was nothing. He heard a sound behind him. He spun round, moaned in terror and dropped the knife. Eyes, like burning coals, glared at him through the darkness.

Words between the pilgrims

'Heavens above!' Mine Host exclaimed. 'Sir Priest, you tell a frightening tale!'

'Is it true?' The Summoner edged nearer the fire, glancing fearfully over his shoulder as if he expected some sprite or goblin to jump through the door of the ruined church.

'Pilate asked: "What is truth?"' the Poor Priest declared. 'He did not receive an answer but Christ said he was the Truth, so I leave that matter to him.'

'But ghosts?' the Pardoner mocked. 'Do you really believe in ghosts?'

'I believe in ghosts,' the Wife of Bath spoke up from where she sat on the cushions on the far side of the fire, her great cloak pulled around her. 'In my pilgrimage to Cologne, I and my companions,' she simpered, 'had to take refuge in a castle high in the mountains: Falkenstein Castle. Yes, that's what it was called.'

'I have been there,' Sir Godfrey intervened. 'When I fought with the Teutonic knights in Prussia.'

'In which case, sir, you know my story,' the Wife of Bath retorted. 'A dreadful place.' She continued in a hoarse whisper, 'The good Count allowed us to sleep in the hall. He told us that, once the doors were locked and barred, we were to ignore anything we heard or saw.'

'And what did you see?' the Summoner joked.

He stood up, clawing at his codpiece. He rearranged his cloak on the ground but, in doing so, made an obscene gesture in the direction of the Wife of Bath.

'Don't you get filthy with me!' she screeched, half rising to her feet. 'I knocked three husbands flat on their backs. I'll do the same to you!'

'Come, come!' Mine Host intervened. 'We were talking about ghosts!'

'A terrible night,' the Wife of Bath continued, glaring across at the Summoner. 'Roaring all around us! Strange lights could be seen through the windows! Knocking on the door! Running footsteps and dragging chains! In the morning we asked our host what was the matter: he took us up into the tower. It was summer but, I tell you this, good sirs and ladies, that place was the coldest on God's earth. At the top of the tower was a chamber, all bare and white-washed, its floorboards painted black. In the centre of the room was a four-poster bed with a large tester, a canopy stretching up to the ceiling. One of our party lay on the bed and the Count then showed us how, if he pulled a secret lever, a swinging axe would come down over the bed and slice whoever slept on it. Then he pulled another lever, hidden behind the arras, and trapdoors opened on either side of the bed.'

'Oh heaven save us!' Dame Eglantine the Prioress broke in. 'So, if you weren't cut to ribbons on the bed, you fell to your death in the oubliette?'

'Oh yes,' the Wife of Bath replied. 'A horrifying death. The Count explained how one of his ancestors used to butcher pilgrims who dared to stay at the castle. The terrible noises we heard were their ghosts who, at night, wailed through the castle looking for vengeance.'

The Wife of Bath would have continued but Sir Godfrey grabbed her wrist. She looked across to where the Poor

Priest was standing, staring into the darkness, as if he had seen something and had forgotten all about them.

'Do you think this is true?' she whispered.

'Good mistress, I think it is. I know Scawsby and I have met the Montalt family on many occasions.'

'Hush now!' The Ploughman, who had overheard them, lifted a hand. 'Sir Godfrey, let my brother finish his tale.'

'It's true,' the Cook spoke up.

Everyone looked at him. Usually the Cook was one of their more boisterous colleagues, ready to joke and parry with Mine Host or the Miller. However, since they had arrived at the church, he had become cowed. Indeed, he spent most of his time peering at the Poor Priest and his brother as if he couldn't decide whether he recognised them or not.

'It's true,' he repeated.

The Poor Priest abruptly broke from his reverie. He glanced at the Cook who now sat feverishly scratching the sore on his leg.

'Yes,' he declared. 'I am, sir, who you think I am. Nevertheless, hold your peace and let me continue.'

PART II

Chapter 1

The next morning, although Edmund and Stephen were up eager to start the day, Philip was dull-eyed and heavy-headed. He had fled from the church the night before and felt he could not share his experiences with his companions. He could not decide whether he had been tired or had drunk too much wine. Or was his soul now stuffed full of ancient legends and mysterious curses? Philip found it difficult to return to the church but, when he did so at mid-morning, he found it dull and cold, dark and dank. However, he was soon distracted by the parishioners who clustered through the rood screen and around the altar whilst he celebrated the Mass of the day. Edmund, who had celebrated a dawn Mass in the Lady Chapel, officiated as his server. Afterwards a few of the old parishioners remained to shake his hand and welcome him into the parish. Philip smiled at them but his eyes kept going to the back of the church, where the coffin woman crouched near the baptismal font. One of the parishioners, Simon the blacksmith, followed his gaze.

'Oh, don't worry about her, Father,' he declared. 'She always likes to sit at the foot of the pillar. We always invite her to join us but it's of little use.'

Philip thanked him and went into the small sacristy where he divested and hung up his vestments. Edmund caught his sour glance.

'It's untidy,' Edmund explained, gesturing at the albs, amices and other priestly vestments which lay about the room whilst half-burnt candlesticks littered the table.

'I thought we had a parish clerk!' Philip snapped.

'So did I.' Edmund smiled back. 'But Adam Waldis seems to have disappeared like the mist. Roheisia and Crispin knocked at his door this morning but his house was all shuttered up.'

Philip closed his eyes and breathed in slowly. Wasn't anything going to go right here? he thought. He told Edmund to stay and tidy up and went across to the priest's house. The day was a fine one and a strong sun in a clear blue sky had burnt off the frost. Even the graveyard looked pleasant and, in the soft breeze, Philip caught the first fragrance of spring. Roheisia was waiting for him. She had been busy at the ovens and the air was fragrant with the odour of meats and bread. She now bustled around the kitchen as busy as a bee whilst her son Crispin sat humming in the ingle-nook, mending battered, leather reins. Philip sat down and broke his fast on watered ale and a fresh meat pie.

'And Waldis hasn't arrived yet?' he asked.

'No,' Stephen declared, coming in, his cloak around him.

The master mason sat down opposite. He pushed his blond hair away from his face which looked flushed and excited.

'You are really pleased to be here, aren't you?' Philip asked.

'Of course!' Stephen smiled. 'You are going out to High Mount with us?'

Philip shook his head. Stephen's smile faded.

'Stephen! Stephen!' Philip exclaimed. 'There's a lot to do here!'

'But you need to see the new site,' Stephen insisted.

'Let Edmund go with you.'

Stephen was going to argue the point when there was a knock on the door. Roheisia answered it and a young man, thin and wiry, dressed in a green tunic and brown leggings, sauntered into the kitchen. He carried a bow with a quiver of arrows across his back: a dagger was stuck into his belt. He came up and extended his hand.

'Piers Bramhall.' He scratched nervously at the scrawny moustache which covered his upper lip. 'I am verderer of the manor. Sir Richard sent me down. I am to be your guide.'

'That was kind of Sir Richard.' Philip rose and clasped the stranger's hands.

'I am also here to protect you,' Piers confessed, plucking at the bow string. 'It's a fine day but, if you stay out late and the mists seep in, it is easy to get lost. And, of course, there's the French . . .'

'Is Sir Richard still receiving reports?' Stephen asked anxiously.

'Oh yes, all the coastal towns and villages are on a war footing. Sir Richard maintains that if the bastards steal horses, they may well ride further inland.'

Stephen drew the verderer into a detailed conversation about High Mount. Philip sat half listening, picking at the food on the pewter plate. Edmund came in. He, too, broke his fast and then, amid shouts and farewells, all three left. Philip sat moodily at the table. Now and again he caught Roheisia glancing furtively at him but he refused to be drawn, deciding that he would be most discreet in what he said.

Philip yawned. He felt tired. Last night was a nightmare

and, in his soul, Philip realised that what confronted him at Scawsby was something he had never prepared for. He saw himself as a priest. Now, he quietly conceded that he was arrogant, patronising to those he was supposed to serve. He had always tried to improve himself. He wished he could pray more fervently, that he had a deeper faith, that he could be a true shepherd and not a wolf. Now, in the presence of evil, of real wickedness, he understood why other priests had simply walked away. Philip closed his eyes and remembered his mother: she had been so proud of her two sons. When they had stood, either side of her death bed, she had grasped the hand of each of them.

'Be good priests,' she whispered. 'Do not lose faith in God and he will not lose faith in you.'

'Father, are you well?'

Philip opened his eyes. Roheisia was staring at him.

'Oh, it's nothing.' He shook his head. 'I just wish Waldis was here.' He tried hard not to sound petulant. 'I mean, he is our parish clerk.'

'Never been the same since he worked so closely with Father Anthony,' Roheisia retorted.

Philip, not wishing to be drawn into conversation about such matters, got to his feet.

'I'll be in my chamber, Roheisia. I didn't sleep too well last night.'

As soon as he was back in his own room, Philip immediately began to sift through Father Anthony's papers and books. He found the calfskin ledger specially made by a stationer in Norwich. This was the parish journal, kept by the vicar and handed over to the bishop or his officers whenever a visitation was made. It stretched back over a hundred years and Philip immediately leafed to the section filled in by Romanel. The ink was faded but the hand was firm, the writing cursive and elegant. Most of the items were of little importance: births, deaths, marriages, the failure of corn. Romanel bemoaned his lack of income but then, abruptly in the spring of 1309, the writing became more feverish; the script less delicate, letters unformed, words not finished. Philip, fascinated, watched this slow disintegration of a soul. Romanel was clearly agitated, trying to hide something, torn between a desire for secrecy and a wish to confess. Most of the entries were mundane but then they'd break off, slip into phrases, expressions which made no sense: THE EYES ARE WATCHING. *They are always there. Montalt's no help, the demons chase me.* Then a misquotation from the Book of Ecclesiastes: *Some spirits there are who are bent on vengeance and lay on with furious strikes.* This was followed by a paragraph from the prophet Isaiah: *In the ruins of Babylon, demons dwell.* Philip turned the pages over. Now there were gaps as if Romanel hadn't even bothered to write. However, under the year 1312, Philip read: *On this day was buried Lord George Montalt, he asked to be buried in sight of the altar but this will not save him from the demons of hell. He died without God and without God he will remain.* A few lines later: *The Watchers are back! I hear their whispers on the breeze and, when I look out of my casement window, I see them, hands stretched out. Perhaps I should kill her? Perhaps she should die too? Ah Veronica, who wiped the face of Jesus, wipe my soul of sin. Reparation, reparation but what reparation?* And, finally: *Montalt is gone. The treasure is gone with him. I should be gone too, deep into the madness of hell.*

For a while Philip just sat. There were no more entries but, those he had read, what did they mean? He understood about the watchers and the whispers. He had witnessed these himself. But who was Veronica? And who was the woman Romanel wished he might kill? He turned to the front of the ledger. Romanel had sketched a drawing of the old Saxon ruins at High Mount. Philip could make out the shape of a priory but what fascinated him were the crude drawings of coffins which filled the sketch. Each was carefully numbered. Philip turned to the back of the ledger, leafing through the pages since 1312. Sometimes the entries were short and ordinary but, now and again, Philip sensed the fear of some of the priests who had stayed too long.

'This is a terrible place,' one of them had written. 'The very gate of hell.'

'Something is wrong here,' another had inscribed. 'There is a lingering sense of evil, of wickedness, yet the people are good. The lord of the manor is kind and generous but, here in the church and in the house and the cemetery beyond, something is very wrong. Should it be exorcised?'

After that Philip found nothing until he came to a vicar called Father Norbert. He had only stayed fourteen months. He had made the usual entries about parish life but, now and again, there were slips: 'Last night was fearsome, why do I feel as if I am always being watched? Should there be an exorcism?' Then this priest's last entry: 'Yesterday afternoon I began an exorcism, too frightening, too dangerous to continue. I have asked his Lordship to be moved. I am a sick man, I am a priest not a wonder worker.'

At last Philip came to the tenure of Father Anthony Holness, the previous incumbent of the parish. Once again the ledger began with the usual parish events. Philip leafed through the pages. So ordinary were the entries that he got the impression that Father Anthony knew about the mystery but remained so long because he turned a blind eye to it. Only now and again was there a sign of what was coming, as the deceased priest mentioned, time and again, his growing friendship with the parish clerk Adam Waldis. Philip looked up.

'And I wonder where he is?' he whispered.

He returned to the ledger: an abrupt change occurred just after Easter two years ago. Father Anthony described a visit to High Mount accompanied by Waldis. He wrote excitedly about the legends and the possibility of hidden treasure. He, too, copying Romanel, had drawn a plan of the old Saxon priory at High Mount, marking with crosses the site of graves in the nave and sanctuary. There was an elliptical entry about something they had found: bones where they are not supposed to be. Philip noted references to 'Veronica?' '6?' 'And 14?' 'Letters of the alphabet?' 'Treasure in High Mount?' Then there was a gap for about three months. By mid-summer, however, Father Anthony was making further entries but the handwriting had changed: shaky, sometimes illegible, sentences not completed. In the margin of the ledger, the dead priest had copied out the eyes inscribed in the church. Father Anthony seemed fascinated by these: 'What are they watching?' 'Where are they looking?' 'Are they guarding something?' Father Anthony's disintegration became more apparent as he referred to the Watchers, to the whispers and the nightmares he was suffering. All entries ceased about six months before his death. Philip looked down at the blank page. He just wished Waldis was here. He could tell him more surely?

Philip then turned to the Blood Book. Most parishes kept such a record to indicate lines of consanguinity and affinity, so a priest could agree to a marriage provided the young man and young woman were not within the forbidden degrees of relationship. The Blood Book also contained the dates of births, deaths and burials. Some of these registers were kept meticulously depending on the priest. Philip found St

Oswald's no different. If the priest was of a clerkly mind and hand, the entries were full and carefully written. Sometimes there were gaps. He turned to the section by Romanel. Philip noticed nothing untoward except in the spring of 1309 where the vicar had written 'mortuus' beside certain entries. Against another, 'Corpus non inventur, body not found'. Philip recalled his conversation with Lord Richard the previous day, about the curse affecting certain families in the village. Due to the haphazard nature of the entries, Philip was unable to trace any pattern except in two families where, generation after generation, the young wife died after childbirth. He noticed that one of these was Bramhall, the verderer's family.

Philip put down the Blood Book and listened. The house was very silent. He went to the door and called for Roheisia but there was no answer. Philip remembered that she had mentioned something about going to the small market in the village. He closed the door and listened to the sounds of the house creaking around him.

'I should really go,' he murmured. 'To High Mount. Stephen and Edmund will be waiting for me.'

He felt tired, still confused; he seized a quill, took a piece of parchment and began to write down what he had learnt.

Item – In the winter of 1308, a group of Templars, fleeing from their church in London, and probably carrying treasure, had been ambushed and killed out on the marshes. Their assailants were from Scawsby led by Sir George Montalt and the priest Romanel.

Item – All the Templars had been killed but where were their bodies buried? More importantly, where was the treasure? What did the inscription on the tomb mean? UNDER THE HIGH MOUNTAIN LIES THE TREASURE OF THE SON OF DAVID. Was that a reference to Solomon and that the treasure came from the Temple in Jerusalem? Did the high mountain refer to the old Saxon priory? Was that why Romanel and Father Anthony had been drawn to these ruins? Why Romanel never went out there, as he regarded the place as cursed? Was the Templar treasure buried there?

Item – Who were the watchers, the 'Spectantes'? Why the eyes? Was this a reference to the Ghosts?

Item – What did the name Veronica mean? Or the numbers 6 and 14? And why did Sir George Montalt talk of reparation? Reparation for the murder and the theft? And the Blood Book? Why the question mark against the word 'Mortuus' – dead? And, 'Body not found'?

Item – If there was a curse on Scawsby why did it appear, at least on the surface, a happy and prosperous place? Or did the curse and the haunting only affect those who had either a hand in the slaughter of the Templars or, like Father Anthony, tried to discover the secret behind it?

Philip yawned, put his pen down and went to lie down on the bed. He stared up at the thick cloth canopy stretched between the four posts, studying the faint emblems there: a cross, a unicorn. He rolled over and drifted into sleep. When he awoke, he felt dreadfully cold, as if someone had opened a window, and the room smelt like a midden-heap, rank rot and corruption fouling the air. Philip pulled back the curtain on the bed: a hooded figure, a horrid spectre, stood there.

Philip stifled a cry as the cowl fell back revealing a face white as snow, a balding head, eyes, upturned at the corners, black as night, thin lips curled in a sneer.

'Kill her!' A claw-like hand jabbed the air. 'Kill her!'

Philip broke from his reverie and screamed, lashing out with the bolster he plucked up from behind him. He heard sounds in the passageway outside.

'Father Philip! Father Philip!'

He hurried to the door and threw it open: Roheisia, cloak still about her, stood there.

'Father, are you all right? Your face, are you sick?'

Philip let go of the door. He turned slowly, as if the phantasm might still be there waiting, those lips hissing their command, yet there was nothing: only the bolster he had hurled, lying against the wall. He ran a hand through his hair.

'Roheisia, I am sorry, I had a bad dream, a nightmare. I'm tired.'

Roheisia offered him some food but Philip shook his head. He thanked her and, when she had gone, walked across to the lavarium to splash water over his face. Was it a nightmare? A dream? He went and studied the small table which stood beside his bed. It was covered with a veneer of dust. Roheisia had promised a proper clean of their chambers would take place once they had unpacked. Philip's mouth went dry; there was an imprint of a hand, the palm small, the fingers long. He placed his own hand down and realised it wasn't his imprint. Seizing his cloak Philip went downstairs. The afternoon was becoming grey, a weak sun setting. Philip walked out into the cemetery. There was a mist seeping in. Philip shivered but, his mind set, he walked through the trees to where he thought the coffin woman had her hut. He found her, a piece of embroidery on her lap, sitting on a stool outside: she didn't even glance up at his approach.

'Are you well, Father Philip?'

She lifted her head and smiled. Philip could detect no malice.

'I've come to talk to you.'

'Talk is cheap,' she replied.

She carried on with her stitching, a piece of snow-white linen. Philip was surprised at how clean it was.

'What are you doing?'

'Making my own shroud.'

'Do you expect to die?'

'Why, Father, don't you?'

Philip grinned and crouched down beside her.

'I make my own shroud and I say my prayers,' she declared.

'What do you pray about?'

The corpse woman paused, needle held up. 'For salvation, Father: that my life in heaven will be happier than that on earth.'

'Have you ever married? Look.' Philip brushed the back of her hand. 'You are a human being, a woman, a member of my parish, a sister in Christ. I can't keep calling you the coffin woman. What did Romanel call you?'

'He called me Priscilla.'

'Priscilla, why Priscilla?' Philip exclaimed.

'I asked him that once. You know that malicious way of his?'

Philip withdrew his hand, the coffin woman flinched.

'What do you mean?' Philip snapped. 'How could I possibly know a man who has been dead over seventy years? You know I've had a vision, don't you?'

The old woman sighed. She pulled the linen up into a bundle onto her lap. She leaned closer. She smelt sweet, of lavender and other herbs, and Philip noticed how clean her fingers and nails were.

'They've all seen it.'

'Seen what?' Philip replied evasively.

Priscilla stretched forward and touched him on the tip of his nose.

'I like you,' she declared. 'You talk to me. You don't call me a dirty, old hag and throw me your scraps. Or look at me

as if I am a witch ripe for the stake. Priscilla,' she repeated.
'It's a Roman name, isn't it?'

'Who was your mother?' Philip asked.

'God rest her, I never knew. Some local girl. I can't
remember. Romanel never told me.'

'And your childhood?'

She closed her eyes. 'I remember being here,' she said. 'I
always remember Romanel but sometimes, sometimes . . .'

'Sometimes what?' Philip asked.

'Sometimes there are other,' she tapped the side of her
head, 'other pictures.'

'Do you know where your mother's buried?' Philip asked.

'Yes, come with me.'

She put the piece of linen down on the stool and, without
waiting, walked into the trees, gesturing for the priest to
follow. He did so. They entered the cemetery. She stopped
for a moment, fingers to her lips. She went across to a
gnarled yew tree.

'Romanel told me she's buried beneath here. This is where
I come to pray.'

'Did anyone in the village talk to you about her?' Philip
asked.

A shake of the head. 'I leaves them alone, they leaves
me alone.'

'And your father, the priest Romanel?'

'Came out of hell and went back to hell, Father. He
should never have been a priest. A man of great lechery,
hand in glove with the old lord he was. They did everything
together: hunt the deer, carouse and drink till the early light.
Romanel was good to me.' She walked towards the corpse
door of the church. 'He was always good, Father. I mean,
he bought me dresses and taught me. But . . .'

'But what?'

'Sometimes I'd just catch him watching me. You know, like a cat does a mouse or a bird.'

'The treasure?' Philip intervened. 'Did your father ever tell you about the treasure?'

'Oh, there were rumours.' The old woman rubbed her face. 'There were rumours that he had done something terrible. I can't remember what. Indeed, I can't remember much, Father. You talked about the village. I remember, after Romanel had died, I went down to the tavern, one of the few occasions I did. It was very hot and I was thirsty. There was no fresh water so I wanted a pottle of ale to wet my lips and slake my throat. I went into the tavern, just within the doorway. They didn't really like me there. Well, I asked for my pottle of ale. I thought I'd a penny but I hadn't so the landlord told me to go away.' The coffin woman looked up at the sky. 'That's it.' She whispered, 'A kind man, long dead now. He bought me a tankard of ale. Told me to sit on a bench outside and watched me sup it. He asked me questions. Simple ones about the weather, how I was feeling? I hurried my ale because I was getting frightened but, just before I left, the kindly man, he took my hand.' She closed her eyes. 'One of the few times any one really touched me.' She opened her eyes. 'I am a virgin, you know, Father: born a maid, I'll die a maid.'

'What did the man say?' Philip asked curiously.

'He just said it was pleasant to hear me talk as, when I was small, when he first met me, I never said a word!'

Philip smiled and realised the old woman was beginning to ramble. She stretched out and grasped his wrist, her nails digging deeply into the skin.

'I'm not witless, Father. I'm not witless. I just thought it was strange that people can remember times whilst I cannot.'

'The treasure?' Philip asked.

'Oh yes, as I was saying, the treasure. There were rumours. I once asked my father. He just laughed but, as his mind slid into madness, he always laughed. One day he was sitting on the steps of the church. His face was grey. His eyes, well, he looked as if he hadn't slept for years. He was muttering to himself. I asked him what was the matter? He replied, "If they only knew what the treasure really was!" That's all I know, Father. But come, I wish to show you something.'

She led him through the door of the church along the dank, middle aisle past the Montalt tomb and into the Lady Chapel. She lit a taper from a candle and, beckoning Philip, went up to the left side of the statue of the Virgin. She crouched down, holding the flame against the wall.

'Look, Father, can you see something?'

Philip, crouching beside her, studied the wall carefully. There was a faded painting, a crucifix surrounded by people, faces lifted, hands outstretched in supplication towards it.

'Study each of them, Father.'

Philip did so. He gasped, almost knocking her aside as he pointed to one face.

'Romanel!' he exclaimed. 'That's Romanel!'

'How do you know, Father? How could you possibly know a man who has been dead for over seventy years?'

Philip got to his feet and walked out of the Lady Chapel.

'You've had a dream, haven't you?' She followed him.

'Yes,' he replied. 'I had a dream: Romanel's face looked ghastly and he was whispering at me, "Kill her! Kill her!"'

'Kill whom?'

Philip turned round but the coffin woman had gone.

Chapter 2

Philip arrived at High Mount just before dusk. His journey through the woods from Scawsby had been uneventful. The priest was lost in his own thoughts, wondering how to cope with the difficulties facing him. As the trackway left the trees, Philip, once again, appreciated Stephen's good judgement. True, there was a distance between the village and High Mount but Scawsby was so prosperous it would eventually break out of its confines whilst the new church would have plenty of room to expand and develop. Parishioners would have to travel a little further but this was no bad thing. Father Philip had talked to Diocesan officials and his own bishop about his dream; they had concurred. There was a growing apprehension that if a church was part of the village, its buildings and cemetery might be used contrary to the rite of consecration. Philip had seen this happen in other towns and villages in Kent: the church was often regarded as the personal property of the powerful burgesses. Markets were held in the cemetery, church sales in the nave, whilst the porch could be turned into a tavern where people gathered to claque and gossip.

Philip reined in his horse at the bottom of the hill and looked up. Not too steep, he thought, and it would give the church a certain prominence. He looked up at the sky. Already the evening star could be seen and the faint outlines of the moon. It had grown much colder. Philip urged his horse on up the narrow trackway. On either side he passed remnants of the old priory, the ruins of what must have been outhouses. He heard voices from the top of the hill. When he reached there, Edmund and Stephen, faces flushed, came running towards him like two boys. Piers the verderer was crouching against the wall as if seeking protection against the cold breeze.

'Well, Brother?' Edmund, cloak off, tunic hitched, sleeves rolled up, stood before him, hands on hips. 'What do you think?'

'It's going to be a splendid church,' Stephen broke in. 'We'll build along the outlines of the old walls.'

Philip smiled in reply. He had been here on previous occasions when he visited Scawsby. Then he had just seen High Mount as a good place to build his new church, an old ruin which would soon disappear. Now, knowing what he did, this derelict priory with its crumbling walls, desolate sanctuary, and, above all, those grave slabs laid out before him, assumed a sinister, eerie atmosphere.

'What happened here?' he asked.

Edmund's smile faded. Philip looked pale and drawn, dark rings under his eyes.

'We expected you sooner,' Edmund replied. 'But all we've done is walk around, measure the width and length and try to draw Piers into conversation. However, he's not as friendly as he was this morning.'

'I heard that.' The verderer got to his feet. He walked over using his long bow as a staff. 'I don't like it here,' he declared. 'There is something about this place, it's cold and empty.'

'What happened?' Philip repeated. 'No, I don't mean

what have you been doing?' He dismounted and hobbled his horse. 'What happened to the priory?'

'It's an ancient place,' Piers broke in. 'Founded after the legions left, or so one of the priests told us. The Norsemen sacked it long before the Conqueror came to this country. It was a ruin then, it's been a ruin since.'

'And these graves?' Philip asked.

'Oh, they house brothers of the priory,' Stephen replied. He gazed up at the sky. 'I think I'll stay out here tonight.'

'No you won't!' Philip snapped. He forced a smile. 'I don't think you should stay here.' He winked at Edmund. 'I have something to tell you tonight when we sup.' He recalled the entry in the parish journal about bones being found. 'Is there a ditch here? A pit?'

Stephen pulled a face.

'There's the well,' Piers broke in. He pointed to the far end of the priory. 'It's there, behind the chancel wall: a deep well.'

Philip gazed around.

'How do you see it, Stephen?' he asked. 'How do you see our new church?'

'Well, the hill is not steep,' Stephen replied. 'And there's a broad enough plateau. I think the church and cemetery should be built here on the top: the rest of the hill being used, in time, as a further place of burial. The priest's house could be built either at the foot of the hill or, if there's room, here, linked to the church through the sacristy.'

'I wonder if it should be built here?' Philip murmured.

'What?'

Philip felt himself spun around. Stephen was glaring at him, he had never seen the mason so angry.

'You might not build it here? What do you mean?'

'Stephen, Stephen.' Philip put his hand on his shoulder. 'I have doubts about this place.'

'But you haven't seen my plans.' Stephen was still glaring at him. 'You asked me a question and I am replying. There's more than one scheme that can work. We can have the church on the top of the hill and the cemetery below. Lord Richard has promised High Mount and the fields around.'

'Yes, yes, I know,' Philip replied wearily. 'It's called a Deodandum: a gift to God. But, if we are going to build a church here, we must make sure it is right.'

Stephen slunk away. Philip, now intent on finding out about the well, walked through the ruins. He turned at the entrance to the sanctuary and looked back down at the nave. Stephen was now whispering to Edmund. Piers, bored, was shuffling the arrows in his quiver. Philip sighed. Sweet Lord, he prayed, let me keep my temper. He paused. Was this what happened to the other priests? he wondered. Tempers becoming frayed? Harsh words, a growing sense of unease?

'Come on!' he called. 'Come on, Stephen, you'll have your church here. Let's see this well!'

He went out through a gap in the wall and flinched at the cold breeze which caught him. He walked across to the edge of the hill: the mist was creeping in but something caught his eye: a smudge of smoke against the horizon, black and thick.

'What's that?' he called out and pointed.

Piers came up, narrowing his eyes. 'There's no place there, Father,' he declared. 'Only some outlying farms. Perhaps they are burning the fields?' The verderer moved restlessly. 'But it's getting dark, here's the well, Father.'

It lay to the other side of the church. The brick wall around it was crumbling the brick and the peat-wooden roof had long gone; only a battered upright remained. Philip crouched and stared down the well but he could see nothing. He took a pebble, threw it and heard a splash.

'Has anyone ever been down?' he asked.

Piers pointed to the steps built into the wall, thickly covered with moss and lichen.

'It's possible,' he declared. 'But it could be dangerous.'

'I'm going down,' Philip retorted.

'What?' His brother caught his sleeve. 'Philip, are you mad?'

'I want to go down now.'

Philip took off his cloak and, despite the protests of his companions, lowered himself into the well. He found the steps deeply cut but the slippery moss was dangerous. Philip moved slowly, marvelling at the skill of the mason who had dug these ancient steps.

'It's quite safe.' He called out, his voice echoing round the walls. 'The stone is very firm. The well can be used again.' He glanced up at the three faces peering down at him. 'Don't worry, Edmund,' he joked. 'If I slip, you will be parish priest.'

He went further down, keeping his mind on the task, feeling for each foothold before he moved. On one occasion his boot slipped and Philip cursed his own stupidity but he wanted to see what lay at the bottom. If he stopped to think, he would never find out. He continued on down, the rim of the well above him growing smaller, the faces of his companions indistinct. Philip paused and sniffed. The air was remarkably fresh, which meant the well must be built over some underground spring, the water flowing in and out. At last he reached the bottom. There was a ledge about a foot wide and he carefully stepped on to this. It was dark but, by scrabbling around, he could feel the water beneath him. On either side of the well, two culverts allowed the water to run in and out. He moved round the well, counting as he did so, he did not want to forget where the steps were.

'If anything happens,' he whispered, 'it's not too deep: a rope and a horse can pull me out.'

His foot hit something which fell into the water: his boot touched something else, he felt it break under him. A branch? Philip crouched down, hand out. His fingers caught something, round and smooth with holes. Philip, keeping his back against the wall, picked it up. At first he thought it was a stone but it was too thin, then he realised. It was a human skull and what he was standing on were other bones. He fought hard to control his panic. He opened his tunic, put the skull carefully in and began to move back, careful lest he crush it against the wall. Voices shouted from the top. Philip looked up and panicked. He could see no one. He began his climb, drawing himself up, ignoring the aches in his body. He stopped for a moment. He wondered if the dead, the ghosts of those skeletons who now lay at the bottom of the well, were rising up to pull him down. He cursed himself as a fool, whispered a prayer and continued to climb. When he reached the top, Edmund helped him over the rim. Philip sat with his back to the wall, gasping, waiting for the aches in his arms to subside. Stephen and Piers stood a distance away talking to a new arrival. Philip rubbed his eyes and recognised Crispin, Roheisia's son. He took the skull, yellow with age, and put it on the ground beside him.

'What's the matter?' he shouted.

Stephen led Crispin across.

'Very bad news. A journeyman going through the forest found Adam Waldis' corpse bobbing on the top of a marsh. He dragged it out and went into the village. The corpse has been collected and taken back to the church. Lord Richard has come down, the villagers are gathered.'

'Was he murdered?' Philip asked.

'We don't know,' Stephen replied. 'Common report says that Adam, who was born in the area, would know the woods like the back of his hand. They find it difficult to believe he became lost.'

'Mystery piled upon mystery,' Philip murmured. He scrabbled behind him and brought out the skull. 'The remains of Adam Waldis are not the only ones discovered.'

'You found that?' Piers exclaimed, coming up.

'Aye, on the ledge at the bottom of the well.' Philip held it up. 'God knows how this poor being died. I suspect a violent death.' He placed the skull back on the ground. 'For the time being, it can stay here. But, before I get much older, that well has to be searched, there's more below.'

'To whom can they belong?' Edmund asked. 'I mean, the venerable monks who lived her would hardly be guilty of murder.'

'If the place was sacked,' Stephen broke in, 'perhaps the corpses were thrown down the well?'

'I doubt it,' Philip replied. 'But,' he got to his feet, 'it will have to wait. We have more pressing matters to attend to.'

They collected their horses and rode back through the gathering darkness towards Scawsby village. Torches had been lit in the cemetery: the village folk were gathering round the death house which lay on the other side of the church. Lord Richard Montalt came out to greet them.

'You'd best come.'

He took them into the grim, dank-smelling hut. Waldis' corpse had been stretched out on the trestle table. Tallow candles burnt at his head and feet. Pitch torches, fixed to the iron brackets, filled the death house with dancing shadows.

The coffin woman had already been busy. Waldis had been stripped of his clothes and she was now washing away the dirt and slime of the marsh. She paused as Philip knelt beside the corpse and, trying to ignore the stricken face, whispered the words of absolution.

'I shall anoint him later,' he declared, getting to his feet. 'How did he die?'

'There's no mark of violence on his body,' the coffin woman announced. 'No sign of a knife or arrow.'

Montalt called out over his shoulder. The journeyman who had found the corpse came out of the shadows, his fardel still on his back.

'I was coming through the wood,' he explained. 'It was late afternoon. I decided to take a short cut. I wanted to be in Scawsby by nightfall.' He scratched his unshaven cheek. 'I don't like it out there. Anyway, I passed the marsh. I know the path round, I have taken it many a time. Something colourful caught my eye. I went across, it was Waldis.'

'You knew him?' Philip asked.

'Well, he is the parish clerk,' the journeyman replied. 'I often travel to Scawsby, have done for years. He was just bobbing there, face down, so I dragged him out. I then raised the hue and cry and he was brought here.'

Philip went back to study the corpse: touching the hand and arm, he found the flesh cold and hardening.

'He's been dead some time,' the coffin woman replied. 'Well over a day and the marsh water's cold.' She looked up, in the candle-light her face seemed youthful. 'If you go down into the marsh,' she continued, 'it closes in around you.' A faint smile crossed her face. 'But, sometimes, it spits you back.'

Philip caught her veiled allusion. He was sure this old woman knew more about the history of Scawsby than she had revealed. Stephen came and stood in the doorway. Philip recalled his friend's anger when he had hinted at the possibility of the church being built elsewhere. Did Stephen also know more than he showed? Was that why he was here?

'I have the power of coroner,' Lord Richard broke in. 'I am supposed to view the corpse and deliver a judgement.' He went across and put his hand on a crucifix which hung on the wall. 'My judgement is that Adam Waldis died a death, accidental by nature.' He let his hand fall. 'Though God knows what he was doing there and why he was running?' Lord Richard pointed to the parish clerk's spindly legs. 'Look,' he said. 'The cuts, bramble and gorse did that. Now, why should Waldis be running for his life, so terrified that he ran into a marsh and drowned?'

Supper in the Priest's house was a sombre affair. Roheisia heaped their traunchers with vegetables and a rich rabbit stew, put a jug of wine on the table, a pie on a platter and said she would be leaving. Philip, who had eaten desultorily, locked the door behind her and came back.

'I am concerned,' he began, 'by Waldis' death. Quite extraordinary events have happened, and are happening in Scawsby.'

He then told them everything which had occurred since his arrival. Stephen kept pulling faces. Edmund sat fascinated.

'I am a mathematician,' Stephen declared abruptly when Philip finished. 'I deal with shapes and measurements. I cut stone and fashion buildings which will be of use as well as a glory to their builder. Oh yes, I believe in God and his angels. However, Philip, if what you describe is true,' he added, 'then this is not a matter for us. You should despatch a messenger to Rochester for an exorcist. This is the bishop's problem, not ours.'

'Didn't you believe in anything I've said?' Philip asked. 'Haven't you experienced anything yourself?'

Stephen put his wine cup down. 'I admit Scawsby is a pleasant enough village,' he replied. 'But I agree, this house, the church and its graveyard are eerie. What is more, I don't like that old woman. She's a nuisance and impertinent.'

Philip looked up in surprise. Stephen sounded petulant yet his friend was usually charming and easy-going.

'There is a presence here,' Edmund declared. 'Like a nagging pain you try and tell yourself doesn't exist but it comes back, forces its way in. I haven't seen anything,' he continued, 'or I don't think I have, except last night after I went to bed: I heard you go out into the cemetery so I opened a shutter and looked out. You went across to the church, yes?'

Philip nodded.

'Well, it was dark. I could only make out your shadow but I am certain someone was following you.'

Philip swallowed hard.

'I believe terrible murders were committed here,' Edmund continued. 'Those poor Templars were ambushed out on the marshes, slaughtered and their treasure taken. Perhaps it was their remains we found at the bottom of that well? Perhaps their souls do hang between heaven and earth seeking retribution? It would be tragic,' he added wistfully, 'if something should happen to Isolda.'

'After we bury Waldis,' Philip replied, 'tomorrow morning, I am going to go out to High Mount: that well is to be rigorously searched.'

'Why?' Stephen asked.

'Why not?' Philip replied. 'It's the best place to begin.

Edmund might be right. If the Templars' remains are tossed down some well or pit, they deserve honourable burial. Perhaps that's what the word 'Reparation' means? Though who Veronica is, or what the numbers six and fourteen signify is beyond me.'

'I've found something,' Edmund offered. 'Tonight, before we came down to sup I thought I would search this house. The cellars hold nothing but have you been in the garrets?'

'Nothing but bits and pieces lie there,' Stephen replied. 'They're draughty and bleak.'

'Bring the candles,' Edmund ordered. 'I want to show you something.'

They followed Edmund up the stairs on to the top gallery. The small garret lay just under the roof. It was bitterly cold, almost like jumping into icy water and the candle flames danced in the draught seeping in between the roof and the walls. The ceiling was low and they had to be careful of the beams. More candles were brought and lit. Philip glanced round. Broken stools, cracked pots and bowls, a flesher's knife, waiting to be sharpened; a large, battered chest with its clasps broken. Against the wall stood a squat aumbry or cupboard. Its doors hung loose, the top was cracked and dented.

'Drag the chest out,' Edmund said.

They did so.

'I came here,' Edmund replied, removing the dust from his hands, 'because I needed something to put my own clothes in. I examined the chest and the cupboard.'

'What's so special about this?' Stephen asked.

Philip now joined Edmund in removing the dust. As he did so, he realised that, in certain places, the leather had been scraped off and that in its pristine state the chest must have been a place where valuables were stored. It was fortified with four locks and bound by iron bands and metal studs. Beneath the lid were two wooden slats, once held together by three clasps, each of which would have carried a padlock. These now hung loose. Philip pulled them back and felt inside: the lining was smooth but beginning to crumble. Curious, he moved the candle along the bottom of the chest.

'This was silk,' he declared. 'Silk with fleur de lys stamped on it. It must have been used to carry something very, very precious.' He replaced the wooden slats. 'Three locks inside, four locks outside and reinforced with a steel band and metal studs.' He tapped the side. 'This is the finest wood and leather.'

Stephen also crouched down, peering round the chest, studying where the leather had been deliberately scraped away with a knife.

'I know what this was,' Philip declared. 'It's not the property of some priest, more like a royal chest used by the Exchequer to transport precious objects.'

Philip opened the lid again and glanced in. He noticed a dark stain had appeared at the bottom where he placed the candle.

'I thought it was interesting,' Edmund said. 'And there's something else, Brother: something to do with the Veronica you mentioned.' He led them back to the garret. 'I thought the chest could be repaired and this cupboard too.'

Philip smiled at his brother's well-known love of carpentry. Edmund had already offered to carve statues in the church and had been pressing his brother to buy the best wood. Edmund put the candles along the top of the cupboard.

'You said Romanel was a warlock?'

Philip nodded.

'Perhaps he was,' Edmund replied. 'He definitely had an interest in the stars. Look at the ceiling.'

Philip did so: he noticed that part of the plaster between the beams had been removed.

'A trap door was once there,' Edmund declared. 'Perhaps Romanel used it to study the stars? He may have had a warlock's dedication to astrology.'

Stephen began to laugh. 'This is all conjecture.'

'But this isn't.'

Edmund removed the candles and pulled the cupboard away from the wall. The painting behind was faded but, by holding the candles up, Philip began to see why this had attracted Edmund's attention. At first sight, it appeared as a tawdry attempt to depict a scene from Christ's Passion. The artist had not been good: the figures were clumsily drawn, the colours crude but that was why the plaster had retained it, a finer painting would have been more easily brushed off by the cupboard or crumbled in the passing of time.

'Look!' Philip explained, tracing it with his finger. 'There's Christ carrying his cross. Here are the women of Jerusalem.' He pointed to another woman holding a piece of linen in her hands. 'This is Veronica wiping Jesus' face.' He moved the candle further up. 'However, this scene is not mentioned by any spiritual writer: the second painting was more stark.'

Philip could make out horsemen riding, what appeared to be Our Lady carrying the Infant Jesus on a donkey and, around them, people with swords, clubs, spears and axes. He noticed that one of the riders had dismounted, or fallen into what looked like a river or a pit, only his head and arms were above the surface. More importantly, following the Virgin and Child, was a sumpter pony carrying a chest.

'Lord and His saints save us!' Edmund breathed. He

almost pressed his face against the wall, so close the candle nearly singed his hair. 'When I first pulled the cupboard away, I only saw Veronica and Jesus but what's that?'

Stephen went out into the gallery as if listening for something. Edmund looked worried as if he, too, had a premonition of danger.

'I believe this garret was used by Romanel,' Philip spoke. He wanted to break the oppressive silence he felt gathering round them. 'This was a special chamber, well away from snooping eyes where he could do what he wanted. He was a priest with certain gifts. You, Edmund, like working with wood. Romanel liked painting. You can see his work in the Lady Chapel where he had the impudence to portray himself praying to the Virgin Mary.' He gestured round the garret. 'But this is different. I believe Romanel did this painting just before he died. For some strange reason the story of Veronica meeting Jesus and wiping his bleeding face has something to do with this mystery.' Philip pointed to the other crudely painted figures. 'Gentlemen, I think this is Romanel's confession. It depicts his attack upon the Templars as they crossed the marshes. He drew it here, an attempt to exorcise his soul. If we had been the priests who immediately followed him, we would have found many such drawings about the house: on scraps of parchment or the blank pages of some folio.'

'Listen!' Stephen came out into the garret, hand on his dagger-hilt. 'There is someone downstairs.'

Philip tried to calm the blood beating in his head. Stephen was right: someone was moving on the gallery below. He handed the candle to Edmund and hurried down: the moon-washed gallery was empty. He went into his own room, opened the window and looked out towards the church. An owl, hunting in the gardens, rose in a light flurry of wings and made him start. He wetted dry lips, staring through the church. He saw it again, the same glow of light as the previous evening.

'In God's name!' he whispered hoarsely into the darkness. 'Who are you? What do you want? Tell me and reparation will be made!'

Nothing but an owl hoot answered his question. Philip was about to close the shutters when he heard another sound: the clink of harness, the whisper of voices and those words again. 'Spectamus te, semper spectamus te: We are watching you. We are always watching you.'

Philip hurried down the stairs and fumbled with the key in the lock. He threw open the front door and ran out but there was nothing there. Only the rustle of the leaves though the light from the church had grown brighter. He had the keys in his wallet so he strode across, this time going in through the main door. The light glowed in the sanctuary behind the rood screen. Philip, summoning up all his courage, walked down.

'In God's name!'

Philip stopped. Waldis' corpse lay in the parish coffin before the high altar. Funeral candles glowed all around whilst the figure kneeling beside it was clearly Priscilla. She didn't even turn round but, resting back on her heels, she seemed absorbed by the red sanctuary lamp.

'Priscilla!'

She opened her eyes and glanced up at him.

'Father, what is it?'

'Nothing, I saw the light in the church. What are you doing here?'

'Father, I always do the corpse vigil, if there's no one else. Somebody has to pray for the soul, as the angels and devils fight over it between heaven and hell. The more you pray, the stronger the angels become.'

Philip smiled at the old legend.

'Who told you that?'

'Why, Romanel did!'

'No, I mean who told you to pray beside the corpses? You wash them and prepare them, that's sufficient.'

The old woman's eyes gleamed. 'Romanel told me to, as an act of reparation.'

'Did he ever say for what?'

The old woman's fingers went to her lips. 'Only once, Father, I asked him why. He said I should pray for being alive.'

Philip crossed himself and stared at the pyx which held the Blessed Sacrament above the high altar. Despite these sacred surroundings, he felt the power, the ugliness of that long-dead priest who had blighted this woman's life.

'I am sorry I disturbed you. Is there anything you wish to eat or drink?'

'Tomorrow a fresh pitcher of milk, thick and creamy, not watered down.'

Philip sketched a blessing over the old woman's head, then he bent down and kissed her gently on the brow. He was about to leave the sanctuary when she called his name. He turned.

'What is it, Priscilla?'

She was now kneeling, staring straight at him.

'You are a good man, Father. You shouldn't stay here. You should go like the rest. Some of the men were good but you are kind. One day, one day I'll take you into my hut. I want to tell you about my nightmares, Father. Don't worry about Romanel.'

'What do you mean?' Philip came back.

'He haunts this place,' the old woman replied. 'But he is not truly dangerous.'

'What is dangerous?'

'To hunt for the treasure. Leave it be! And, if you do hunt for it, Father, never, ever go out in the marshlands where the corpse candles can be seen. Pinpricks, the devil's lights in the mist. I dream about them a lot.'

'You should sleep,' Philip replied.

He genuflected towards the sacrament and, walking down, locked the main door behind him. He realised that Priscilla must hold a key to the corpse door which led in directly from the cemetery. Philip went round to check this. Sure enough it was open.

'Some former priest must have given her a key,' he murmured.

Philip closed the door, turned round and recoiled in terror at the figure standing before him. The same white face shrouded in its black cowl, the evil eyes and sneering lips. Philip closed his eyes even as the most piercing shriek came from the house on the other side of the graveyard.

Philip fled through the graveyard. He didn't bother to turn to see if that awful apparition was pursuing him. He reached the house and sped like an arrow upstairs. Stephen and Edmund were standing over the trunk, their faces white, staring at Edmund's left hand which was dripping with blood.

'In God's name!' Philip hissed, gasping his breath.

Edmund just shook his head and pointed to the trunk. Philip knelt down and felt inside but, when he brought his hand out, there was no mark, only grains of dust.

'It's gone!' Edmund whispered. He showed his hand, any trace of blood had vanished.

'What happened?' Philip asked.

'We were here examining the chest,' Stephen explained. 'Edmund was searching for a secret compartment: he felt something damp and pulled his hand out. It was soaked, absolutely soaked in blood, as if he had been slashed by a sword.'

Philip closed the chest and pushed it back into the room. 'Enough is enough!' he declared, coming back out of the gallery. 'I will not flee from here!' He raised his voice, shouting at the presence he had glimpsed in the graveyard. 'I will not be pushed or hounded out! Let's go to bed,' he said. 'But, first, I am writing a letter to His Grace the Bishop of Rochester. He must send an exorcist to help us!'

Chapter 3

Adam Waldis' funeral took place at noon the following day. Philip and his two companions slept late and busied themselves preparing the church. It being a Saturday morning, most of the villagers attended and Lord Richard Montalt whispered to Philip that perhaps now was the best occasion to hold a meeting, introduce himself as well as talk to the villagers about the new church. Philip agreed and, once Waldis' body had been interred in the graveyard, he divested and went up into the pulpit. He stood there for a while until Montalt and the others, returning more slowly from the graveyard, packed into the nave. Lord Richard sat in the sanctuary chair next to him facing the villagers. Beside him on a bench, young Henry and Isolda sat whispering, heads together.

'In nomine Patris.' Philip made the sign of the cross.

Silence ensued as the parishioners copied him, then made themselves comfortable along the nave. Philip stared down the church. It didn't seem so forbidding now. Children chattered in the transept: one even wandered up and patted Lord Richard on the knee whilst two more climbed on to the great sarcophagus which housed the remains of Montalt's ancestors. Philip studied his parishioners who gazed expectantly up at him: brown, weather-beaten faces. They were all dressed in their best attire though some still had muddy hands and their boots were caked with dirt. A number of women had babies suckling at their breasts.

'Brothers and sisters in Christ,' Philip began. 'By now you know that his Lordship the Bishop has agreed to provide not one priest but two to the Parish of Scawsby. You are, therefore,' he added wryly, 'twice blessed.'

'Aye and twice taxed!' someone murmured.

Philip joined in the laughter. 'I promise you.' He held his hand up. 'I have already given my word to his Lordship that my brother and I will not increase the tithes. We are here to care for Christ's sheep not to shear them!'

This time the laughter was even louder.

'Lord Richard Montalt,' Philip continued, 'has kindly agreed to pay the stipend my brother Edmund will need, for, as it is written in scripture: "the labourer is worthy of his hire".'

He now had his congregation's attention and he remembered the words of an old vicar. 'A priest should be able to preach, Philip. If he can't hold his people's attention then, how on earth, can he attract God's?'

'Are you going to build a new church, Father?' a voice shouted out.

'The church,' Philip replied, 'constantly renews itself not only with souls but also with buildings. My dear people, look around this church! The roof is beginning to decay, the walls are cracked, the light is poor. Once again Lord Richard's generosity has been manifest: we do plan to build a new church at High Mount. He will provide the money. The materials will be quarried locally and we hope that all in the village will assist in its building. I have brought my friend, a master mason from London who has worked on the church of St Bartholomew's in Smithfield.'

He paused at the 'Ooohs' and 'Aahs': some of the

more wealthy peasants had made the journey to the capital. They now began whispering what a great church St Bartholomew's was.

'What about the cemetery?' A man in the front stood up. 'Everything you say, Father, makes sense. We are glad there are two priests here. Now, this church has never been popular with the people. Isn't that right?' He turned to get the reassurance of his fellows.

Philip suddenly realised how, in all the churches he had visited, the priest often had a battle to keep children from playing amongst the tombs or traders using it as a market place. Yet, even in his short time here, Philip had never seen anyone, man, woman or child, in the graveyard.

'Our people are buried here,' the man continued.

'Give the priest your names,' Lord Richard shouted.

'Brodkin!' the stout fellow replied. 'I own three fields, two ploughs, forty sheep . . .'

'And that doesn't include his wife!' someone shouted from the back.

Philip used the laughter that followed to look down at Sir Richard Montalt, who nodded approvingly. A fight would have ensued between Brodkin and his taunter but Lord Richard stood up and an immediate hush fell on the group.

'Church law,' the manor lord declared, walking forward, 'is quite clear. Those buried within living memory, and that includes poor Waldis whom we have just returned to Mother Earth, will be exhumed and moved to the new cemetery. This will be done at night. The children will stay away. Many of the bodies will be nothing but dust and ashes. Others,' he added, 'might not smell so sweet as they did in life . . .'

A general discussion followed. The parishioners got to their feet. Some declared they wanted their loved ones re-interred. Others that their kinsfolk were now with God so where they were buried was of little import. Questions were asked about when all this would happen. Philip, at a sign from Lord Richard, used this to bring the meeting to an end.

'We will pray,' he declared. 'God will send us a sign.'

And, before any further points could be made, Philip raised his hand in benediction and the parishioners teemed out of the church. Henry and Isolda followed, eager to be away from the watchful eye of Lord Richard who stayed behind.

'You look pale, Philip,' the manor lord began.

In a few, pithy words the priest described what had happened the previous night. Lord Richard whistled under his breath and crossed himself. Philip brought out the letter he had written to the bishop.

'I am a simple priest, Lord Richard,' he declared. 'These things are beyond me. I have asked his Lordship for an exorcist. Could you send one of your couriers to Rochester with this?'

'Of course. Of course.' Lord Richard took the letter and slipped it into his wallet. 'If it helps.'

'What do you mean?' Philip asked.

'I am not too sure, Father. However, years ago when I was knee high to a sparrow, an exorcist was brought from London. My father mentioned it once: he refused to elaborate. Anyway,' he sighed, 'I'd bring a legion of angels here if I could.'

He bade his farewells. Philip joined Edmund and Stephen back in the house to break their fast. Roheisia bustled around chattering about the meeting.

'Everybody's pleased, Father. No one really likes that church.'

Philip interrupted her to ask if she would leave out a pitcher of fresh milk for Priscilla. Roheisia looked back in puzzlement.

'The coffin woman,' Philip explained. He glanced at Edmund and Stephen who were eating heartily enough after their chilling experience the night before. 'We'll go out to High Mount,' he announced.

'Piers is waiting outside,' Stephen interrupted.

'He hasn't told anyone, has he?' Philip asked.

Stephen shook his head, refusing to meet Philip's eye.

'He'll say nothing about what we found there yesterday. I swore him to silence. I also gave him a silver piece. I said there would be more if he kept his mouth shut.'

'I should have told Lord Richard,' Philip mused. 'But, come on, the day is drawing on, the light will soon be poor.'

In the event it was a fine afternoon. The sun kept the mist away and, when they reached High Mount, they went immediately to the well. Piers had brought a rope ladder, rings of cordage and two large canvas sheets all piled onto a sumpter pony. Stephen volunteered to go down the well first and, before anyone could stop him, he was over the crumbling wall, lowering himself quickly down the ladder. Philip realised that Stephen, working on buildings, would be used to making his way up and down ladders with no fear of heights. Under Philip's directions, and Stephen's shouted instructions from the bottom of the well, a simple pulley was arranged. A large leather bucket was lowered. Philip could hear Stephen splashing about below.

'It's like a charnel house down here!' Stephen shouted, pulling on the rope. 'Bones and skulls!'

The leather bucket was raised time and again, with its grisly cargo: skulls, parts of rib cages, legs, arms, the small bones from feet and hands. Towards the end, a few artefacts: a crude, wooden cross crumbling with age formed in the Celtic fashion; a length of cord; a piece of sandal strap.

Eventually Stephen said he could find nothing else and climbed back, his face and hands covered in mud. They now spread out the canvas sheets; ignoring Piers' grumbling about ghosts and ghouls, they laid out what they had found. Philip tried to arrange the bones as decently and appropriately as possible. When they had finished, the sun was beginning to set as Philip counted the remains of at least sixteen corpses.

'Where did they come from?' Edmund asked.

Philip squatted down. He studied the artefacts, then scrutinised the bones, especially the skulls.

'I'm not a physician,' he declared. He picked up a skull. 'Nor am I a soldier but I've been told that most wounds are to the head. I can see no mark of violence on any of these. Whilst the bits of cord, the cross suggest that these remains belonged to monks who once lived here. Now all this begs further questions. True, the monks could have been stabbed in the chest or belly, even beheaded by those marauders who ravished this area hundreds of years ago. However, I doubt if such godless men, having killed monks, would bother to toss them down a well which they themselves would use whilst any Christian soul would give them a decent burial.'

'But,' Edmund asked, 'we still found them at the bottom of a well?'

Philip got to his feet. He remembered those drawings he had seen in the parish ledger marking the tomb stones here at High Mount.

'I think,' he said, 'that someone pillaged their graves, perhaps looking for valuables or . . .' Philip shivered. He

114

looked down the hill at the mist seeping across the fields. Or what? he thought. He was sure these bones had been known to Romanel and Father Anthony. He walked back through the ruins, shouting at the others to follow him. He paused where the high altar stood and tried to remember the drawings of the graves.

'Ah yes, there's one here.'

He crouched down beside the grave slab on the far side of the sanctuary, examining the earth around it. 'Someone has been here before us,' he remarked. 'Look, they've moved this stone, then replaced it whilst trying to hide any sign of what they'd done. Piers, fetch those poles you brought.'

The verderer did. Philip and his brother began to lever them under a stone. In the end, the slab moved easily. Philip expected to find the grave empty but a skeleton sprawled there. He knelt down, in the poor light he could just make it out. He said a prayer so that the Lord would realise he intended no blasphemy.

'This man was not meant to be buried here!'

'What do you mean?' Stephen asked.

'Of course!' Edmund whispered. 'He's buried the wrong way. His head should be towards the east.'

Philip picked up the skull, there was a jagged hole in the back. He then scrutinised the rest of the skeleton: two ribs bore hack marks. He then searched the earth around, there was nothing.

'I don't believe this man was a monk,' Philip declared. 'He was killed in a most ferocious fight. The cut to his body brought him to his knees and someone smashed his skull. It's no monk,' he continued. 'Any man of God would be buried with a cross, or Ave Maria beads whilst his head would lie in the direction of east, facing the altar.' Philip glanced at his companions. 'There's not a shred of clothing, nothing, which means the corpse was completely stripped before being put here.' Philip paused. 'I believe this grave was ransacked, the skeleton thrown down the well and this one was hurriedly placed here.'

'But why?' Edmund asked. 'Why open a grave, take one skeleton out and put another in?'

Philip was about to answer when he heard the jingle of harness. A shiver of fear went down his spine and he crossed himself. Edmund, too, had caught his unease. Piers the verderer lifted his bow, notching an arrow to the string.

'Didn't you hear that?' Philip asked.

Again the jingle of harness, this time from the far end of the church. Stephen strode down but shouted back he could see nothing. The mist was coming in thicker now. The light was beginning to fade.

'It's time we were gone,' Philip declared. 'Tomorrow we'll come back early.'

They replaced the tomb stone. Going back to the well, Philip ordered the remains to be wrapped in a canvas sheet and then hidden just inside the priory walls. They collected their horses: these were so skittish, Piers said he was glad he had hobbled them. The sumpter pony lashed out with his legs and, if Piers had not held on to the rope and its bridle, it would have panicked and galloped away. They left High Mount, riding a little faster than usual, on to the path through the woods to the village.

'I suspect,' Edmund drew his horse alongside that of Philip's, 'our deceased clerk, Adam Waldis, had a hand in the opening of that tomb.'

Philip looked around: Waldis was coming back from High Mount when something frightened him off this path so he became trapped in a marsh. Philip reined in, calling Piers forward.

'Do you know where Waldis was found?' he asked.

'Yes. What we call the woodland mere.'

'And could you tell where Waldis left the path?'

Piers' face broke into a craggy grin. 'I can follow a rabbit at night, sometimes I have had to. I'll go first.'

Piers was about to ride on when Philip restrained him.

'Tell me, Piers, you are a married man?'

The verderer's smile faded. 'No, Father, a widower.'

'Let me see.' The priest continued, 'You have a child?'

'Yes, a little girl. My sister looks after her.'

'And your mother?'

Piers blinked, fighting back tears. 'Died just after I was born. And, before you ask, Father, her mother likewise. I know, I know . . .' He gathered the reins in his hands. 'Life is like the seasons. It takes a time before a pattern emerges. Already people in the village are beginning to chatter and gossip. They talk of some curse or malediction.'

'Do they gossip much about the past?' Philip asked. 'The legends about the Templars, their hidden treasure?'

'No, Father, they don't. It's strange, in any village such legends would be handed down and passed from one generation to another but people here don't like talking about them. So, what they don't like, they choose to ignore: the way you priests never stay long: the wickedness of Romanel. Oh, we know about him, Father, and poor Father Anthony. Aye, I could tell you plenty about him but I'm freezing cold.'

Piers rode on. A few minutes later he came back.

'I've found the place, just as you enter the trees and then a little further on.'

When they reached the place, Philip could tell how someone had left the track, charging mindlessly through the bracken and bushes. Piers even found pieces of cloth on a winding bramble bush. They left their horses hobbled on the road, Stephen volunteering to look after them. Philip and Edmund followed Piers deeper into the woods. As they went, Philip began to quietly curse his own impetuosity. The light was failing, the mist now curling like steam amongst the trees. An awful, dreadful silence lay over the woods, as if some presence was watching them and, in so doing, killed the clatter of the birds and the scurrying of the smaller animals through the undergrowth. Piers stopped and grinned over his shoulder.

'Don't worry, Father. I know these woods like the back of my hand. We won't follow Waldis into the marsh!'

They went on. Piers held his hand up. The undergrowth gave way to hard caked mud. Philip saw how the mud suddenly became a light, attractive green, like some grassy path in a sun-lit forest glade. Piers picked up a branch.

'Watch, Father!'

He threw it in front of them: the branch hit the top of the marsh: it stayed for a few seconds and then quickly sank.

'What was Waldis so frightened of?' Philip whispered. 'To run into that?'

Piers, who had walked closer to the edge, studied the ground carefully. He came back, shaking his head.

'I can see the marks Waldis made and those who came to drag him out but nothing else.'

'Let's go back,' Edmund murmured. 'This place is haunted. I don't like it.'

They all froze at the jingle of harness, that same harsh metallic sound they had heard up on High Mount. Piers unslung his bow, notching an arrow to the string. Again the jingle of harness, loud and clear, like fairy bells pealing deep in the woods.

'Let's get back to the horses,' the verderer declared.

Philip, to his dying day, never knew why he ignored

such sensible advice. However, he suddenly had a picture of himself attending school, of excelling in the Halls of Cambridge in Logic and Theology, so, why should he run from a mist-soaked wood just because he heard a jingle of harness? He was tired of being frightened.

'I am going to find out.'

And, before they could stop him, Philip began to run at a half-crouch along the marsh. He saw firm ground ahead of him and heard once again the jingle of the harness. He ran into the trees not caring about the branches which scratched at his face or the brambles which caught at his legs. He heard a sound and spun round. Piers was following him, a stubborn look on his face.

'If I lose you, Father, I can't go back to Sir Richard.' The verderer smiled bleakly. 'This is strange, it's not the place for horses.'

Again the jingle of harness. Philip hurried on. The trees began to thin. They both stopped to catch their breath.

'Be careful now, Father. The trees thin, the ground dips to a broad dell, then the woods roll on, stretching west.'

Philip nodded. They proceeded more slowly. Philip stopped and sniffed the air. He had caught the smell of cooking, wood smoke. Piers, too, smelt it but shook his head.

'There are no cottages here. Haven't been for years. The woods of Scawsby are not liked.'

Philip approached the rim of the hill. He could now hear voices. Peering over the top, he stared down in disbelief, his heart in his mouth. The dell was full of armed men. For some strange reason the mist wasn't as thick here. Philip reckoned there must be at least two hundred and, straining his ears, he realised they were not English: faint words of French, orders being shouted out. The men themselves were dressed in a garish collection of rags and ill-fitting pieces of armour. Studying them carefully, Philip realised they were wearing what they had looted from different farms and villages. One young man wore a woman's green smock. Another had a visored helmet but, over his chest, he had the chasuble stolen from some church. Beside him Piers was already beginning to withdraw.

'A French raiding party,' he whispered. 'They have circled in from the coast, kept to the heathland and come in from the west through the woods.'

'But why here?'

'Father, it will be dark in an hour. They'll stay tonight but they will be in Scawsby by dawn, then ride like demons for the coast. This probably was their real destination. Scawsby and the Rockingham Manor are wealthy whilst the sheriff's men would never dream of looking for them here. By tomorrow night, they hope to be back at sea. Come on, we must warn Sir Richard!'

'But their horses are not saddled?' Philip murmured. 'We heard the jingle of harness?'

'Never mind that!' Piers snapped.

They ran back, Philip going in front. At first, when the figure loomed out of the gloaming, he thought it was Edmund but then he stopped. The man in front of him was small, olive-skinned with glittering eyes: the fellow behind, slightly taller, raw-boned, red-faced. The small one was already drawing his knife.

'Qu'est-ce que? Qu—'

Philip threw himself upon the Frenchman before that long knife could reach him. They both crashed to the ground, turning and writhing. Philip could smell the man's sweat, the odour of olives and rich red wine. The Frenchman pushed him away and, rising in a half-crouch, was about to close again when Piers' arrow took him full in the mouth. He dropped like a stone. Philip tried to control his trembling. Piers was already rifling though the wallet of the second Frenchman whom he'd despatched with an arrow in the throat. He did the same to Philip's assailant: the priest had to admire the verderer's cool, detached manner, muttering with pleasure at the silver coins he slipped into his own pouch.

'Spoils of war, Father. The bastards had to die.' Piers grasped Philip's arm. 'Come on, Father, say a short prayer, then we'll bury them in the marsh.'

Philip tried to recall the words of the De Profundis but he stumbled. Piers was already dragging one corpse along the path. Philip heard a splash, then the verderer returned for the second. Both bodies disappeared within a twinkling of an eye. Piers then went back, doing his best to thoroughly remove any sign of a struggle or bloodstains from the ground.

'Let's pray they'll think their scouts got lost. We should leave, Father.'

They found Edmund crouched beside a tree. He said he had heard something but decided discretion was the best part of valour. Philip ignored his questions about why his robes were dirty. They returned to the pathway, where they informed an impatient Stephen what had happened. They quickly mounted their horses and galloped into the village, not stopping till they had reached the Priest's house.

Piers said he would warn Lord Richard. He ordered Philip not to sound the bell or raise the alarm but, on his advice, Philip sent Edmund and Stephen, together with Crispin, to gather the men who were now coming in from the fields. Philip went into the kitchen. He removed his cloak and sat whilst Roheisia, who had the sense not to ask questions, served him a bowl of steaming hot stew and a goblet of watered wine. Philip ate slowly, trying to make sense of what had happened. He'd been out at High Mount and, when they were coming back, God knows why he had entered the woods or why he had insisted on finding out who those horsemen were. He had heard it, and so had Piers, that harness jingling, as if mounted men were moving amongst the trees. Philip rose, thanked Roheisia absentmindedly and went up to his chamber to change. He sat on the edge of his bed and, through the window, watched the darkness gather. He knelt at his prie-dieu before the crucifix.

'So far, Lord,' he prayed in a hoarse whisper, 'I have experienced nothing but evil here. Yet there, in the woods . . .'

Philip stopped, distracted. He had always prided himself on his love of reason, the dictates of logic, yet he was sure that, somehow or other, he had stumbled upon those French because he had been warned. But by whom? He heard Edmund calling him from downstairs.

'The men are gathering in the church, Brother. Sir Richard will be here soon!'

It took about an hour before everyone arrived at the church. When Sir Richard appeared, Philip repeated what Piers had already told the manor lord. Sir Richard bristled like a fighting dog and clapped the verderer on the shoulder.

'There's a reward for you, Piers my boy. What you say is true. The French have swung in through the woods. They are waiting to attack.'

'Won't they come tonight?' Edmund asked anxiously.

Philip looked around. Stephen seemed hardly alarmed by the crisis: he was more interested in Sir George Montalt's tomb, crouching down, studying the Latin inscription.

'No, they won't attack tonight,' Sir Richard replied slowly. 'That's as dangerous for them as it is for us. In the dark, you can't tell friend from foe. No Frenchman would want to be cut off, any who were captured would be summarily hanged.'

'But why are they waiting?'

'What's the day today, Father?'

'Why, Saturday.'

'And what happens on a Saturday evening?'

Philip pulled a face.

'Oh come, Father.' Sir Richard laughed. 'The men have worked hard and tomorrow is their rest day. They'll drink deep, sleep heavy and, tomorrow, rise and put on their best apparel . . .'

'Of course,' Philip broke in. 'And come to church. All the villagers will be here for morning Mass.'

'They've done it before.' Piers spoke up. 'When they were raiding Rye and Winchelsea they always tried to trap the people in the churches. Men are away from their houses, they don't carry arms. The French would simply bar the church and fire it. Afterwards, they can loot and kill to their hearts' content.'

'Won't they attack the manor?' Philip asked.

'No, Father. You've seen the walls and gates. Why should they go there and raise the alarm? No, they'll sack Scawsby first and then come looking for me. They'll enter the village by the high road.' Sir Richard continued, 'Scouts will go first, doing what they always do, killing the old, the infirm, silencing the dogs. However, we'll be ready for them!'

Sir Richard strode up into the pulpit and clapped his hands. In a few pithy phrases he told his tenants what Father Philip and Piers had seen in the woods. He clapped again for silence.

'If we had not known,' he declared, 'we might have all died. Now we do, the tables are turned. I will send a rider, for what it is worth, through the night, to see if the sheriff and his men can be raised but, tomorrow morning, no one leaves the village or goes out into the fields. The French do not know Scawsby. Father Philip will, an hour after dawn, about seven o'clock, ring the bell for morning Mass. You must all come here, bring your wives and your children. The old and the bed-ridden. No one must be left at home. They can shelter in the church. But us, all men between the ages of fourteen and sixty, must come fully armed. Bring bow and arrow, staff and sword: any weapons you can lay your hands on. My retainers will bring what we have from the manor. I tell you this: we will teach the French to come to Scawsby!'

His short, fiery speech encouraged the villagers. Sir Richard then repeated his advice. No one was to leave the village whilst he would post scouts on the outskirts to make sure the French did not come at night. He then invited Philip to offer a prayer of thanksgiving and a petition for God's help. As the priest did so, he also added a quiet word of thanks to those mysterious riders in Scawsby wood who had warned him of this terrible danger to his parish.

Chapter 4

Philip felt a relief, the French incursors were a physical threat, something which could be dealt with. This pressing danger allayed some of his fears. He slept fitfully so he got up, put his cloak around him and went out into the high street. Sir Richard had posted guards, men who moved quietly as cats, grizzled veterans from the French wars. They were used to stealing food at night and dealing, so they told the priest, with French pickets. Philip gave them his blessing and went back to the house where he knelt and prayed. At last, peering through the window, he saw the first streaks of dawn. He heard a sound from below as people, anxious to be away from their homes and wishing to be together, began to arrive early for church. Mailed horsemen, the hooves of their mounts muffled by rags, also appeared. A party of Montalt's retainers pushed carts, the wheels of which were covered in straw, down the high street. Philip shaved and washed. He put on his best robes, went down and broke his fast on some bread and ale. Edmund and Stephen, white-faced and anxious, were already waiting for him.

'Keep out of the fighting,' Philip warned. 'None of us are soldiers: that's not cowardice, it's just common sense. If the French break through and enter the church, that will be different.'

Beneath his cloak, Philip wore his sword and a long Welsh stabbing dirk. Edmund carried a long arbalest he had found in one of the chambers upstairs. It was still workable and lashed to his belt was a leather quiver containing ugly, barbed bolts. Stephen wore his sword and said he would try and borrow a long bow and a quiver of arrows. They left the house and made their way across the cemetery to the church. Women and children were already flocking in. Sir Richard stood on the steps. He was dressed in half-armour, a conical steel helmet on his head, its broad nose-guard covering most of his face. He looked a fighting man born and bred. He gruffly greeted Philip. Beside him his son was similarly attired but more nervous, shuffling from foot to foot. Philip went into the church, moving round, talking to the women and children, encouraging the latter that here was some new game they had to play. Outside he could hear the preparations for battle. Sir Richard was shouting orders: there was the creak of harness and the rumble of cart wheels, the sheering clash of swords being sharpened. Sir Richard cursed, telling everyone to be as quiet as possible. Philip remembered the coffin woman. He went out and across the cemetery. She was already up, collecting sticks: Philip almost had to drag her into the church. She protested volubly and said she didn't care but Philip heartily reminded her that freebooters were respecters of neither age nor sex. She was one of his parishioners and he would protect her. She seemed rather flattered and, before he left, she grasped his hand and kissed it.

'Ring the bell!' Sir Richard ordered, coming into the church. 'Ring it loud and hard! Let the French know we are at prayer, though a different service than they intended.'

Edmund went into the tower. Stephen, who had borrowed a bow and quiver from Piers, followed him up the steps but

Sir Richard had already placed men there so he came down. Instead he took a position near an arrow slit aperture facing the main porch. Edmund rang the bell for all his worth. Philip, standing beside Stephen, suddenly saw all the men disappear. The front of the church became as silent as the graveyard. Behind him the children played and chattered whilst their mothers pretended to listen. The bell stopped tolling and Philip began to pray. Time passed slowly. Philip wondered if they had made a mistake when he heard a dog, one of the mongrels who roamed the village, start to bark raucously, then suddenly go quiet. Philip peered through the window – nothing, only a bundle of grass and twigs being rolled by the early morning breeze. When he looked again his heart stopped. A man was standing there, a leather mask covering his face. He carried a shield and sword. He turned and waved. Philip heard the sound of running feet and shouts, doors being broken into. More of the attackers poured into the broad space in front of the church. Stephen notched an arrow to his bow string as one came in under the lych-gate. Suddenly, sharp and clear, the sound of a horn shrilled. Silence reigned for a few seconds. The horn blew again and the battle began.

At first Philip couldn't see what was happening. He heard a whirl, as if some giant hawk was flying through the sky, and the French began to die. Some were killed outright, others writhed in agony as the arrows took them in the face, chest, neck or stomach. Stephen loosed at the man standing by the lych-gate; the arrow missed but the man, alarmed, retreated back into the high street. Philip went up the tower steps, pushed aside one of the archers and stared out. His view was limited but he saw how sound Montalt's tactics were. The French had been allowed into Scawsby. However, in the houses further down the high street, including his own and in the church tower above him, archers had been placed. In the fields behind the hedges other men had been hidden. Their tactics were the same as the English armies had used to such devastating effect in France. The archers simply found their aim and loosed: if the French ran forward they went into a hail of arrows. If they went back, or to their right or left, the same threat met them. Philip had heard about the skill of the long bow but now he saw why it was so fearsome. An archer, a few steps above him, was loosing arrows more quickly than the priest could finish a Pater Noster. Philip went down. Most of the fighting was taking place further back in the village but, even from where he stood, the sound of screaming and shouting was like that from some infernal nightmare. The enemy in front of the church disappeared, most of them killed or wounded, others retreating back to join the main battle. Piers, who had been left in the church as Sir Richard's officer, now ordered the doors opened.

'I am to collect all the archers and move them to the village,' he said. 'Make sure the French are sealed in. I will leave three men to guard the church.'

'I'm coming with you!' Philip declared. 'Edmund, you stay, Stephen too!'

Piers was already hurrying down the path, shouting at the men in the church and the cemetery as well as those behind the hedgerows to join him. At first Philip kept stopping by every corpse.

'There's a man wounded here!' he shouted.

'Ah, so there is.' An English archer knelt down and, before Philip could intervene, the wounded man's throat was slit from ear to ear.

More corpses littered the highway. Piers now formed his archers into a line. They moved slowly down the high road back into Scawsby. Now and again they would stop to despatch a wounded assailant. Occasionally, very rarely, some of the French attackers tried to run to the outskirts of the village. The verderer's archers made short work of them. Up came the bows, the archers wagering where they would hit their victims. Philip lowered his eyes. When they turned the corner, the scene in front of them was unbelievable. Sir Richard had sealed the village off with carts, full of burning tar and pitch. The French were now forced to fight in a tightly enclosed square. The houses on either side were packed with English archers whilst others, a mixture of retainers and peasants, stood behind the carts and simply loosed over the French milling about. Now and again the occasional attacker would break free from the trap only to be cut down. As Piers' group approached, they heard the horn sound again. Sir Richard, leading a line of horsemen, came out of a side street: grappling hooks were placed on the carts, which were pulled aside, and then Sir Richard charged. By the time Philip had reached the bloody mêlée it was apparent that the French had been utterly defeated. Corpses lay sometimes two, three, deep in places. Others were fighting desperately with the horsemen swirling about them. Eventually the cry went up.

'*Ayez pitié! Ayez pitié!*'

Frenchmen dropped their arms and knelt, hands extended. Philip was horrified to see the killing still continue: heads pulled back, throats slashed; horses tumbling across prostrate men. Sir Richard charged about on his great destrier. Young Henry rode behind him carrying a pennant bearing the Montalt insignia and motto: IN MONTE ALTO, SUMMUM BONUM: In the high mountain lies the supreme good. A pun on the family name? Philip ran through fighting men and grasped Sir Richard's knee.

'My Lord! My Lord!' he cried. 'This is murder! They have surrendered! This is butchery!'

Sir Richard lifted his visor. Philip recoiled at the blood lust in the old man's eyes.

'They would have killed us, priest!' he rasped. 'Men, women and children and they would have hanged you from the door of your church.'

'For the love of God!' Philip declared. 'Surely, Sir Richard, there's more to life than an eye for an eye and tooth for tooth? This is murder and you know it.'

Sir Richard dropped his sword. He then shouted at Henry who blew three long blasts on his horn. Already more merciful feelings were making themselves felt. The English hit and cuffed the French but the hot-blooded slaughter ceased. The French were pushed together; there must have been about sixty still standing and another score wounded. Hands and ankles were tied. They were formed into a line and led down towards the church. News of the victory had already reached there. Women and children came running up and, if Philip had not intervened, rocks and sticks would have been hurled. Eventually the French were led into the cemetery and forced to sit under the yew trees whilst their wounded were laid on great stone slabs. Sir Richard now sent out riders to see if anyone had escaped. Piers led another force into the woods to discover where the French had hidden their plunder when they had camped the night before.

Philip was pleased to see some of the women, the coffin woman included, begin to tend the wounded French. Wine and herbs were brought to dress the terrible wounds, clean rags being used as bandages. These were assisted by Montalt's veterans who used their long misericordia daggers to force out arrow heads or cut the hard-boiled leather which the French had used as armour. After the excitement, exhaustion set in. Men, women and children sprawled everywhere. Aidan Blackthorn, the owner of the village tavern, brought down a hog's head of ale and victuals to eat, Sir Richard promising that he would pay for everything that he provided. The old lord took his helmet and chain mail off. He slumped on the church steps, bathing his face and neck with a wet rag, taking great sips from a blackjack of ale which Aidan always kept full.

'Well, Father?' Sir Richard stared into the priest's face. 'Our young King and Commons will be pleased. My Lord of Gaunt,' he referred to the Regent of the kingdom, 'will make his pleasure known.'

'And what about the French?' the priest asked.

'I know that was a bloody business.' Sir Richard gestured further down the high road. 'But these are pirates. When they attack they take no prisoners. I've seen women and children impaled on spikes, priests hacked and skinned like animals. By all the laws and usages of war they should hang and be dead within the hour.' He sighed. 'But you are right. I'm a soldier, not a butcher.' He held Philip's gaze. 'And we need God's blessing here, don't we, Father? Only those who grant mercy can receive it. It's been a good day, not one Scawsby villager was killed, a few nasty wounds but nothing that won't heal.' He stood and pointed to the prisoners. 'They'll be taken to Rochester or Canterbury. The French hold English sailors as prisoners. They'll be exchanged or ransomed. What I want to know is why they came to Scawsby?'

'But you said the manor and village were rich?'

'Yes, Father, but it's a good ride from the coast. Marauders very rarely cross country unless they are looking for something. As I've sat here, supping Aidan's watered ale, I've been wondering what? So, perhaps it's time we found out. You'd best come with me.'

They walked into the cemetery. The French, those unwounded, had now clustered together talking and jabbering at a tall, blond-haired man who had a nasty slash across his right cheek. He was dressed differently from the rest. The chain mail was of good value and, on the empty scabbard which hung from his war belt, was the insignia of a noble family. The young man stared coolly as Sir Richard and the priest walked towards him.

'I can speak French,' Lord Montalt began. 'But this is England and these are my lands. You are pirates. I have every right to hang you like a farmer would rats and there are enough trees in Scawsby to do it.'

The young man's blue eyes stared impassively back, one finger going to dab at the cut on his cheek.

'Can any of you speak English?' Philip asked.

'I can speak it as well as you,' the blond-haired man replied, bowing slightly to Sir Richard. 'I am Sir Tibault Chasny.'

'I have heard of that family!' Sir Richard exclaimed.

The young man smiled and picked up his scabbard. Across the family insignia was a black bar sinister.

'I must make it very clear,' Tibault said liltingly, 'that I am a by-blow, illegitimate; how you English say, born on the wrong side of the blanket.' He smiled. 'And you?'

'Lord Richard Montalt. This is my priest, Father Philip.'

The young man, hands on his stomach, sketched a bow.

'Sir Richard, I must congratulate you. If I had known Scawsby was such a prickly hedgehog I wouldn't have come.' He gestured to his men. 'They think we were betrayed. Why were you waiting? Such a clever trap!'

'You weren't betrayed,' Philip replied. 'I and others stumbled on your camp yesterday evening. We killed two of your scouts.'

The Frenchman closed his eyes and laughed. He then translated what was said to the rest of his men. Tibault made his way through them to stand before Sir Richard.

'I thought they had got lost. I really did. My lieutenant, he said we should search for them.' He blew his cheeks out. 'He was right and now he's dead. I was wrong and I am alive though not for long, eh, Sir Richard?'

'Your treasure, your harness and your horses,' Montalt replied, 'are already ours. But you won't hang. The priest here,' he smiled grimly, 'won't allow it. You have my word, you won't be killed. It's to Rochester and Canterbury for you. Weeks in some cold dungeon, then you can either be ransomed or exchanged for Englishmen in France.' Sir Richard drew in his breath. 'It doesn't really matter to me but tell your men that if any of them try to escape they will be killed on the spot!'

The young Frenchman translated quickly to his companions. There were smiles and sighs. Philip, studying them more closely, was glad that he had intervened. They were French, the enemy, but they were men with wives, sisters, lovers, families. They had probably come to England to wreak revenge for what had happened in France.

'You'll be well looked after,' Philip declared. 'But I beg you, Monsieur, tell none of your men to try and escape. They will be cut down or hanged out of hand whilst the marshes of Kent trap the unwary.'

'Why did you come here?' Sir Richard asked. 'Oh, I know Scawsby is a prosperous place but there are many such villages in Kent. Why this one? Why now?'

'We carry letters of Marque,' Tibault answered. 'From

the Provost of Boulogne. Our task is to harass English shipping in the Narrow Seas and attack the enemy wherever possible.'

'Yes, yes,' Sir Richard replied testily. 'But why Scawsby? Monsieur, I am no fool. I have served as a soldier. I have shown you great compassion. I deserve a better answer.'

Apparently one of Tibault's men could also understand English and, relieved that he wasn't going to hang, abruptly shouted at Tibault. Philip could only fathom a little French but he caught the word 'treasure', as did Montalt.

'What treasure?' Philip asked abruptly. He seized the Frenchman's wrist. 'Sir, you dabble in waters you know little about. What treasure could possibly lie in Scawsby? Don't lie, you owe us your life!'

'Not here,' Chasny murmured.

Sir Richard agreed. He and Philip escorted Tibault out of the cemetery and on to the porch of the church. Tibault sat down, stretching out his legs.

'It's good to be away from my men. If you English don't kill me they probably would. This has been a disaster. We were supposed to attack Scawsby, then ride fast, eastwards, back to the coast. We have three galleys and further out at sea stands a cog waiting to accompany us.'

'The sheriff will seize your galleys,' Sir Richard answered drily. 'And I doubt if you'll spend Yuletide in France.'

'Can I have something to drink?'

Philip went outside, got a blackjack of ale and brought it back. The Frenchman drank it greedily.

'I never thought your ale would taste so sweet.'

'I am tired,' Philip spoke up. 'Monsieur Tibault, I am tired of waiting, why did you come here? What is this about treasure?'

'Ah, very well, what does it matter? I am of the Chasny

family, albeit a by-blow. Ever since I was a boy, in the
Chasny family there have been stories, vague rumours,
legends about a great treasure which should have come
to our families but didn't.'

'Continue,' Philip ordered, sitting down opposite him.

Tibault looked round the church. 'This is a strange place,
gloomy and dark, just like the story we were told. Anyway,
according to this, in 1308, Philip Capet King of France
launched an attack upon the Templar Order. Any soldier
monk belonging to it was arrested, imprisoned, tortured and
killed. There was, at the time, a leading French Templar in
England. His name was Sir Guillaume Chasny or, as you
say, William Chasny. You English were not so speedy in
the destruction of the Order. Sir William was supposed to
leave the Temple in London, make his way across Kent
and take ship to France. Apparently there was a plan to
bring the treasure from London with him and hand it
over to the Chasnys in France for safe keeping.' Tibault
pulled a face.

'Of course, he never reached the coast,' Philip intervened.

'No, he did not. Now the French king, through his secret
agents, not to mention the Chasny family, tried to find
out what had happened.' He smiled thinly. 'I believe the
English Crown was equally curious and equally frustrated.'
He paused. 'However, one thing became apparent. In all
the documents I have seen, both in the royal archives
in Paris as well as those letters held by my family, Sir
William reached, or was on the road to, Scawsby when
he suddenly disappeared. We also know that the English
Crown believed,' he glanced up at Sir Richard, 'that your
ancestor and either some or all of the men of Scawsby
were involved in the destruction of Sir William and his

135

entourage.' He shrugged. 'The end of the legend is this: here in Scawsby lie the treasures of the Temple which,' he spread his hands and grinned boyishly, 'by God's right, and by all that is legal, should be ours!'

'Aye,' Sir Richard replied tartly. 'And I understand that it is snowing in hell and the Lord Satan will sing "Sanctus, Sanctus".' He stood up over the Frenchman. 'You, sir, are a pirate and a freebooter. You came to pillage and to burn.'

'True, Richard, yet didn't you do the same in France? I have seen the work of the English écorcheurs there. Yes, my men were here for profit but I was here for a treasure that belongs to my family. I was born a bastard but I'll die a Chasny. Can you imagine what would have happened if I'd returned to France with this great treasure?' He pulled a face. 'If a man succeeds who cares about his origins?' He clambered to his feet. 'That is all I can tell you.'

'You'll be kept in the manor,' Sir Richard spoke up. 'You and all those who are able. I have your word you'll not try to escape?'

Sir Tibault held a hand up. 'I swear to God in this holy place.' He glanced round. 'Or perhaps not so holy. I have never been in a church like this. Anyway, the corpses of my dead?'

'I will take care of them,' Philip replied. 'They will be buried in the common grave but I will sing a Mass for them and bless their corpses. What happens to their souls is up to God.'

Sir Richard and Tibault left. Philip went and sat at the foot of the pillar staring into the darkness. He always believed that heaven ruled and God, in his infinite way, guided even the minute affairs of men. So it was with this terrible attack. Philip was certain that he had been guided into Scawsby woods, that he had been meant to discover the Frenchmen's camp.

'So, what do we have here?' he murmured. 'On the one hand, a presence of evil, but on the other God-saving work. If I had not gone into the woods, Scawsby would now be a sea of fire from one end to the other.'

'Are you talking to yourself, Brother?'

Philip turned. Edmund and Stephen stood in the doorway.

'Just saying a prayer: thanksgiving for deliverance.'

Stephen pointed with his thumb over his shoulder. 'Your parishioners are already celebrating. The French have been led off. Sir Richard says that today the people can celebrate. Tomorrow will be a boon day. There will be no work in the manor or in the fields, only a Mass of celebration followed by a feast.'

'Sir Richard's shrewd.' Philip got to his feet. 'Come on, Brother, we have other work to do. The French dead must be collected and buried.'

'Where?' Stephen asked curiously.

'Why,' Philip replied. 'In the cemetery. The people asked for a sign of God's approval for building the new church. Now they have it. The French dead will be buried and left in the old cemetery. The parishioners will be given a new one.'

'They are already calling you the Saviour of Scawsby,' Edmund joked.

'I suppose they'll call me a lot of things,' Philip replied drily. 'But the burial of the dead is a great corporal act of mercy. I want it done before the corpses begin to stink and my parishioners are too drunk to wield a shovel!'

As it was, Philip found little trouble in getting his parishioners to help him. The flush of victory had now receded. Sober minds prevailed and the parishioners were as eager as he to collect the corpses and bring them into the cemetery. The women and children were kept indoors and it was dusk before the sorry business was finished. Philip watched the line of corpses grow. He forgot about the mystery and the curses, the legends and the fables. The sight of a long line of dead young men was pitiful. Some of their wounds were terrible: throats slashed whilst many bore the devastating and terrible effects of the long bow, arrows in their heads, faces or buried deep in their bellies and chests.

Piers the verderer returned from Scawsby woods. He announced that the horses of the Frenchmen and their treasure had been taken to the manor. The verderer and some of his companions stayed to help the priest search for corpses. Late in the afternoon, Philip ordered a rest and Roheisia brought out jugs of ale and some bread which she'd baked. The men sat around joking and laughing, oblivious to the corpses. They ate and drank to celebrate their own survival. Philip returned to the Priest's house and took down the parish ledger. He turned to the section written up by Romanel, those curious entries about the dead of 1308. In the margin, as in many such ledgers, the priest also indicated in what part of the cemetery these corpses had been buried. Philip satisfied himself and went out. He took the labourers to the eastern part of the cemetery, not far from the coffin woman's hut, and ordered a large, broad trench to be dug. Ignoring Edmund's questioning look, Philip ordered the trench to be dug deeper and broader than need be.

'It will cut a swathe across the cemetery,' he whispered. 'Any coffins that have to be removed, will be.'

Torches were lit. The labourers put mufflers across their

noses and mouths and began the work. Darkness fell. The digging continued. Now and again they would come across a coffin, the crumbling remains of some long-dead parishioner but no questions were asked. This was regarded as a derelict part of the cemetery.

Grave stones and crosses had long disappeared. No one could remember a parishioner being buried there in living memory. As the pit broadened and began to move across the cemetery, Philip put on his stole, brought out his Asperges rod and bucket and ordered the corpses of the dead French to be interred. Every so often the digging stopped, Philip would intone the 'De Profundis' and the 'Requiem', sprinkle the corpses with holy water, order the earth to be filled in, then the labourers would go back to their work. The night drew on. It was a garish sight. The cemetery, usually so lonely, so sombre, especially at night, was now lit by flickering pitch torches and echoed to the noise of axe, pick and the shouts and grunts of men. No one objected. They all knew, from the days of the Great Plague, how necessary it was for the speedy burial of the dead. The coffin woman came out. For a while she sat and watched them but then she went into the church to continue her lonely vigil before the altar.

Sir Richard Montalt also came down. Philip explained what he was doing.

'It's best if we act quickly,' he declared. 'No questions asked. This is an area once used by the priest Romanel to bury his parishioners, so God knows what we might find.'

Sir Richard agreed and then, almost as if to echo the priest's words, Piers came running over.

'Father, Sir Richard, you'd best come and see this!'

'What is it?'

'Empty coffins!'

Philip and Sir Richard hurried across. Three coffins had been pulled out of the trench.

'They were so heavy,' Piers remarked. 'One of the lids fell off.'

Philip ordered torches to be brought and crouched down. The coffins were empty of any human remains but full of rocks and soil.

'Corpus non invenitur,' he muttered.

'What was that?' Sir Richard asked.

'It's in the parish ledger,' Philip replied, getting to his feet. 'It's Latin for a body could not be found. But why all this mummery? Why bury a coffin with rocks and soil in it? Three in number?'

Edmund and Stephen came over to join them. Sir Richard told Piers to tell the labourers to continue digging.

'Why should Romanel do that?' Philip asked. 'Why should he go to such lengths?'

'It sometimes happens,' Edmund replied. 'If a man is lost at sea, or believed to be dead and his corpse cannot be found, the family will still have a requiem Mass.'

'Yes, I've heard of that custom,' Philip replied. 'But usually they place some of the dead's personal belongings in the coffin as a token memorial. Wait a minute now.'

Crouching down, he studied the three coffins carefully. Many times the poor could not afford a coffin but were buried in canvas sheets. Philip studied the wood; it was good and thick, able to withstand age and decay. He noticed the coffins were uniformly oblong.

'They are not coffins,' Philip declared. 'They are arrow chests.'

Helped by Sir Richard, Stephen and Edmund, the priest pushed one of the coffins sideways until the earth fell out.

They heard a clink. Philip saw something glint in the torch light. He scrabbled amongst the dirt.

'Swords and daggers!' Edmund exclaimed.

The other coffins were emptied. All around them the noise of digging stopped as Piers and his men realised something extraordinary was happening. Philip ordered the weapons, swords, daggers, even a small two-headed axe, to be collected together and brought on to the church steps. Buckets of water were brought to clean the mud off. Piers shouted that they had found another such coffin, two more in fact. The pile of arms on the church steps grew. A conical helmet with a broad, flat noseguard: shirts of chain mail and, despite the decay of the years, a tabard, tattered and rotting, but still bearing the remnant of the Templar cross.

'This is proof!' Philip exclaimed excitedly. 'Don't you realise, Sir Richard!'

'That evil man!' the manor lord exclaimed. 'What a terrible sin. The priest must have led that attack on the Templars. They must have trapped them out on the marshes and killed them – but what about their corpses?'

'I know where they put them,' Philip intervened. 'You can't ride into Scawsby with a dozen corpses. That evil priest had their bodies stripped. The bodies were taken to High Mount. The ancient tombs were emptied of their bones, which were thrown down a well and replaced with the wounded corpses of these soldier monks.' Philip tapped a helmet with the tip of his finger. 'They must have known the English Crown would be searching for Sir William Chasny. Romanel, and probably your ancestor, God forgive him, took the dead men's weapons, put them into arrow chests and buried them deep in the cemetery.'

'Oh no! Oh miserere . . . !'

Philip whirled round. The coffin woman had come into the church and was now staring at the arms piled on the steps. She gave another scream and fled into the night.

Words between the pilgrims

The pilgrims sitting round the fire drew a little closer.

'Devil's tooth!' the Reeve whispered. 'This is a strange tale of heaven and hell.'

The Poor Priest just stared into the flames of the fire. The pilgrims had built this up, the Knight ensuring that dried-out branches kept the flames merry and bright. The Knight swept out, stretching his fingers. Had he not served in the eastern march, fought the fierce Prussians and Slavs as well as the Turks of North Africa? He had hunted and been hunted by the Strigoi, the living dead, along the gloomy, wet valleys of the Danube. The Knight was certainly not a timid man but he was uneasy. Oh, the ruins provided shelter and warmth, the air was still thick with the savoury odours of their meal whilst their breath was sweet with the taste of wine. True, the Poor Priest's tale was chilling but Sir Godfrey's unease was deeper than this. Outside the mist swirled, like some angry malevolent spirit trying to break in, to wrap its tendrils round their throats, to snuff out their lives like the wicks of a candle. And there was more than this: no owl hooted, no nightjar chattered, no frogs croaked in protest. Why? Sir Godfrey scratched his chin. He wanted to draw his sword and go out there. He was sure someone, something was watching them.

The Reeve, however, had been whispering to the Cook, who now looked across the fire at the Poor Priest.

'Is this tale true, Father?'

'Why do you ask?' the Ploughman spoke up.

'I have been to Scawsby,' the Reeve replied. 'There is no church where you describe it, though there is a small monastery of Capuchins.' He glanced quickly at the Friar and the Monk. 'Devout men who pray continuously to the good Lord Jesus. Not like some . . .'

'Yes, yes,' Mine Host broke in. 'You said you'd been to Scawsby?'

'Aye, there's no church there but there's a lovely one at High Mount and the Montalt family . . .'

'Hush!' The Poor Priest brought a finger to his lips. He glanced across at Sir Godfrey. 'You are uneasy, sir?'

'No, no, Father. My son and I know the Montalts. I'll be honest, the fight at Scawsby . . .'

'It happened, didn't it?' the Shipman broke in, waving his hand up and down as he explained. 'About ten years ago. I was on a cog, the *Merry Mary*. We were pursuing the French up and down the coast. My squadron was off the Medway when news came through that a French force had been defeated by peasants and their galleys taken by the sheriff of Kent.'

The Poor Priest just smiled.

'Oh!' the Wife of Bath exclaimed. 'So terrifying, Father!' She pulled her rug closer about her ample shoulders. 'I would not stay in a haunted place.'

'You never know,' the Poor Priest answered, 'what is haunted and what is not.' He waved round the ruins. 'How do we know the dead don't throng here? Watching us, listening to us?'

'I don't give a fig!' the Summoner retorted, rubbing his

stomach. He felt slightly sick after the wine he had drunk. He stretched out his legs, waggling his toes in front of the fire. He didn't care that his leggings were dirty whilst his feet hadn't seen water for many a week. 'I don't give a fig,' he repeated, 'about ghosts or demons! I don't believe all this. A lively tale, but fable not fact.'

'So, you don't believe in ghosts?' The Man of Law pushed back his hood. 'Well, that doesn't matter.'

'Why?' the Summoner asked suspiciously.

'Because ghosts may well believe in you,' the Poor Priest replied.

'And this is true,' the Cook added, scratching the ulcer on his leg. 'It's true, isn't it, Father?'

'Oh yes, Bartholomew,' the Poor Priest replied. 'Of course it's true. You know it is.'

PART III

Chapter 1

The entire village slept late the next morning. During the night Sir Richard's messengers rode furiously up and down the roads of Kent. By dawn the sheriff and a posse of his men arrived to take the prisoners and march them off to the prison hulks at the mouth of the Medway. The dead had all been collected, the burials completed: a great, broad swathe of freshly turned earth now ran across the cemetery like a scar. The Templar arms were hidden under a canvas sheet in an outhouse behind the Priest's house. Philip slept well and awoke refreshed, despite the previous night's hard labour. He rang the church bell and, at noon, celebrated a Mass of thanksgiving. At the end, he and Sir Richard led the congregation in thundering out the verses of the Te Deum. Afterwards the villagers swarmed up round the priest, slapping his shoulders, thanking him for his work.

'God's will has been done!' the blacksmith shouted on the steps of the church. 'And it has been seen to be done. Our priest, as far as I am concerned, can build a hundred churches!'

His words were greeted by a roar of approval and the rest of the day was given over to a village celebration. Sir

Richard's munificence made itself felt. Tables were laid out. Carts arrived from the manor house with hogsheads of ale, vats of wine and a huge ox gutted and ready to roast. The blacksmith built up a huge fire in the centre of the village and soon the air was thick with the smell of roasting beef. Bread and sweetmeats were piled high in baskets. Everybody contributed what they could: apples, slightly rotten where they had been kept all winter; rounded pieces of marzipan, sweet-bread, whilst the ale and wine flowed like water. There was dancing on the green from where young couples, hand in hand, stole off into the woods.

'I just hope they are careful,' Philip remarked to Edmund. 'Otherwise, in late summer, we're going to have a crop of weddings and be busy at the baptismal font.' He glanced around. 'Where's Stephen?'

'Gone to High Mount,' Edmund replied.

Philip glanced away so his brother would not catch his annoyance. Philip was concerned about Stephen. His friend was not his merry self: he had become taciturn and drawn. Philip was growing increasingly suspicious. High Mount could wait, so why was it so important to go there today? Did Stephen realise Philip and Edmund would be busy in the village? Did Stephen know more about the legends of Scawsby than he admitted? And was he more interested in the hidden treasure than building God's house?

'Come on, Father.' Piers swaggered over. He thrust a blackjack of ale into the priest's hand. 'Hard knocks yesterday, eh, Father? Grisly work digging up those graves. What was that armour we found?'

'Nothing,' Philip murmured. He pulled a face. 'Well, in time, I'll tell you.' He toasted the verderer with the blackjack. 'But you, you were going to tell me a story? About Father Anthony?'

'Oh yes. Have you met Walkin?'

'Who?'

'Walkin the stone-cutter. He's very old and venerable. Some people say he was here when Romanel was vicar.' Piers glimpsed the interest in the priest's eyes. 'Come on, Father. You'd best come and talk to him before he gets too drunk.'

They found Walkin on a table which had been laid out before the tavern. He was small and wiry, neck as scrawny as a chicken, popping eyes and red, flushed face, the lower half of which was hidden under a wispy moustache and beard. Piers made the introductions.

'Sit down. Sit down.' Walkin patted the bench beside him. He smiled in a display of toothless gums. 'Sit down, Father. I've been longing to meet you. This is my helpmate, my grandson, Bartholomew.'

He pointed across to a dirty-faced boy whose hair was so greasy it hung in rat's-tails to his shoulder. The lad had his foot up on a bench, scratching vigorously at his leg.

'Stop that, Bartholomew!' Walkin snapped. 'He has a sore on his leg which never heals.' He indicated over his shoulder with his thumb at the tavern. 'He works there. He wants to be a cook. If I were you, Father, I wouldn't eat a thing he's touched.' Walkin sniffed the air like a dog. 'It will be dark before the beef is done. I want a nice, crisp piece. I've got some salt in my pocket and I'm going to sit and chew it.'

'Good for you, Walkin,' Philip replied. 'Piers tells me you knew Father Anthony?'

'Well, of course I did,' the old man retorted. 'I've known a lot of the priests. I always go to church on Sundays and Holy Days.'

'Did you know Romanel?'

'Oh Father, I was only a boy, a mere stripling, but I remember him.' He shook his head. 'We children didn't like him. He was a bad bugger. Mysterious, out in the cemetery there at the dead of night. Aye, I've heard what you've found. I bet if you dug a bit more you'd find something else.'

'What do you mean?' Philip asked.

Walkin leaned closer and tapped his red, fleshy nose. 'He was a leader, was Romanel. Men feared him. He would often come down to the tavern here. He could drink any man under the table and often did. Now those were the bad old days, Father, when our King's great-grandfather, Edward II, married the French woman. Times were hard. The Scots were raiding under Bruce. The royal commissioners were collecting stores and harvests were bad. Famine sat at many of our tables. Do you know, Father, further west, away from the towns and villages, they said men turned to cannibalism?'

'Romanel,' Piers interrupted.

'Ah well, yes. With the crops failing and the livestock dying, some of the villagers became outlaws. You've ridden round Scawsby, Father, even today it's a lonely place.' He drank from his jug of ale and once again told Bartholomew to stop scratching his leg. 'Anyway, Romanel and the old manor lord, they used to take men out in the marshes and attack the unwary.'

'But you were talking about the graveyard?'

'Ah, yes, so I was. Now, you've heard about the Templar treasure and all that nonsense? Well, I tell you this, Father, one night they did go out but not all of them came back. Those who did were all dead within the year.'

'A curse?' Philip asked.

'Aye, you could call it that, Father. Now Romanel also

150

claimed to be a leech, which made him such a lecher.' The old man smiled at the pun he had created. 'There were rumours that Romanel helped members of his gang into the grave: a potion here, a touch of powder there. Whatever, every man-jack of them died. As I have said, he was an evil bugger.'

'And Father Anthony?' Philip asked.

'Oh, he was different. He was a gentle, old soul. He loved the antiq—'

'Antiquities,' Philip finished the sentence for him.

'Yes, that's it, Father. Always coming down here asking people about the history of Scawsby. He was a good priest, until he met up with that idle bugger Waldis.'

'And what was your involvement?' Philip asked.

'Father Anthony came down to see Grandfather,' Bartholomew suddenly spoke up, as if to distract himself from scratching. He wiped his nose on the back of his hand. 'Didn't he? He came down to the tavern. He was strange by then, white-faced, unshaven and he smelt to high heaven.'

'A case of the pot calling the cauldron black!' Walkin snapped.

'He wanted to see Grandfather,' Bartholomew continued. 'Asked us would we come to the church.'

'You see,' Walkin interrupted. 'In my youth, Father, I was a very good stone-cutter. Anyway, Father Anthony took me up to the church. He led me down to the crypt and pointed to the pillars. "Walkin," he asks, "would it be possible to dig into this stone?" Well, I thought he was madcap and witless to boot. "Father," I replied. "You could spend eternity hacking at that stone and hardly make a dent. And if you did, well, you'd cut away the supports of the church. The crypt would cave in." He then asked about the flagstones on the floor. I said they could be lifted but what was the use? The old priest just smiled, he said it was a problem which was vexing him. He gave me a coin and that was it.'

Philip questioned him again but the old man couldn't give any indication of what was in Father Anthony's mind.

'I never saw him again, Father. Well, not till they cut his poor corpse down from the tree in the graveyard.'

Philip thanked him. He picked up his blackjack of ale and walked along the village high street, stopping to talk to this family or that. By the time he returned to the church he felt a little embarrassed; his parishioners regarded him as a hero. But, now the danger from the French had receded, Philip looked up at the stark tower of his church. He was truly convinced that the best thing he could do was destroy this place and not even wait for the new one at High Mount to be built. He was certain that in the cold, bleak winter of 1308, Romanel had massacred those Templars, left their corpses at High Mount, desecrated the old graves there and then buried the Templars' armour in his own cemetery. Philip stared at the gravestone: armour was difficult to hide. Fresh holes out at High Mount or discovered in the woods might create suspicion. Or did Romanel intend, at a later date, to dig the armour up and sell it? Anyway, by doing this, Romanel hid any evidence of the Templars disappearing on the marshes outside Scawsby. No eagle-eyed royal commissioner would be able to collect a scrap of proof which would indict him. Romanel hadn't finished there. He knew that those who had joined him, guilt-ridden, eager to confess or greedy to gain a reward, were also a danger. Philip knew enough about physic to realise that the fields around Scawsby contained deadly herbs. These could be collected, crushed and dried ready to dissolve in his accomplices' ale or wine. Of course, when they fell sick who would visit them? Their parish priest, pretending to bring more medicine but, in fact, hastening them all towards their graves.

Philip remembered the coffin woman's excitement the previous evening. He went through the lych-gate and across the cemetery. When he reached the grave which had been freshly dug the previous evening, he was surprised to see small candles had been pushed into the earth and lit so they formed a shape of a cross. On the other side of the newly turned earth, Priscilla knelt, eyes closed, praying her beads. Philip knelt opposite her. She opened her eyes.

'They are rejoicing, aren't they?' Her face seemed more youthful.

'Why did you scream last night when you saw the armour?' Philip asked.

'It was the violence,' she replied. 'Men of war with their bloody swords and the screams of the dying.' She sat back on her heels. 'Always the swords, the flying arrows, shapes in the darkness.'

'Have you seen the armour before?'

'In my dreams, yes.'

'These dreams, what happens in them?'

'I am on a lonely moor. The wind is cold. There's no moon, only clouds. A huge, white owl, with wings which fill the heavens, swoops over me. A harbinger of death.' She screwed up her eyes. 'Last night I dreamed again and it was more clear. There are men around me, they are tired. I can smell the sweat and boiled leather. They are good men. They are warriors but they are kind to me: gentle-eyed and gruff-voiced. There's one in particular. He has a moustache and beard. A wise man. Is he my father?' She opened her eyes. 'What do I mean by that?' she asked as if talking to herself. 'What am I saying? Romanel was my father, wasn't he?'

A shiver ran down Philip's spine and his mouth went dry.

'You were there, weren't you?' he asked. 'You were there when the Templars were attacked? What on earth, child, were you doing out there? Was Romanel so evil as to include you in his nefarious affairs?'

'I don't know.' The reply was sing-song. 'Father, I don't know. Sometimes I dream and it's terrible. Sometimes I draw pictures.' She beckoned with her hand. 'Would you like to see those pictures?'

Philip got up and followed her across into her hut. It was neat and tidy and smelling fragrantly of herbs and wild plants. The floor was earth-packed and strewn with fresh grass from the cemetery. The walls were of plaster recently painted. Philip surmised that the old woman had probably done that herself. A small hearth stood beneath the chimney piece, a crude affair. In the far corner was a ladder which led up to a bed loft. She made the priest welcome, sitting him on a stool whilst she wearily climbed the small ladder and came back with yellowing rolls of parchment. She handed these to the priest.

'I drew those myself,' she said shyly. 'Sir Richard, whenever he asks me what I want for Yuletide, I always say parchment and some sticks of charcoal.' She smiled. 'And, of course, fresh milk. Look at them. You are the only person who has seen them.'

Philip unrolled the parchment. Some were cracked and dried. Others were still clean and soft to the touch. At first he could make little sense of them. He moved to catch the light from the window and realised they were drawings, simple yet possessing a vigorous life of their own. He lay them out on the floor.

'Others have been lost,' she murmured. 'On one occasion

I burnt a few by mistake.' She tightened her lips. 'And, Father, I confess, sometimes I grow tired of it all.'

Philip just nodded, fascinated by the drawings. They seemed to depict the same scene. A group of men on horses crossing the countryside. He could tell they were knights. They wore pointed helmets, carried shields and spears and, in the middle, a small figure riding a palfrey. Like all the people in the drawings, the body was stick-like but Philip realised it was a small girl with long hair. The next pictures were black as if the woman had just rubbed and filled every available space with a piece of charcoal, except for the small drops of red ochre daubed onto the parchment, like pitch torches flickering in the dark. Philip recalled the wall paintings he had glimpsed in the garret: these were just the same.

'What are these?' he asked, pointing to the red drops.

'Corpse candles, Father. At least, that's what they call them. They are fires out over the marshes. Some people call them jack-o'-lanterns: to me they are corpse candles.'

'And what do they signify?'

'Death. The Devil's lights. Satan is coming through the darkness, Father. He misleads souls and he misleads bodies. He takes them onto the marsh where they die.'

'And have you seen these corpse candles?' Philip asked.

'Oh, no, Father. I am too afeared. I never leave the church. I never go out of Scawsby.'

'What?' Philip exclaimed. 'You must be well past your eightieth summer and you've never left the village?'

'No, I am too afeared. The corpse candles will be there.' She shivered and hitched the coarse blanket she had put across her shoulders closer round her. Lifting her head, she sniffed the air. 'They are roasting an ox, aren't they?' She wetted her lips. 'I'd love a piece of meat. Soft and juicy and maybe some to dry, to keep for another day?'

'You will have your meat,' Philip murmured. 'Priscilla, don't you know that these corpse candles are only fires, gases from the marsh.' He smiled. 'Or so I have been told.'

'To you, Father, they can be, but, to me, they are corpse candles, the Devil's lights.'

'But, if you haven't been out to the marsh, how can you remember?'

'It's like here. When the mists come and curl up around the trees and stones in the cemetery, I see the corpse candles and I know Romanel is about.'

Philip put the drawings down. 'Romanel!' he exclaimed.

She smiled slyly at him, turning her head sideways.

'You've seen him: wicked in life, wicked in death! I tell you this, when you see the corpse candles in the graveyard, Romanel is about. He will haunt this place until reparation is made.'

'Reparation for what?' Philip asked.

'I don't know, Father. But he was an evil man. He killed those Templars and he killed others.' She shook her head. 'Or I think he did.'

Philip returned to the drawings. The more he looked at them the more convinced he became that this old woman had witnessed the attack on the Templars in the marshes outside Scawsby. Each drawing told the same story.

'Why were you with the Templars?'

She shook her head. 'Was I? Was I really?' Her eyes filled with tears. 'I don't know!' she sobbed. 'Oh Lord, I wish I did!'

Philip collected the drawings together and handed them back.

'Thank you.' He got to his feet. 'Do you have anything, Priscilla, anything else from your early life?'

'Nothing at all, Father. All I have is what Romanel gave me.'

Philip helped her to her feet and kissed her vein-streaked hand.

'Then leave it all here. That ox must be well roasted by now. Come, my pretty, I'll have a piece cut for you.'

Philip led Priscilla by the hand, out across the cemetery. The day was drawing on. He stopped by the yew tree.

'You say your mother was buried there?'

'That's right, Father. That's what Romanel told me!'

Philip led her back out along the high street. He found her a place beside old Walkin who was now much the worse for drink. Young Bartholomew was despatched to cut a slice for her whilst Philip went into the tavern and brought her back a jug of milk. He then went along the street. He passed Edmund who sat at a table, being teased by some of the young maidens. Of Stephen there was no sign. Philip's face hardened: he had already decided, at the earliest possible moment, to confront his friend who, he believed, was more interested in hunting for the treasure than building a new church.

'You look angry, Father.'

The priest turned. Piers stood there, a blackjack in one hand, his other around a comely, fresh-faced, young woman.

'Come on, Father. A few cups of wine and you can dance with the rest of us.'

'Piers, I'd like to ask you a favour.'

'No, find your own girl.'

Philip didn't smile. Piers' hand fell away from the young woman's shoulders.

'What is it, Father?'

The priest excused himself: the girl smiled, Philip led Piers out of earshot.

'I want you to help me dig once more in the graveyard.'

'Oh, Father, not now.'

'Please. It won't take long.'

Piers swore under his breath.

'What are you looking for, Father?'

'A grave, the skeleton of a woman.'

Piers shrugged. 'Ah well, as they say, a labourer's work is never done.'

A short while later Philip, gown off, his sleeves rolled up, helped Piers to dig beneath the yew tree where Priscilla said her mother was buried. The earth was soft, easy to break. Piers' spade struck something hard. He crouched down, brushed away the dirt and laughed.

'You'll find no bodies beneath here, Father.'

'What do you mean?'

Piers stood up, wiping the sweat from his brow with the back of his hand.

'Father, you are tired and I am half-drunk. If I was sober I'd have told you. You can't bury anyone beneath a tree. We have just hit the roots. No corpse is buried there: never has been, never will be.'

Philip apologised. They both refilled the hole. He then apologised once again but Piers just waved his hand.

'You are a good man, Father.' He clapped him on the shoulder. 'I saw what you did in Scawsby wood and I've told the rest. You've got a fire in your belly, you and your brother. I'm glad you are here.'

Philip, slightly flattered, took the mattock and hoe back to the small enclosure behind the Priest's house and rejoined the revelry. He drank a cup of wine more quickly than he should have done. He was tired but still fascinated by what the coffin woman had told him. He went back to the Priest's house, climbed the stairs to his chamber and took down the missal which was kept there. He turned to the front and looked down the index of saints arranged in date order. He found it: Saint Priscilla's feast day, February 9th. Philip closed the missal and lay down on his bed.

'You were a wicked man, Romanel,' he whispered. 'That old woman in the graveyard, she was never your daughter. But, for some strange reason . . .' Philip paused. Yes, he thought: when that coffin woman was a very young girl, she had been with those Templars. The soldier monks had been slaughtered to a man but some spark of decency must have saved the girl from having her throat slit. Romanel had brought her back to Scawsby, an easy task: she must have been very young and frightened out of her wits. So terrified, the shock unbalanced her: Romanel simply put it about that she was some by-blow of his.

'That's why you called her Priscilla,' Philip spoke into the gathering darkness. 'You gave her the name from the day you found her in February 1308, the feast of St Priscilla.'

Philip closed his eyes. He was certain that old woman could only vaguely remember that terrible night so many years ago. Being of tender years, the shocking event would have removed any memory from her mind, burying it deep in her soul: hence her dreams, her drawings and those terrible screams last night when she saw the armour of the Templars: men who had died around her, led to their deaths by the corpse candles on Scawsby marshes.

When Philip woke up it was dark. He calculated that he must have been asleep for at least an hour. Darkness was falling and, even from where he lay, he could hear the sound of the revelry in the village. When he opened a window overlooking the cemetery, he caught the faint smell of cooking. Philip went downstairs to check all was well, ensuring the postern door at the back was locked, the fire in the kitchen dampened down. He drank some watered ale to clean his mouth and tasted the oatmeal Roheisia had prepared for the following morning. He went out and looked across the cemetery. His stomach curdled, for the mist had swept in.

'Priscilla!' he called. 'Priscilla, have you returned?'

Silence. Philip walked across to the church. The main door was locked and, standing on tiptoe, he peered through the window. He could see no lights. He was halfway back across the cemetery when he heard a crackle as if someone had stepped on a dry twig. The mist swirled about and his stomach clenched in fear as he saw a small glow of light, yellowish-red, as if someone was holding up a shuttered lantern: turning it now and again so he could glimpse the flame. Philip hurried back into the house, slamming the door behind him. It felt colder now, unwelcoming. Had he left his candle alight in his chamber? Philip was halfway up the stairs, when he heard the whisper.

'Priest!'

Philip whirled round. He breathed in and gagged at the terrible stench.

'Priest!'

The voice was now in front of him as if someone was in the gallery above.

'Who are you?' Philip called. 'Stephen, is this some jest?'

'Meddling, meddling priest!' The voice was a whisper, yet hoarse with malice. 'Aren't you interested in the treasure? Why question the woman?'

Philip went up the stairs. The voice was now behind him, chuckling like the giggling of some spiteful child. Philip decided to ignore it. He walked into his chamber; it was in darkness. He had extinguished the candle. He made his way carefully across the room, picked up a crucifix and a small stoup of holy water he kept there, and walked out into the gallery.

'In the name of Christ Jesus!' he called and threw some water onto the floor. 'In the name of the Lord Jesus, I order you to return whence you came!'

As if in answer, he heard the ghostly clapping of hands: slow, measured as if whoever was there was mocking him. Philip walked to the top of the stairs. He took a deep breath, then went down, casting the water before him, letting it spill out of the stoup. The crucifix was clenched so tightly between his fingers, the wood stuck to his flesh. His heart jumped: from the gallery above somone was dancing on the spot. Then a faint humming, slow footsteps behind him as if the person was coming down the stairs, but taking their time, singing under their breath. Philip reached the door and put his hand on the latch. He felt his shoulder gripped. He was spun round and held fast against the door. He screamed in terror at Romanel's face, white, skull-like, cadaverous, the red lips parted in a rasp of stale air.

'In Christ's name!'

Philip felt as if the hand round his neck was going to strangle him. Romanel brought his hand back, struck him across his mouth and Philip gratefully sank into unconsciousness.

Chapter 2

'Ite Missa est. Go, the Mass is finished.'

Philip raised his hand and sketched a blessing in the air though not many of his parishioners were present to receive it. The revelry had gone on well after midnight and most of the villagers were still abed. Philip returned to the sacristy. He quickly divested. Edmund was watching him curiously but Philip had said nothing about the previous night's visitation. He had regained consciousness very soon. There was no mark on his face and anyone would think he had, perhaps, just tripped and fainted. Nevertheless, Philip had no doubts about what had happened. After regaining consciousness, he'd left the Priest's house, losing himself in the rejoicings of his parishioners. He had later retired to bed, laughingly refusing any further attempts to make him stay. Stephen must have returned, slipping into the village, because Philip had glimpsed him sitting at one of the tables. Now Philip was bent on a confrontation. He found his friend at the table breaking his fast, sipping hungrily at a bowl of sweetened oatmeal.

'Roheisia!' Philip exclaimed. 'I'd be grateful if you would leave us for a while.'

Edmund, who had slipped into the room, sat down. He was fearful for his friend who had changed since they had arrived in this parish. Yet, because he was so close to his elder brother whom he adored, he also realised that Philip was not happy with Stephen and that a friendship, built over the years, was beginning to crumble.

'I missed you at Mass, Stephen!'

'Ah, good morning, Philip.' Stephen put his horn spoon down and stared defiantly back.

'I missed you at Mass,' Philip repeated. 'And I missed you yesterday at the festivities. You were out at High Mount, weren't you?'

'I am Stephen Merkle,' his friend replied sarcastically. 'A master mason. I am here at Scawsby to build you a church. High Mount is the new site. I went down yesterday to draw up plans. I have my notes upstairs.'

'Oh, I know who you are and why you are here!' Philip snapped. 'But do not lie to me. The Stephen Merkle I know can't resist any gaiety or revelry. True, you are here to build a church but you are also searching for the treasure, aren't you? I can see it in your eyes.'

Stephen's gaze fell away. Philip leaned across and gripped his shoulder.

'Stephen, believe me when I tell you this: that treasure is cursed. Whatever it is, it's drenched in innocent men's blood! Everyone and anyone who has tried to find it comes to grief.'

Stephen opened his mouth.

'Don't lie!' Philip shouted, drawing away, jabbing a finger at his friend. 'Don't sit there . . . !'

'Philip, what is the matter?' Stephen half rose. 'You accuse me of hunting for the treasure. Yet, since you've arrived at St Oswald's, you, too, have changed: sour-faced, secretive.'

'Oh, for the love of God!' Edmund intervened. 'Stephen, you saw what happened the other evening, the blood in

163

the chest.'

'I can send you away.' Philip drew back on his stool. 'I am parish priest here. Sir Richard Montalt is my patron. We can always hire another mason.'

As soon as the words were out of his mouth Philip regretted them, and knew he always would. He caught a look, a mere glance from Stephen: he saw the fury seething there just before the master mason forced a smile and held his hands up.

'Confiteor. Confiteor,' he declared. 'I confess. I confess. The legends of the treasure do fascinate me.' He leaned across the table. 'Philip, you know I was born near here. The stories about the Scawsby treasure are famous. So, yes, it's tempting to know that somewhere out at High Mount might lie a king's fortune.'

'In my view,' Philip replied, getting to his feet, 'the only thing that lies out at High Mount are the remains of murdered Templars. We are going out there this morning. I have sent Crispin to Sir Richard to ask for Piers, a good cart and some canvas cloths. I am going to transport the remains of both the monks and those Templars to hallowed grounds. You are going to help me.'

'Of course! Of course!' Stephen got to his feet and came round, his face genial. He clasped Philip's hand. 'I am sorry,' he apologised. 'Philip, I will do whatever you ask. Whatever you say.'

Edmund visibly relaxed. Philip drew Stephen to him and clasped him firmly. You are lying, he thought: I saw the look on your face, the fury in your eyes. You are lying. You are only coming to High Mount because we might discover something. Nevertheless, he stood back and smiled his appreciation at Stephen's words. He recalled Roheisia back in the kitchen. Despite the agitation in his stomach,

Philip sat down, put a bright face on matters and ate a hearty breakfast. He finished and was about to go to his chamber when Crispin returned with a rather sorry-looking Piers. The verderer's sallow face was now white, his eyes red-rimmed. He clutched his stomach and groaned.

'Father, I confess I ate and drank too much yesterday. Now I'm paying for it. However, a jug of watered ale and some of that oatmeal . . .'

In a twinkling of an eye, Roheisia, who had become all shy and coy when Piers came into the kitchen, ushered the verderer to the table. A bowl of oatmeal, laced with nutmeg and honey, and a large blackjack of ale were set before him. Despite his inebriation of the night before, Piers had the good sense to keep his mouth shut until Roheisia and her son had left the kitchen.

'Sir Richard read your letter,' he began, putting his spoon down. 'He agrees: the remains of the Templars, as well as those of the monks we fished from the well, are to be decently shrouded and buried in the crypt beneath the manor chapel. Sir Richard believes it should be done immediately. I am to give you every assistance. He would have sent more men but he thinks this matter should be kept as secret as possible.' He stirred his oatmeal. 'Already tongues are clacking and people are beginning to wonder. Sir Richard also says you are to bring the armour you found the previous night: that, too, is to be buried with them.'

They finished the meal. Philip collected his cloak. Edmund would have preferred to stay but Philip said they would need every available pair of hands. So, with Piers driving the cart and Philip and his companions riding behind, they left the Priest's house and went out of the village, through the woods towards High Mount. The day was a fine one, the sun growing strong in a cloudless sky. Scawsby wood seemed to have lost its menace: birds sang and swooped overhead. The bracken on either side was noisy as small animals scurried about. Squirrels, high in the branches, chattered in protest at being driven away by the clop of hooves and the crashing of the steel-rimmed wheels of the cart. Piers soon recovered his good spirits, describing how the French had been taken away as well as the different mishaps during the previous night's revelry. Philip, riding beside him, half listened, Romanel's ghastly visitation still haunting him.

'Do you think this will end it, Father?' Piers looked at him narrow-eyed. 'I mean, Sir Richard is pleased. You've done more than any of the other priests have: you've proved the Templars were murdered out on the marshes. Perhaps, if they are now given hallowed burial?'

Philip smiled at the verderer's weather-beaten face.

'You are a good man, Piers,' he replied. 'I would love to say, yes, all is ended. But,' he urged his horse forward as they reached the bottom of High Mount, 'I have a feeling that it is only about to begin.'

It took some time for the cart to reach the top of the hill. Once they had assembled, Philip insisted on kneeling before where the high altar had stood and recited a psalm. He then called on the Virgin Mary, all the Saints and Angels as witnesses, loudly declaring that what he was about to do was not out of desecration, greed or any other base motive but to give innocent men hallowed burial. He had scarcely finished when a cold breeze, which seemed to come from nowhere, whipped their faces. Philip stared round. The sun still shone. The ruins were desolate, peaceful, yet he was sure he caught the whisper: those words inscribed so many times around the church: 'Spectamus te, semper spectamus te.' 'We are watching you, we are always watching you.'

They spent the first hour taking the bones and remains of

the monks who had been thrown down the well and carefully laid them in the canvas cloths Piers had brought. Philip also took from a leather bag, placed in the back of the cart, a large stoppered flask of holy water. Before each canvas was bound up, he blessed the pathetic bones, sprinkling them with water and intoning the 'Dona Eis Requiem'. All the time he watched Stephen. The master mason was very attentive and helpful. Nevertheless, Philip could sense his excitement as if Stephen could hardly wait to remove the grey slabs from the priory floor and see what lay beneath. After they had eaten some bread and dried bacon as well as generous cups of claret from the wineskin Roheisia had also provided, they began to move the gravestones. Piers had brought poles but, in the end, this did not prove difficult. In each grave they found a skeleton, very similar to the one found in the sanctuary. Not a shred of cloth or any insignia betrayed their origins, though it was apparent that all had died violent deaths. Blows to the skull, broken ribs, a shattered arm or leg. Philip realised what a desperate, bloody fight must have occurred out on the marshes.

'A terrible act,' Piers whispered. 'They were killed in cold blood!'

'What do you mean?'

Edmund overheard Piers. He came up and stared down at the skeleton they had just removed, the bones of the arm shattered and splintered.

'Well,' the verderer replied. 'This must have been a dreadful fight. However, I doubt if these men were killed in the cut and thrust of battle.' He crouched down and pointed to the skeleton's arm. 'What I suspect has happened is this. These men were knights, yes? Close up, fighting back to back, let's say at a place like High Mount, they would have taken all comers. But, what I suspect happened . . .' He held his hands up. 'Can you imagine out in the marshes at the dead of night? Arrows whirling out of the darkness! Horses going down! Men slipping in the mud! The arrows would wreak terrible damage but then the attackers would close in, as you saw in the fight against the French, battering the wounded to death.'

Philip shivered. He stared at the sagging jaw of a skeleton. Piers pointed to a hole in the side of the skull.

'That's how this man died. Probably his horse was killed under him. His helmet comes off, an arrow takes him in the body. He was then finished off, battered with a club.'

'Why didn't they just leave the corpses in the marsh?' Edmund asked.

Piers grinned wolfishly. 'The marshes are not what you think, good priest. Oh, I have heard of quagmires which drag a man down but the marshes here are not all that deep, not like you get in the Fens. The marshes of Scawsby are, perhaps, only a yard, maybe two yards deep. Like Waldis the parish clerk, the man is sucked in but eventually he'll rise to the top again. No, no,' he continued, 'these men were probably attacked at night and then their assailants waited until daybreak. They took each corpse out, stripped it and brought the bodies here.'

'Of course,' Philip murmured. 'And they would pile the armour in the cart?'

'Yes, that can be hidden. But you can't hide a dozen corpses.'

'And the horses?' Stephen asked. 'They must have had horses?' He glanced apologetically at Philip. 'Sumpter ponies to carry the treasure?'

'Oh, they would have killed them,' Philip intervened.

'It can easily be done,' Piers added. 'Try and sell a horse that's stolen and you'll soon find yourself at the foot of the gallows. Most of the Templars' horses would have been lamed or wounded. They would have been slaughtered, driven into some lonely glade and had their throats cut.'

'But there was one thing missing,' Philip intervened. 'Clothing, the saddles, the harness of these knights?'

'Buried elsewhere,' Edmund replied. 'God knows, Brother, and I mean no disrespect, but God knows what else that graveyard in Scawsby holds!'

They lifted the skeleton up and placed it on a canvas cloth and continued their macabre task of opening the graves. In the end, they unearthed the remains of fourteen men. Some of the graves lay outside the church, though most were in the nave or sanctuary. They replaced the slabs carefully lest any curiosity seeker came on to High Mount and discovered what had happened.

'Though there is little chance of that,' Piers remarked. 'Only the hardy hearts come up here. It's always had a reputation for being an eeric place.'

'What will happen in the new church?' Edmund asked. 'I mean to the graves?'

'Oh, I plan to move them anyway,' Stephen replied absentmindedly.

Philip could see Stephen was fighting hard to conceal his disappointment. They had found nothing in the graves to give them any indication about the treasure or where it could be hidden.

'The foundations of the old priory,' Stephen continued, 'are probably firm and we will build over them. All this,' he gestured round the nave, 'will disappear. But, Philip, there are other graves.'

'Where?' Philip asked.

'Just two, over here.'

Stephen led them into a far corner just within the ruins.

Both walls had bushes and weeds growing up the sides. Stephen pulled these aside with his mattock: crouching down, Philip looked through and glimpsed a paving slab.

'How long do you think these bushes have been growing?' he asked. 'Perhaps the poor monks who are buried here have been allowed to rest in peace. Ah, yes.' He rose slowly. 'I can now see two paving stones.'

Philip was sure that these graves had not been disturbed but he wished to humour Stephen, so he began to hack at the bushes and grass until the area was clear. The graves' slabs were much more difficult to move than the rest, their rims caked with hard-packed earth. The first tomb held that of a monk, Philip could deduce that by the wooden cross buried with him. The second grave was deeper. At first they thought it was empty until Philip stretched down into the grave. He clawed away the dirt and drew out the remains of battered leather saddlebags. Seven or eight in number. Stephen was beside himself with excitement. They laid them out on the priory floor. The straps were rotting, the buckles rusted.

'They are made of good Cordovan leather,' Philip remarked. 'Otherwise they would have rotted away long ago.'

'They emptied the saddlebags. A few pathetic items: horn spoons, a knife, Ave beads, fragments and shards of clothing, cloaks, surcoats, baldrics, belts, even a broken spur. When they climbed into the graves they found other items also buried there. Yet, in the end, the saddlebags proved to be a disappointment. Only one thing caught Philip's attention: a rolled-up piece of tapestry with what appeared to be cambric round the cuffs and neck. He held it up: it was thin and dirt-stained.

'I'm not too sure,' Philip remarked. 'But I'd say this was the remains of a girl's dress.' He decided to hide what he'd learnt from the coffin woman. 'But what has this to do with Templars fleeing through the dead of night?'

'What apparently did happen,' Edmund added, 'is that Romanel must have brought the corpses here, piled their arms into a cart, then buried the bodies and all the clothing where no one could find it.'

'I suspect,' Philip declared, walking to the edge of the ruins and peering through what had once been a doorway, 'that the remains of the horses and the harness are somewhere on the Scawsby moors. If anything, Romanel was thorough. The bodies and their effects stayed at High Mount: the harness tossed elsewhere whilst the armour was the most dangerous thing. Clothes, harness, horses might be found but armour would provide more positive proof of what had happened to the Templars. So, it couldn't be hidden out here at High Mount: metallic and cumbersome, someone might notice it.' He beat the heel of his boot against the earth. 'It would be difficult to dig here. There are foundations and any new hole, either here or in the forest, might be noticed. The arms were taken to Scawsby, probably at night and buried deep in the graveyard, the safest place for them. Ah well.' He came back. 'Place all this into one of the canvas sheets. Let's eat and drink.' He glanced up at the sky. 'Edmund, Stephen, I want you to take the cart to the manor house. Sir Richard will know what to do. On the way collect the Templar arms, tell Sir Richard I'll sing the requiem Mass tonight. Only we will attend.'

'What are you going to do?' Edmund asked.

'Piers can borrow your horse. I want him to ride with me out along the marshes. I want to see where this terrible tragedy began.'

They all agreed though Stephen's disappointment was obvious. Whilst the rest ate and drank, he paced restlessly

171

round the ruins as if they might have overlooked something. Philip sat by himself, his back to the wall, face up at the sun to catch its warmth. Piers lay down and fell fast asleep like a child whilst Edmund, now also suspicious of Stephen, insisted on following the master mason around the priory. Philip closed his eyes. He could now visualise what had happened so many years ago. The slaughter out on the marshes; the burial of the corpses; the desecration of the graves. Romanel and his conspirators slipping back into Scawsby village. But what was the treasure they had brought? Where was it buried? Surely they wouldn't leave it out here at High Mount? Romanel, a ruthless man, would be intent on keeping a close eye on it. Philip stirred, stretching out his legs. Something dreadful had happened but no more terrible than other incidents Philip had heard about. Innocent men died every day. People were robbed. True, Romanel may have been a necromancer, a warlock, but other priests had been steeped in wickedness. Did they haunt their churches? What was so horrible, so blasphemous in what they had done that Lord George Montalt had hidden himself in the cellar, scrawling the word REPARATION so many, many times? And what did the numbers 6 and 14 mean? Who was Veronica? And where did the coffin woman come from? Was she with the Templars as a child? Philip recalled what he knew about that fighting order of monks. They were bound to celibacy and chastity. True, accusations of sodomy had been laid against them but there had never been any allegations about consorting with whores or bringing paramours into their houses. Romanel had definitely lied about the child he called Priscilla. The girl's mother was not buried in the graveyard and she seemed to have certainly witnessed the attack as a child. Was she a daughter of one of the assailants who'd been killed and Romanel had taken her into his care? Philip sighed and wondered what to do. In a way he had begun to regret sending that letter to Rochester asking for an exorcist. Would the bishop think that he had lost his wits? That he was scarcely a week in his new parish and he was already causing trouble, seeing sprites and goblins in the trees? Philip heard the clink, the sound of hoof beats. At first he thought it was some traveller passing along the road. But it came again, as if mounted men were gathering at the foot of the hill. He opened his eyes. Piers was already on his feet, an arrow notched to his bow. Stephen and Edmund came running across.

'Did you hear it?' Edmund cried.

Philip got to his feet. The sun didn't seem so strong now. He could definitely hear the sound of horses as if a group of men were massing at the bottom of High Mount. He went over to the walls and stared down the hill. There was nothing. He ran to the other side: nothing except sun-dappled fields, the woods in the distance, smoke coming from the hearths of Scawsby village. He looked along the trackway; a journeyman with his sumpter pony was making his way into Scawsby.

Philip stalked along the ruined nave and into the sanctuary. He passed one of the open graves where they had yet to return the slab. Something caught at his foot. He looked down – it was a bony hand snaking out to grasp him. Philip kicked out but, when he looked again, there was no hand at all and he cursed himself as a dreamer. He went out through the ruined wall and stood on the brow of the hill. Birds swooped, trilling their hearts out. A large fox, his bushy tail held high, trotted across the foot of the hill and disappeared into some bushes. Philip swallowed hard: his throat was dry, his lips and mouth sour as if he had eaten something rotten.

'Lord Jesus,' he whispered. 'Keep us safe from the noonday devil. Protect us against the barbs and arrows of the enemy.'

'Help me!'

Philip jumped round. There was no one.

'Help me!' the voice whispered. 'Oh, help me!' The voice seemed to be coming from the well. 'Oh, help me, please!'

Philip went across and crouched down. He peered over the rim and stared straight into the corpse-white face of Romanel. The phantasm gave a great sigh, his hand came up to clutch Philip's jerkin, dragging him down. Philip fought hard, trying to break his gaze from those devil-eyes, that leering mouth, the smell of rottenness.

'Help me!'

The ghost was imitating the voice of a child: the mouth then curled into an angry snarl. Philip fought hard, struggling to keep a grip on the stone rim, yet Romanel was pulling him down. He tried to scream but couldn't.

'Oh, St Michael,' Philip prayed to his patron. 'Oh, St Michael and all the Angels.'

Suddenly he felt himself lifted up and pulled away. Romanel was falling, down into the blackness of the well. Philip lay on the grass gasping and spluttering. He looked around. No one was there. Edmund, Stephen and Piers were now running towards him.

'Brother, what's the matter?'

Philip rose to a half-crouch, pulling back his jerkin.

'Nothing,' he gasped. 'I felt a little faint.'

Piers, however, was quick. He caught Philip staring at the rim of the well. The verderer walked across, an arrow notched to his bow and peered down.

'It's nothing,' Philip murmured. 'Come!' He got to his feet.

They pushed back the remaining gravestone and cleaned up the site. Edmund climbed into the cart, Piers advising him what paths to take to the manor.

Philip watched them go, noticing that Stephen hung back on his horse as if reluctant to talk to them. He and Piers mounted their horses. The verderer was silent but, once they had left High Mount, he pulled his horse back to ride alongside.

'Something happened up there, didn't it, Father?'

'Yes, Piers, it did. Something demonic, spat out from hell.' Philip sighed in exasperation. 'What I can't understand is why do I experience this? If I rode into Scawsby and told them what was happening they'd think I was witless.'

'No, Father, they wouldn't!' Piers retorted. 'I told you the tongues are already beginning to wag. My wife's death, the death after childbirth of other women married to certain men in the village. A terrible evil lurks in Scawsby. Now I've been ordered by Lord Richard to give you every help. I am not a lettered man, Father. I can barely read and write. However, I know what happened here and I believe one of my ancestors, God forgive him, had a hand in it.' Piers hawked and spat. 'You say the people of Scawsby would mock you.' He shook his head. 'It's not like that, Father. Scawsby is a pleasant village, good people who fear God and honour the king: that is the truth. Nevertheless, Father, we are really like children playing by a snake pit. As long as we don't go near the edge we are secure. As long as we have nothing to do with trying to discover that treasure, we are safe.'

'But I am not trying to search for the treasure.'

Piers smiled. 'I know that, Father, and so does Lord Richard. If you were, you might have been killed on High Mount.'

Philip rode on silently. He still felt sick at that terrible vision he had seen at the well. He couldn't dismiss it as some trick of the mind but, there again, he wondered who had dragged him back? Freed him from Romanel's clutch? Someone had. He'd felt himself lifted up. An angel of light? Or were those whispers true? Were there others watching him? Constantly studying what he was doing? Whatever, he concluded, if he had not been freed from Romanel's grip, it would have been just another unfortunate accident. Poor Father Philip who had gone out to High Mount and, by accident, fallen down a disused well. Philip closed his eyes. He prayed that Stephen had told him the truth.

'So, Father.' Piers took another swig from his wineskin. He offered it to Philip who seized it greedily and took two generous mouthfuls.

'Take a little wine for the stomach's sake,' Philip smiled, quoting from St Paul.

He handed it back. Piers lowered the wineskin over his saddle horn.

'So, Father,' the verderer repeated. 'Where do you want to go?'

'I want to go to the marshes, Piers. You are a soldier. I want you to use your imagination. You are leading a troop of men fleeing from London. It's dark and in the dead of winter. You have to stop at villages to eat, drink and rest the horses. Scawsby is in your line of march but you want to keep well away from the main paths and trackways. You want to be safe until you reach the coast.'

Piers rode on, thinking about what the priest had said.

'We are travelling north,' the verderer declared. 'There are many paths to Scawsby, Father. I know the line of march the Templars would have followed but we have some riding ahead of us.'

He urged his horse into a canter. Philip followed.

They rode for an hour, then stopped by a small brook where they shared out the last of their provisions, drank some wine and allowed their horses to rest before continuing. They left the main trackways. Slowly, almost imperceptibly, the countryside began to change. No sign of any farms or men working in the fields. Philip realised they were on the marsh lands, a veritable wilderness, broad and dark. Piers told him to be careful as they threaded their way past dark, stagnant water, foul rivulets which curled their way around small islands of weeds, tummocks and thickets. Above them curlew and snipe flew against a sky becoming rapidly overcast. A cold, dark place, lonely and flat, bereft of any sign of human habitation. Piers seemed to know his way. Now and again they would dismount but, at last, they came to a broad trackway which seemed to cut through the wilderness. They rode a distance down this, then Piers reined in. He dismounted, hobbling his horse beneath the outstretched arms of a blighted oak tree. Piers indicated with his hand along the path.

'I suspect, Father, that the Templars came along this road. If you follow it south you'll come to other villages. Now, if we were travelling to Scawsby, we would follow the route we have just ridden along, passing High Mount, through the woods into the village. If we were riding fast it would take us just over an hour.' He smiled impishly. 'I'll confess, Father: for a short while I became lost. So it will take us less time to travel back than it did to arrive.'

'What would happen then?' Philip asked.

'Well, it's a spring day, Father. Think of yourself here at night with freezing sleet and snow. Pretend you are the Templar commander. You know the path.' Piers tapped the side of his head. 'Before you left London you'd study the paths and trackways. However, your horses are tired and your men are starving. Suddenly you see lights out on the marsh.'

'Corpse candles!' Philip exclaimed.

'Ah yes, Father, corpse candles, the devil's lights.'

'Devil's lights they were,' Philip breathed back, patting his horse which had grown restless in the eerie silence. 'Somehow Romanel and his gang knew that the Templars were coming along this path. They used the old smugglers' trick, luring people off the pathways with torches.' He stood high in the stirrups and looked out over the marshland. 'A terrible place,' he murmured. 'Oh, there are trackways and paths of firm grass but, for the ignorant and unwary, it would be a death trap.'

Philip sat back on his horse and, closing his eyes, fervently intoned the 'Dona Eis Requiem'. He then looked up at the sky.

'Come on, Piers. I have visited the place.' He sketched a blessing. 'I have satisfied myself and Lord Richard will be waiting.'

Piers untethered his horse, mounted, and they rode back along the pathway. The daylight was fading. Philip felt cold. He even regretted coming here. He heard a sound to his right and looked across the wild heathland: his heart seemed to leap into his throat.

'Oh, sweet Lord!' he whispered.

In front of him Piers just rode on.

'I know, Father. I can see them,' he called out. 'It's best if you continue your prayers and we keep riding.'

Philip, however, had to look again. Away to his right, as if following some invisible path along the marshes, a line of horsemen, shadowy, dark, were also riding, keeping them under close scrutiny.

Chapter 3

Darkness had fallen by the time they reached the Montalt manor house: the line of mysterious riders abruptly disappeared just before they approached High Mount. After such a journey, Philip was pleased to see Lord Richard, Edmund, Henry and Isolda waiting for him in the parlour. He refused any wine or food.

'I'll be breaking my fast,' he declared, 'for a Mass should be said.' He gripped Piers' shoulder. 'Lord Richard, I would like to thank you for Piers. If I had to choose, I couldn't have selected a better man.'

Piers blushed with embarrassment: he shuffled his feet, muttering under his breath that it was nothing.

'Ah well.' Lord Richard clapped his hands to break the silence. 'I'd best show you what I've done.'

He led them out along a ground-floor gallery to a small chapel at the back of the manor. A jewel of a chamber; dark, wooden wainscoting covered the walls. The altar stood on a wooden dais at the far end under a small rose window. Niches on either side held statues of the Virgin Mary and of St George killing the dragon. The paving slabs in front of the altar had been lifted, the remains interred; servants were re-planing the broad, thick flagstones.

'They can lie in the small crypt there,' Lord Richard declared, taking Philip aside. 'Until, perhaps, the new church is built. I have told my son and his betrothed that they are just the remains of poor monks from High Mount.' He paused, fighting back the tears. 'I wish this business was over,' Lord Richard whispered. 'Young Henry and Isolda came to see me this morning. Henry acquitted himself so well against the French,' he forced a smile, 'he now sees himself as the new Sir Galahad.' His smile faded. 'He wants to become handfast, betrothed to Isolda. They have chosen the feast of the Assumption, the fifteenth of August.'

'And they cannot be persuaded differently?' Philip asked.

Lord Richard shook his head. 'No, I've already postponed it twice and they are beginning to wonder why. Can't you see, Father? If they marry in August, and Isolda becomes pregnant, that beautiful girl could be dead within eighteen months.'

Philip looked over his shoulder at Isolda and Henry standing so close together, hands clasped, laughing and chattering to each other.

'They probably think,' Lord Richard added, 'that we are discussing their nuptials.'

'August has not yet come,' Philip replied. 'Let us put our trust in God. These matters will surely come to a head soon.'

Edmund had brought vestments down from the church: black and gold chasubles and amices, the colours for the Mass for the Dead. Philip washed his hands at the lavarium. He put the vestments on and, standing before the altar, intoned the entry antiphon: 'Eternal rest grant unto them, Oh Lord.' The service was simple and short. Edmund served as deacon, reading the gospel. In between that and the offertory, Philip blessed the place where the remains had been buried. Once the Mass was ended, he joined Lord Richard and his family in the hall for some wine and a bowl of broth.

'Where's Stephen?' he whispered.

'At the church,' Edmund replied grimly. 'It's the cemetery which now fascinates him. I still believe he searches for the treasure but now accepts that High Mount is, perhaps, not the place.'

Philip, concerned, ate his soup and drank the wine a little more quickly than he wished. He refused Lord Richard's invitation to stay. He thanked Piers again, they collected their horses from the stables and rode back to the Priest's house. Philip was relieved to find Stephen sitting at a table before the kitchen fire immersed in his drawings. They exchanged pleasantries. Philip then walked round the house to ensure all was well. He was about to retire for the night, exhausted and troubled by his visit to High Mount and journey across the marshes, when he heard a loud knocking at the door. Going to the top of the stairs, he sighed with relief that the noise was not caused by some macabre occurrence. A cloaked, cowled figure walked into the hallway. Edmund came to the foot of the stairs.

'We have a visitor,' he called up. 'Brother Anselm. His Lordship the Bishop has sent him.'

Philip came downstairs to greet his guest.

'You are the exorcist!' he exclaimed.

The bald, cheery-faced little friar pulled back his cowl and laughed out loud.

'My name is Anselm Broadbench. I am a Franciscan friar, a priest and, yes, if you want, an exorcist!' He gestured towards the door. 'I've stabled my palfrey.' He grinned. 'I call it Lucifer.'

Philip smiled back. Anselm was of middling stature, broad, well built, his round, cheery face adorned with a grey moustache and beard. The friar patted his bald pate.

'The Lord giveth and the Lord taketh away,' he intoned.

'What I've lost on top, I've gained round the mouth and jowls.' He scratched his luxuriant beard. 'I had a word with his Lordship. He sent me here to help. However, I must warn you.' He took his cloak off and handed it to Edmund. 'In the end, perhaps, I can only give advice. But, first, I must kill one demon.'

'Yes?' Philip asked.

'Hunger.' Anselm patted his stomach. 'I'm cold and I'm hungry and I'd accept anything you have on offer!'

Philip led him into the kitchen. He introduced Anselm to Stephen: the friar plumped himself down at the head of the table. He rubbed his stomach and gazed benevolently at the dishes Philip had served.

'Oatmeal, roast beef, bread, vegetables, some wine. I thought I'd come to Scawsby and, look, I've found myself in Paradise!'

For a while the friar sat and ate, chattering about Rochester, the journey, how the weather was improving. Philip studied him closely: he recognised that the friar was trying to put them at their ease as much as they were him.

'You are surprised, aren't you?' Anselm remarked, pushing away the platter. He stared in mock seriousness. 'What did you expect? Someone cloaked in black from head to toe with a chain of bones around their necks? Pushing a hand barrow full of relics and phials of holy water?' He drummed his fingers on the table. 'Let me explain before I begin. Satan does not like humanity. He fears us. He wants to make us less human, he therefore exploits all our weaknesses. A man who is tired, a man who is starving or dying of thirst or wounded in body or mind – such a person is more vulnerable than a man who feels all is well with himself and God. Satan hates the ordinary things of life: husband and wife making love. He'd much prefer to have them at each other's throats. Two friends sitting in a tavern sharing a jug of wine. Children playing on a summer's day. The sun in God's sky, the stars wheeling at night. These and prayer are the best defences against demons.'

'But here is different,' Philip interrupted.

'I'll come to that.' Brother Anselm sipped from his wine cup. 'I believe,' he continued, 'what Holy Mother Church teaches. Man is part of a cosmic battle: the war has already been fought and won by Christ but each man must play his part. Some of that battle we never see because the world is not only visible but invisible. Some we witness every day: a man being stabbed in a tavern; a woman being raped; a child being abused. Sometimes we can get depressed because it seems we are surrounded by darkness but that, too, is one of the devil's tricks. He wants us to despair, to lose our humanity as well as any hope in God.' He grasped Philip's hand. 'You are not despairing, are you, Father? You still have faith in the Lord Jesus?'

'Lord, I have faith, please increase the little I have,' Philip replied, quoting from the gospels.

Anselm laughed and released his hand. 'His Grace the Bishop told me about you, Philip, you and your brother are good priests. His Lordship also sends his apologies.' He paused and picked at a crumb on the table. 'This is a terrible house,' he whispered.

A shiver ran down Philip's back. The friar had spoken so nonchalantly.

'Terrible evil lurks here,' Anselm murmured. 'I can feel it, sense it around me, pressing down.' He crossed himself. 'In the far corner,' he added. 'Over near the hearth there. No, you won't see it, just a shadow deeper than the rest. A presence watches you.' He forced a smile. 'And that's why his Lordship the Bishop sent his apologies. The records

183

at Rochester list many incumbents who have come here, stayed only a short while, then left complaining about the stench of sin which pervades this place, the oppressive evil of this house. The demonic attacks which may be just nightmares yet no one dare talk about them, lest they be dismissed as possessed or witless themselves.' The friar breathed in deeply through his nose. 'Before the Bishop sent you, he had already made himself a secret promise that, if you complained about Scawsby, he would do something about it.' He spread his hands. 'And that's why I'm here.'

'So, what will you do?' Edmund asked.

'I don't know,' Anselm replied. 'As I have said, we live in a world of the visible and the invisible. Think of our reality as a mirror, we only see what we can but it does not mean that beyond the mirror another world, another reality, does not exist. Most times the two are kept separate. Sometimes, for good or evil, they can merge.'

'And this is happening here?' Stephen asked from where he sat.

'Yes, yes. Perhaps it is.' Father Anselm rolled back the sleeves of his gown, emphasising his points on slender fingers. 'Real evil, the work of Satan, can become enmeshed in the affairs of men in a number of ways. First, someone could live such a wicked life that, as the gospel says, the devil finds a home there. Secondly, by direct invocation, by appealing to the powers of darkness, by summoning them through sorcery or the black arts. Thirdly, a violent and evil act can also attract the attention of demons. It can be a house where a terrible murder has taken place. And,' he paused, staring across the chamber.

'And?' Edmund asked hastily.

'The worst phenomenon of all, a combination of all three.'

The friar shook himself as if he was trying to clear his mind. Philip noticed how subdued he had become. His eyes had lost their twinkle of merriment. Now and again the friar's lips moved wordlessly as if he was quietly and earnestly praying. Sometimes he glanced quickly at Stephen or stared into the darkness as if he already sensed what was waiting for him. The friar picked up the wine jug and filled his cup to the brim. He closed his eyes and sipped.

'His Grace the Bishop,' he continued, 'told me something about this place. But, Philip, tell me everything you know.' He opened his eyes quickly before closing them again. 'And I mean everything!'

Philip did so, haltingly at first, then as he relaxed, the words came out in a rush. He told the friar everything he had experienced since his arrival in Scawsby. He ignored Edmund's and Stephen's gasps at those incidents he'd never told them about, particularly what had occurred at High Mount when he'd almost been dragged down the well. He finished with the description of his ride out across the marshes and that mysterious line of horsemen who had shadowed his journey home. When he finished, Brother Anselm rose slowly to his feet. He opened his pouch, took out a large string of rosary beads and put them round his neck.

'I would like a stoup of holy water,' he said. 'That and an asperges rod. Do you mind if I bless the house?'

'You are going to perform the exorcism now?' Edmund asked.

'I didn't say that,' Anselm replied. 'But I will reflect on what your brother has said. I would like your permission to walk the church, the cemetery and this house. What I have to do, I will do tonight! There's little point in waiting.'

Philip jumped as he heard a loud clattering in the gallery

above and the sound of someone coming down the stairs banging their feet. Then from the graveyard came the howl of the dog whilst the feathery wings of some bird dashed against the window glass.

'Ignore it,' the friar murmured. 'Just ignore whatever happens. Whoever is here knows what is about to occur.' He shrugged. 'Naturally they don't like it. But first we will pray.'

At his bidding they knelt on the kitchen floor and said a decade of the rosary. Brother Anselm then began his walk round the house, praying fervently and sprinkling the holy water to left and right. He had given instructions that all three should remain in the kitchen. Philip found this hard to do as the noise and clamour grew: rappings on the walls, the sound of charging feet along galleries and up and down stairs. Invisible hands rapped at the windows. Edmund was sure he saw the shape of a cat scurry across the kitchen floor, the howling of a dog now seemed to come from the chambers above. The air grew very cold: sometimes the stench was offensive as if a pot full of rottenness had been opened, its unsavoury stench seeping through the house. Brother Anselm, however, continued his prayers. He ignored such phenomena as a parent would the mischievous pranks of a child. He went upstairs praying and sprinkling the holy water. When he came down Philip rose to meet him but the friar just shook his head.

'But, Brother, you look ill,' Philip gasped, alarmed at how white and drawn the friar's face had become.

The friar seemed unable to walk forward as if some invisible wind was buffeting him, pressing him back. At one point he had to sit down, gasping for some meat and wine. Philip hurriedly served these. Brother Anselm then continued his task, ordering them to remain.

'Can't I come with you, Brother?' Philip pleaded.

The friar turned his sweat-drenched face. 'Stay here and pray,' he replied. 'But when I call, Philip, and only when I call, you come and join me wherever I am. Do not obey any other summons. I will say to you, "Come in the name of the Lord Jesus." Whatever else you hear, whatever else you see, close your eyes, close your ears but keep your soul open to God.'

The friar went out of the front door which he slammed behind him. As he did so Philip was sure he heard a voice growl obscenities. He and Edmund needed no second bidding. They knelt on the floor. Stephen, albeit reluctantly, joined them and they continued the decades of the rosary. In the cemetery beyond, a terrible clamour arose. The clash of arms, the beating of a drum, the screeching of some terrible bird, hideous yells and then silence. Philip stopped praying and opened his eyes.

'Perhaps it's finished?' he murmured.

'Philip! Philip, where are you? What are you doing there? You and Edmund, come now!'

Philip stared at his brother.

'That's Mother's voice!'

For a period of time, Philip and Edmund, their faces soaked in sweat, stomachs churning, had to hear different voices from the past, some demanding, others pleading for them to leave the house. In the end, when Philip found it difficult to control the tensions seething within him, the door opened and Brother Anselm returned. He seemed calmer, more at peace.

'Is it over?' Edmund asked anxiously.

'Oh no.' The friar shook his head. 'Not yet.'

'We were expecting you to call. We heard different voices!' Philip explained.

187

Anselm tapped the side of his head. 'Outside it is as silent as the grave. I knew you would, that's why I changed my mind and came in.'

'You mean there were no voices?'

'Just fears and anxieties that the darkness can exploit.' Anselm sat down at the table. 'It's not extraordinary. Haven't you, in your normal life, experienced memories, calls from the past? A certain smell, a certain type of weather and the memories come tumbling back. That's all that happened now. Just ignore them.'

'So, what have you done?' Edmund asked.

'I've walked the church, the graveyard as well as this house. That's the first part of the exorcism: to identify, to seek out and that's what I have done. There is undoubtedly an evil presence here but not just one, possibly a dozen, even more. They are lost, trapped souls. Their leader Romanel still holds them in thrall. He thrives on their fears and anxieties as well as his own evil. It's really strange, I can feel a malevolent presence in the church porch and in the nave but not when I pass the tomb. To whom does that belong?'

'Sir George Montalt, the Lord I mentioned!' Philip exclaimed.

Anselm looked surprised. 'Strange,' he murmured. 'The demons will not go beyond that.'

'Why?' Edmund asked.

'God knows. Perhaps it's the sanctuary and the presence of the Blessed Sacrament. The same evil presence can be found in the cemetery and in this house.'

'So, this place is haunted?' Stephen exclaimed.

'Oh yes, haunted by evil. But there's something quite extraordinary here, it's also haunted by other powers. These are not evil, they are good. They do not involve themselves but they watch. They stand on the fringe of the darkness and observe.' Brother Anselm spread his hands. 'Try and imagine,' he said. 'A room full of light except for the centre where there is a pool of darkness. The dark does not affect the light and the light does not affect the dark. But they co-exist together, waiting for something.' Anselm paused and gnawed on his knuckles. 'The evil thrives on the wickedness it can find here. You mention poor Father Anthony, his desire for the treasure. The powers of darkness used that and then destroyed him because he allowed them to. He opened his will to them. What you are seeing here, what I suspect has happened, is that the terrible events perpetrated by Romanel still wait to be resolved. The Watchers, those who died with their faces towards God, look for justice and reparation. Romanel, on the other hand, turned his face to the darkness. He still clings to that and holds the others he led into wickedness in his power.'

'So, you cannot exorcise him?' Philip asked.

'I am going to try. I'll just try once. Philip, you will accompany me. Edmund and Stephen stay here. Do not leave the house. But don't worry.' Anselm smiled at the fear in Edmund's eyes. 'The powers of darkness must also bend the knee to the name of Jesus. So, when I summon them, they cannot be elsewhere.'

'What shall I do?' Philip asked.

'Nothing,' the friar replied. 'You have a crucifix on you?'

'Yes,' Philip replied.

'Then come with me.'

They walked out of the house, across the cemetery and in through the main door of the church. Philip was pleased that the coffin woman was not keeping her vigil; perhaps she sensed what was happening. At the friar's insistence, he lit a candle and placed it on the baptismal font. Brother Anselm faced directly down the church.

'Prostrate yourself,' he murmured.

Philip looked at him, surprised.

'Lie face down!' the friar ordered. 'Close your eyes and, whatever happens, do not move!'

Philip obeyed.

'Do not lift your head!' the friar repeated. 'In nomine Patris et Filii et Spiritus Sancti!' Brother Anselm began the exorcism. This was introduced by a powerful prayer to the Trinity, Our Lady, St Joseph and then to St Michael and all the powerful angels who stood in God's presence. Once that was finished, Brother Anselm began the adjuration to the presence. 'I adjure in the name of the Lord Jesus . . .'

Philip, though he kept his face down, suddenly had a picture in his mind's eye of the church filling with cursed spirits, horrid in appearance: huge heads, long necks, scraggy faces; filthy and squalid with shaggy ears, blood-filled eyes and foul mouths. Their teeth were like wolf fangs, their open gullets filled with flames. They shrieked and were harsh of voice. They had crooked shanks, bent knees, spidery arms and shrivelled-up toes.

'Oh my God!' he murmured and made to get up, but Brother Anselm pressed him back gently.

'Children's games,' he murmured. 'Stay still, listen to whatever happens.'

The silence was now oppressive.

'By what name are you called?' the friar shouted into the darkness.

Philip suddenly went cold. He was not sure whether the voice was outside his head or within it. First there was a snigger, an evil, chuckling laugh.

'Piss off, friar!' The voice came like the hiss of a snake.

'By what name are you called?' Anselm repeated.

'Shite and dross. Filth and muck. Get a wash, friar!'

Again Philip tried to lift his head.

'No, no!' Anselm whispered. 'There's nothing here, Philip. You can see nothing. I heard the same voice as you.'

'Fornicating friar!' the voice mocked. 'Foulsome and horrid!'

'This always happens,' Anselm murmured. 'In the name of the Lord Jesus,' he intoned. 'Be quiet and answer my question. By what name are you called?'

'Our name is Legion, for we are many.'

'I adjure you once again, by what name are you called?'

'Romanel, former priest.'

'And I adjure you to tell me the truth. Why are you here?'

'Tied here.' The voice was now tired. 'Tied by sin.'

'By the evil you did?' Anselm asked. 'Answer me!'

'By the evil we did.'

'And what was it?'

'The priest knows.'

'You mean Father Philip?'

'The priest knows: he has been chosen for atonement.'

Other voices now intervened, clamouring, begging for mercy, asking for atonement, then silence. Philip waited, then raised his head. The friar was now kneeling next to him, hands clasped, eyes closed. He made a brisk sign of the cross and got to his feet.

'Is it over?' Philip asked.

'It is over but not finished,' the friar replied. 'You see,' he continued, 'in an exorcism all I can establish is what power inhabits a certain place as well as a very brief reason for it being there. More than that I cannot ask.'

Brother Anselm walked with Philip out of the church.

They stood on the steps and the friar stared up at the star-strewn sky.

'It will be quiet for a while,' he declared. 'But I cannot exorcise this presence. You must do that, Philip. Atonement must be made.'

'What do you mean?' the priest asked.

'It's like here on earth, Philip,' Anselm replied. 'If you attacked me, burnt my house, you would be punished, you would be fined and you'd be expected to make reparation. The same is true of the spiritual life. When great evil is done, it must be undone. The debt must be settled, reparation must be made. That is a matter for you.'

'But how?' Philip asked desperately.

Anselm smiled, linked his arm through Philip's and led him down the steps back across the cemetery to the Priest's house.

'I think you are doing well already. That's why Romanel has pitted himself against you whilst the others, the Watchers, wait and see if they can help.'

'So, what do you suggest?'

'I am going to have some more wine, Philip, then I am going to bed. At dawn I'll be gone. No, no fee, no payment, nothing. I'll go as I came and report what I've done to his Lordship.'

'And?' Philip asked.

The friar stared back at the church. 'You went out across the marshes today?'

Philip nodded.

'And you've been to High Mount, the manor house and, of course, here? Well, I think you should go to where it all started and where it all ended.'

Philip looked at him in surprise.

'London!' the friar exclaimed. 'The Templars came from

their church there. I understand the archives of the Order are still extant. Perhaps you might find some clue, some key to unlock this mystery.' He took a deep breath. 'And then go to St Bartholomew's: that's where Romanel died, didn't he? Raging mad? Perhaps the good brothers kept some record of him. And, if I were you, I would start immediately. In the end, I would also advise two further matters. First, your friend in the house, whatever he tells you, Stephen, that's his name, isn't it?'

Philip nodded.

'Stephen is like the others: he has a hunger for this ill-fated treasure.'

'And secondly?' Philip asked.

'Once you have the key, whatever it is, burn the church to the ground and the house as well. Clean it with fire and then build something else. Something which will help to atone for the dreadful deeds done here.'

Philip started to move on but the friar caught at his arm. Now he looked sad, even fearful.

'This will never leave you, Philip,' he added. 'Whatever you think, whatever you do, you are a priest. You have taken on this church. You have put your hands to the plough and, whatever the cost, you cannot let go. You will make reparation!'

Words between the pilgrims

The Poor Priest paused in his story. He stared round at the rest of his fellow pilgrims. The Cook was now smiling at him, nodding in recognition, whilst the Friar was almost beside himself with excitement.

'I know Brother Anselm!' he exclaimed. 'A truly holy man. Much travelled in the work of Holy Mother Church.'

'Well, I am glad one of your friars is!' the Miller bawled.

'Can such things really happen?' Dame Eglantine the Prioress spoke up.

'Oh yes.' The Pardoner ran his fingers through his dyed yellow hair which hung like flax on either side of his thin, mischievous face. 'I could tell you stories about exorcisms which would make your hair curl, my lady, and frighten the life out of your little lap dog.'

'But this is surely only a ghost story?' the Wife of Bath spoke up. She stared round the ruined church and shivered. 'Do you think it's midnight yet?'

'It soon will be.' The Summoner leered. 'And then, all sorts of goblins and creatures of the night will come crawling out from their secret places.' He edged a little closer. 'But I'll keep you warm and secure!'

The Wife of Bath shook a ham-like fist in his face.

'And I'll make your ears warm and secure!' she spat back.

'Hush, hush, now.' Sir Godfrey got to his feet. All the chatter and gossip died as he drew his sword. 'I don't wish to startle you.' He was glancing through the broken doorway. 'But I am certain I heard a sound outside.'

'We should make sure.' The Squire sprang to his feet, ever eager to follow his father.

'And I'll go too.' The Yeoman picked up his long bow and grinned at the Poor Priest. 'I am as good a shot as any verderer. Even in the dark, I can see like a cat!'

'You can go,' the Poor Priest replied. 'But, I assure you, you'll see nothing there.'

Sir Godfrey, however, was striding towards the ruined doorway, the Yeoman and Squire following quickly behind. The Poor Priest turned to his brother the Ploughman.

'My story seems to have caused some alarm.'

Without answering, the Ploughman got to his feet: he and the Priest went and stood in the doorway.

Sir Godfrey, his sword and dagger out, was moving forward slowly, his son and the Yeoman spread out on either side of him. The Knight felt his mouth go dry. He was sure he had heard someone moving here, softly, as if sheltering beneath some tree or behind a bush, watching the pilgrims as they grouped round the fire. The Knight paused. He was a man who kept his own counsel. He did not accept that the Poor Priest's story was mere fable. He knew the Montalts. Had he not been out there and supped with the family? They, too, had referred to a great mystery, about something which had happened a few years before Lord Richard's death. Moreover, when the Knight passed through Scawsby he had seen no church: Lord Henry had explained how a new one stood outside the village on a small hill called High Mount. Sir Godfrey shivered. He was not just worried about the Poor Priest's story. Had he not devoted most of his life to hunting the Strigoi? Those devils in human flesh who drank the blood of others? Did he not have suspicions about the Monk? With all his blustery good cheer, the Monk's soul was as dead as stone. They had never met before yet the Knight recognised the Monk nourished a burning resentment towards him. The Yeoman came over, slipping softly through the darkness: he was joined a few seconds later by the Squire.

'Sir Godfrey, there is no one here. Perhaps it was some animal? A fox?'

'Then let us return.'

Sir Godfrey turned back. The Poor Priest and his brother were standing just outside the ruin. As they returned to join the rest, Sir Godfrey was sure that the Ploughman whispered:

'Even here?'

To which the Poor Priest replied, 'Yes, Brother, they watch us even here!'

PART IV

Chapter 1

When Philip rose late the following morning, Roheisia informed him that the friar had left.

'Oh, he was very friendly,' she declared as she bustled round the kitchen. 'He said he would pray for you and wished you every happiness.'

Philip sat down at the table. He thought Anselm would do that, arriving with so little fuss and departing in the same manner. Stephen and Edmund also came down. They followed him out across the cemetery to the parish church where he celebrated a low Mass. A few parishioners joined them, just standing within the rood screen. Afterwards all three broke their fast in the kitchen.

'I am leaving today,' Philip declared, putting his horn spoon down. 'I have to travel to London, certain matters require investigation. Edmund, you will be left in charge. Matters should remain quiet here. If they do not, go and stay with Sir Richard Montalt. Stephen,' he glanced sadly at the master mason, 'I would like to see some progress on your drawings by the time I return. I must ask you to heed Brother Anselm's advice. Do nothing to disturb the harmony here.'

Stephen promised; Philip knew he was lying but accepted there was little he could do about it. He gave Edmund more detailed instructions, then went upstairs and packed his saddlebags. Within the hour he had left Scawsby. Philip deliberately avoided the paths and trackways which wound through the marshes but headed east until he reached the Pilgrim's Way which linked Canterbury to London. That night he stopped at an Augustinian priory. The kindly brothers gave him a bed and board in their guest house and he entered London through Bishopsgate late the following morning.

Philip found the city a harsh contrast to the silence of the open countryside. Huddled houses, narrow, winding lanes, open sewers, the bustle and roar of the market place. Different people thronged there: Hanse merchants, seamen from Levant, Italian bankers and, on every corner, crowds of beggars, men and women, pleading for alms. He found the stink and stench, the shifting sea of colour, rather unnerving. He stopped at a tavern in St Martin's Lane where his horse could be fed and rested, whilst he dined on a hearty meal of capon pie and a jug of strong London ale. It was late afternoon by the time he had left the city again, riding down the lanes to Fleet Street until he reached the rounded church of the Templars. He stabled his horse in a nearby tavern where he also hired a chamber for the night. He then dressed in clerical garb and went up into the church. Philip marvelled at the strange architecture and design of this rounded church, built, so it was said, on the model of Solomon's temple in Jerusalem.

For a while Philip just sat on a bench near the door, staring at the different wall paintings. He got up and studied the Templar tombs laid out on the floor of the church. He walked round the walls and noticed with interest that the church had a new devotion, fostered by the Franciscans, whereby Jesus' passion and death were portrayed in fourteen paintings. These began with Jesus' condemnation by Pilate and ended with the dead Christ being placed in the sepulchre.

As he walked round, Philip gasped and returned to one of the paintings. He knelt down and said a quick prayer of thanksgiving. He could not believe his luck and, getting up, he went round again and counted fourteen paintings in all. He then returned to number six. This was a painting which showed Jesus carrying his cross on the road to Calvary: he was stopped by the holy woman, Veronica, who bathed his bleeding face with a cloth.

'Can I help you?'

Philip whirled round. The young monk was dressed in the black and white habit of the Carmelite Order. He had a broad, open, friendly face, snub nose, smiling mouth, though his eyes were watchful.

'I'm Father Philip Trumpington,' he introduced himself.

'So you are, so you are.' The Carmelite came forward, scratching his black, wiry hair. He pointed to a small prie-dieu at the far end of the church. 'I have been kneeling there since you came in. I must admit, Father, at first I thought you were a madcap, walking round, bobbing up and down.'

'A madcap I might be,' Philip quipped back, 'but I am still a priest looking for help.'

The Carmelite grinned. He came forward, they clasped hands and exchanged the kiss of peace.

'Brother Nicholas,' the Carmelite introduced himself. 'Nicholas Overton for my sins, member of the Carmelite order, I also serve in this church. You seem interested in the Way of the Cross?' He led Philip back to the paintings.

'Yes, it means something to me,' Philip replied. 'Brother, it's too long a tale to tell. I've heard of this devotion but never seen such paintings before.'

'Oh, the Templars, when they owned the church, had these painted,' Nicholas replied. 'They took the idea from the Franciscans.' He pointed to the scene of Veronica bathing the face of Jesus. 'You were studying that one. You know it's a legend, don't you? Thirteen pictures,' the Carmelite continued, 'are based on scriptural evidence but nowhere in any of the gospels is there any mention of a woman called Veronica bathing the face of Jesus. It's just one of those stories which has been around since, well, since time immemorial.' The Carmelite paused and scratched his chin. 'Mind you, there is some evidence . . .' He glanced at Philip. 'Am I boring you, Father?'

'No, no, do continue.' Philip pointed to the painting. 'This is the sixth of fourteen, yes?'

'Why yes.'

'And the order has never changed?'

'Never. The devotion is now spreading across Western Europe.'

'And the legend of the veil?' Philip asked.

'Well, as I was going to say, there has always been a tradition that this woman, Veronica, wiped Jesus' face as he struggled towards Calvary. As a reward he left the imprint of his divine features upon the cloth.' The Carmelite stepped back and pointed up at the painting. 'Now the veil was supposed to have travelled around Europe but, eventually, it fell into the hands of the Byzantine Emperors who lodged it in one of their basilicas in Constantinople. In 1204 Constantinople was sacked by the Crusaders, these included a large contingent of Templars. They seized the veil and kept it for themselves.'

'Where?' Philip asked.

'Oh, at their headquarters in Paris but, more than that, I can't tell you.'

Philip breathed in deeply to control his excitement. He could hardly believe his good fortune. He now knew that, somehow or other, the word 'Veronica' and the numbers 6 and 14 referred to this painting and the legend of the veil.

'Brother Nicholas, what happened to the Templar documents?'

'Most of them were seized by the Crown,' the Carmelite replied. 'They were used in the pursuit of the Templar wealth. Eventually, most of them were returned. They are kept in the archives and library. Do you wish to have a look?'

Philip nodded.

'Anything in particular?'

'Oh, household accounts, expenses of the Temple, particularly for those months at the end of 1307 and the beginning of 1308.'

'That's when the Templar Order was suppressed,' Brother Nicholas replied. 'I know something of their history. How can this concern a priest from Scawsby?'

'There's a link between the history of my church and the Templar Order,' Philip replied.

'Ah well,' Brother Nicholas breathed. 'Come, I'll help you.'

He led Philip out by a postern door, through an overgrown garden and into the Templar buildings, much decayed, which lay at the back of the church. The library, however, was well preserved. The walls had been replastered. The floorboards were of polished wood. The air smelt sweetly of leather and beeswax, books and manuscripts were carefully arranged on shelves.

'God knows how long they will stay here!' Nicholas murmured. 'We Carmelites now serve the Temple but no one has really decided what belongs to whom. Until they do, the library is held in trust by us.'

'Not by you, Brother.'

An elderly Carmelite shuffled out from behind one of the wooden stacks which ran at right angles to the wall. He was tall, thin-faced, his cheeks as smooth as a baby's. Tufts of hair stood upright on his balding head, his light-blue eyes had ponderous bags beneath. He came forward, clutching his stick.

'Brother Benedict, may I introduce Father Philip, a priest from Scawsby. He wants to study the Templar accounts.' Brother Nicholas glanced at Philip. 'From 1307 to 1308.'

The old librarian became charm personified, only too eager to help. Philip was sat down at the table, candles were brought and then a large set of folios.

'They are organised according to regnal years,' Benedict claimed. 'So, the winter of 1307 to 1308 will be the first regnal year of Edward II.' He opened the leather-bound folios, leafing through the pages. 'There are other accounts as well,' he added. 'What are you looking for?'

Brother Nicholas also became involved. Philip couldn't resist their good-natured offers of help.

'I am looking for anything,' he said, 'about a Templar knight, William Chasny. He fled from the Temple about the end of January 1308. He may have been carrying his Order's treasures.'

'But that's impossible!' Benedict's head came up. He scratched his scrawny neck. 'That's impossible!'

In any other circumstances Philip would have laughed at such a defiant denial.

'Oh, don't keep us in suspense!' Brother Nicholas exclaimed. 'Why is it impossible, most learned one?'

'Because the Templars here in London had very little treasure: what was left was seized by the king.'

Philip sat, mouth half-open. 'What . . . ?' he stammered. 'But there are legends in Scawsby about a Templar treasure?'

'Is that what you are looking for?' Nicholas asked sharply.

'Oh, no, no. I swear on the cross.' Philip smiled weakly. 'I am the sort of man who would stumble across a treasure trove and it wouldn't change my life. No, a group of Templars led by Chasny were massacred by smugglers out on the marshes near Scawsby. A terrible sin was committed.'

'Then, in that case,' Father Benedict remarked, 'they were killed for nothing.'

He got up and walked into the darkness. He came back carrying a small, golden crucifix with an amethyst embedded in the centre.

'Brother Nicholas, Father Philip, this is part of the Templar treasure left here by the royal commissioners. Hold it!'

Philip did so, surprised at its weight.

'Now,' the Carmelite continued. 'Can you imagine sacks of chests full of such precious objects? The Templars would not get very far, especially trying to struggle across the wilds of Kent in the middle of winter.'

'So, what were they carrying?' Philip asked.

'I don't know but let's find out.'

If Philip had been surprised at discovering the Way of

the Cross and understanding what the figures 6 and 14 meant, he was not so fortunate in his search through the Templar archives. An hour passed but very little was found. Sir William Chasny appeared in the accounts but only as an officer of the Temple. Then Brother Benedict gave an exclamation.

'Here it is!' His smile faded. 'Though I am afraid it's nothing much.'

He passed across a folio, pointing to a list of horse and armour: 'Being prepared for Sir William Chasny and his party'. The writing was barely legible and the entry details minimal.

'You must remember,' Benedict explained. 'By the winter of 1308 the Templar Order was in disgrace. Its organisation was beginning to break down. Entries would be hurried and, sometimes, just omitted.'

Philip perused what the Carmelite had found. Everything pointed to supplies being gathered together for Sir William and a party of knights to leave the Temple in London for some unknown destination: foodstuffs, money for the journey but nothing exceptional. No mention of any treasure or, indeed, anything mysterious. Philip sat back and rubbed his face.

'I'll continue the search,' Father Benedict offered. 'I mean, if you are tired?'

'The day is drawing on,' Philip declared. 'And I have kept you long enough.'

'Nonsense!' the archivist declared.

'Do you have any books about the legend of the veil?' Philip asked. 'I mean, the one Veronica used to wipe the face of Christ?'

'Of course, of course.'

Benedict pushed back his stool and, leaving Philip and

Brother Nicholas to pore over the accounts, he hurried around the library, muttering to himself.

'Ah, I knew we had something.'

He came back, bearing another tome entitled *Sancta Anecdota.*

'Literally holy stories,' he translated. He thumbed through the pages and laid the book before Philip.

The writing was in Latin but Philip had no difficulty understanding it. The story told was no different than what he had learnt from Brother Nicholas. How the holy woman Veronica had helped Christ: she had been rewarded and the veil with the imprint of Christ's face had become a precious relic. Yet there was nothing new to help solve the mysteries confronting him. He handed the book back and was about to leave, when Brother Nicholas exclaimed.

'Look at this!' He pushed back the list of expenses Philip had so summarily dismissed, jabbing a finger at a nondescript heading entitled 'Equi', 'Horses'. This listed the destriers and sumpter ponies Sir William Chasny and his party would need. Each horse was described by colour. At the end was one enigmatic entry, 'Una equa: Pro Virgine'.

'I don't understand this,' Nicholas exclaimed. 'Literally, that means a palfrey or a pony for the Virgin.' He pushed back his stool. 'What would that mean? A palfrey or pony for a virgin? Was it a statue of Our Lady?'

'Virgin can also be translated as maid,' Benedict offered.

Philip went through the accounts again but could discover no explanation. He felt disappointed. The library was growing dark and he felt he had trespassed too much on these good brothers' kindness. He thanked them and made his way back into the church. He paused and peered through the poor light at the picture of Veronica wiping the face of Jesus. Philip then returned to the garret he had hired in a nearby tavern and spent the rest of the evening either pacing restlessly up and down or lying on his bed looking at the ceiling. He felt safe in London. Somehow, he realised, the evil of Scawsby could not reach him here. He sighed, realising it was growing late, undressed and went to bed.

Philip rose early the next morning refreshed and returned to the Templar church. Brother Nicholas kindly allowed him to celebrate Mass in one of the chantry chapels. The Carmelite was waiting for him in the sacristy.

'Come on, Brother Priest,' he joked. 'I know a man does not live by bread alone but at least break fast with us!'

Philip joined the Carmelites in their refectory, where Brother Benedict was waiting for him, flapping his hands in excitement.

'I've been through all the documents again,' he declared. 'And read everything I could about the sacred veil and Veronica.' He smiled apologetically. 'But I could find nothing.'

Philip took out his horn spoon and began to sip at the oatmeal. It was not as thick or as sweet as Roheisia made it but he found the company of the Carmelites soothing and friendly.

'So, why the excitement?' Brother Nicholas teased.

'It was that entry,' the Carmelite continued. 'About a palfrey being hired for a virgin. Well,' he continued in a rush, 'I went back to the life of St Veronica. Now I know it's all legends but, according to those, Veronica was a virgin when she wiped the face of Jesus. After the Resurrection she became a follower of Christ and dedicated herself to a life of chastity. In a word, she became a virgin dedicated to God.' He tapped the side of his head. 'And that awoke other memories. You know the legends of the Grail?'

Philip nodded.

'Well, according to those, the Grail can only be carried by a virgin.'

'And?'

'And the legend of the unicorn, how that fabulous beast can only be tamed by a virgin?'

'Of course,' Philip broke in. 'You are saying that when the Templars left London they were escorting and guarding a virgin? A young girl.' He paused. 'A young girl who was chosen to carry something sacred.'

'I believe so.' Father Benedict straightened up in his chair.

'But would the Templars,' Nicholas asked, 'simply seize a young girl and take her off across the wilds of Kent?'

'No, they wouldn't! No, they wouldn't!' the old Carmelite retorted. 'But you remember the house of St Ursula? It is a small convent,' he explained. 'Not very far away, in the fields near the Bishop of Salisbury's Inn. This was protected by the Templars. Indeed, the Order had given the nuns land and revenue. Early this morning I went across there. Now, the good nuns used to accept in their houses young girls, foundlings or orphans who later would be dedicated to God and, if they wished, enter the Order. According to the register, in January 1308, one of these young girls was handed into the care of Sir William Chasny.'

'The coffin woman!' Philip exclaimed. 'She's an old woman who lives in the cemetery of my church. She claims to be the bastard child of a wicked priest called Romanel. I think she is the child you mentioned, Brother Benedict, from the local convent: the Templars were guarding her but why is a mystery.' Philip got to his feet. 'I don't know how to thank you. One day, I promise you, when I find the truth I will let you know.'

An hour later, having taken further directions from the

brothers, Philip went down to the waterside and hired a wherryman to take him downriver to Westminster. A thick sea mist had rolled in, a chilling reminder of High Mount and Scawsby. The little, rat-faced wherryman, however, told him the only thing they had to worry about was colliding with another boat or barge on the Thames. Philip sat back. He wondered what Edmund would be doing and, once again, if he had been wise to leave Stephen. Philip tried to distract himself: when the mists parted he could see how the river was busy. Royal men-of-war, anchored in a line, were taking on supplies. The traffic between the shore and these was very busy with wherries, bum-boats and barges full of fruit and other supplies.

'It's the bastards!' the wherryman explained, referring to the French. 'There's a fleet been seen off Thanet.'

And the wherryman subsided into a litany of groans and moans about a kingdom being under a child and the ineffectiveness of the Regent to keep the French contained. At last they reached King's Landing at Westminster. Philip paid the wherryman. He went up the steps, making his way through the crowds of lawyers, plaintiffs and tipstaffs, all thronging to the courts. At last he found the Archives room and its custos, a pompous clerk dressed resplendently in a fur-trimmed robe. He peered arrogantly at Philip through an eye-glass and grudgingly conceded the priest's demands. Philip was shown to a table in a small carrel where one of the clerk's assistants brought him the required records, pointing out the relevant places. Philip read carefully. The letters and documents were written in official language but, nevertheless, these showed how, in the spring and summer of 1308, royal commissioners had moved into Kent. They had visited the towns and villages round Scawsby, making careful and diligent enquiries to establish if a Templar party under Sir William Chasny had come their way. There was no doubt that their suspicions had fastened on Scawsby. The commissioners complained bitterly about the attitude and lack of co-operation from both Lord George Montalt and the vicar of the parish church, Romanel. Philip paused. The letters were written in Latin and the clerk, possibly out of ignorance, had transcribed Montalt's name in the Latin, Monte Alto. He had seen that somewhere else.

'Where?' he murmured.

Then he recalled that fierce fight in Scawsby. Montalt's banner bearing the family insignia and motto. He returned to the text. The royal clerk who had headed the commission believed that the Templars had been attacked and massacred but he could find no clue to their whereabouts, who had insti- gated such an attack and, above all, the whereabouts of the 'Magnum Thesaurum' which the Templars were supposed to be carrying. The commissioners had returned time and again but, by the autumn of 1308, the entries became less frequent and more terse. Eventually, the royal searchers had given up the task as fruitless and returned to London.

Philip put his face in his hands. What was this 'Magnum Thesaurum', the 'great treasure', the Templars were carry- ing? And why take a young girl? A virgin?

'Are you finished?'

Philip looked up. The clerk was peering down at him like a schoolmaster would at a scholar taking too long over his horn book.

'Yes, yes, I have.'

He thanked the clerk and left the abbey grounds. The mist was lifting as Philip reached Holborn, the busy thoroughfare which led into the city. Peasants, their carts piled high with produce for the markets; tinkers and pedlars, trays slung round their necks, full of ribbons, pins, amulets, cheap necklaces and brooches. Scholars going down to the school at St Paul's, ragged-arsed but full of life. A group of hooded guildsmen escorting a coffin draped in funeral cloths and placed high on a cart; behind this a priest, dressed in black, chanted the office of the dead. A line of felons, their clothes in rags and chained together by the neck, were being led by a bailiff and two drunken soldiers down to the prisons at the Fleet and Newgate. Philip kept behind these until they passed the Bishop of Ely's inn. He then made a detour round the city ditch, covering his mouth and nose with his hand. This broad sewer, into which all the rubbish of the city was piled, poisoned the air with its foul vapours. Philip kept his head turned away. He did not wish to see the bloated corpses of animals which had been tossed there. A group of labourers, busy sprinkling the ditch with sulphur, called out raucously that he could join them.

At last Philip was free of it and reached the edge of Smithfield, a broad field dotted with copses of elm trees which stretched from the city limits north to the great Priory of St Bartholomew's. Philip had been there on busier days when the great market did a roaring trade but this morning it was quiet: only a small crowd had gathered round one of the elm trees where two felons were being hanged. These were bundled roughly from a cart and hustled up a ladder which was abruptly pulled away. Philip murmured a prayer for them and tossed a penny as a beggar, recognising that he was a priest, came scuttling out from where he had been hiding behind the wooden fence which ringed the execution stake.

Philip paused to let a squire, leading a line of destriers from some lord's stable north of the city, trot by. The trees thinned and Philip saw before him the long, sprawling building of the Augustinian Priory of St Bartholomew's with the red tiled roof of the hospital beyond. A porter at the gates listened carefully to his request. He escorted Philip round, through the herb gardens, to the chancery at the back of the hospital.

'Brother Norbert,' the lay brother explained, 'will be the one to help you. Though the patient you describe . . .' He let his words hang in the air as he knocked at the door.

'Come in!'

The room inside was surprisingly large, the walls painted a soothing green. No rushes covered the floor of dark-red tiles which gleamed, they'd been scrubbed so often.

'Be careful as you step.' The large Augustinian friar rose from his canopied chair behind the table and walked across to greet him.

He shook Philip's hand and dismissed the lay brother.

'I have seen many visitors fall flat on their arses!' he exclaimed. 'Which is not very good for the hospital, is it? Well, who are you?'

'Philip Trumpington, I am vicar of St Oswald's church in Scawsby, Kent.'

The Augustinian looked perplexed. 'Strange,' Brother Norbert declared. 'I have heard of that and I think I know your name.' He scratched his balding head, his rubicund face creased in perplexity. 'Well, bugger that! Anyway, Father Philip Trumpington of St Oswald's in Scawsby, why are you here?'

He led Philip across to a chair and pushed a bowl of rose water in front of him.

'Wash your hands and face.'

Philip, surprised, did so, then dried himself carefully with the napkin provided.

'Do you do this with all your visitors, Brother?'

'Look round the chamber, Father Philip. What do you see?'

The priest did so. He noticed how clean the walls and floor were. The furniture, too, looked as if it was washed regularly, even the brass on the coffers and chests gleamed with polish.

'Clean, isn't it?' Father Norbert declared proudly. 'And that water you've just washed in, is pure rain water; brought in through elm pipes it is. Do you know why, Father? Because I've studied my Galen.' He leaned across the table. 'I've even got a copy of Hippocrates, not to mention the writings of the Arabs. And do you know what they say?' Brother Norbert's broad Yorkshire accent became more apparent. 'Where there's dirt there's disease. You've come from Kent. When the great plague struck Canterbury, nearly everybody died except the monks of Christchurch. They only used to wash and drink pure spring water and they kept everything clean.' He sighed. 'God knows why we always think that dirt and holiness go together. Oh, I am sorry!' He shook himself from his reverie. 'I am always sermonising. Father, why are you here?'

'St Bartholomew's had a patient,' Philip explained. 'Many, many years ago, in the reign of the present king's grandfather, Edward II. His name was Romanel. He, too, was a vicar of Scawsby but he lost his wits, became madcap and was brought here.'

Brother Norbert pulled a face. 'But that's almost seventy years ago,' he replied. 'Oh yes, we have a small house here,' he continued. 'A building divided into cells where the witless, who are either a danger to others or themselves, are kept.'

'And are there records? Brother Norbert, I have travelled all the way from Kent, I would be most grateful for any help.'

'Ah well,' the Guardian exclaimed. 'If you can't help a

brother priest! Stay there. Let me see what I can discover.'

He left the chamber. A servitor came in with a tray bearing a trauncher with manchet loaves, some rather hard cheese and a jug of ale. Philip sat for nearly half an hour eating the food and drinking the ale, then Brother Norbert came back, bursting through the door like the wind.

'I've found something,' he said. 'It's not much. This,' he tapped the small, grease-covered ledger in his hand, 'is the record kept of all the patients, well, like the one you described, who were incarcerated here. Read the entry.'

He thrust the open ledger into Philip's hand, indicating with his stubby finger the entry for July 1312.

'"Today, the feast of St Bonaventure, died Romanel, former priest of the church of St Oswald's in Scawsby, Kent. He died raging against God and man. He believed devils were thronging about his bed, eager to pluck his soul to hell. The said Romanel, who covered his cell with paintings of human eyes, talked of *Those who were watching him* and, in his delirium, said all he could see were a dreadful pair of eyes. Whether he had lost his wits, or was of wicked nature, is not known. He raged constantly, refusing food, drink or any solace, be it corporal or spiritual. In his dying whispers, he said that High Mount held a treasure and that the High Mount was responsible. He died shortly before Vespers and was buried in the common grave near Charterhouse,"' Philip read out.

Philip stared at the entry: written in Latin, this scribe had also used the words 'Mons Alta' to describe High Mount.

'He wasn't talking about the High Mount,' Philip whispered. 'He was talking about Montalt.'

'Father Philip?'

The priest looked up.

'I thought I had heard of your Scawsby before. Our archivist just reminded me. We had a master mason here. What was his name? Ah yes, Stephen Merkle. He, too, was very interested in that entry!'

Chapter 2

In his chamber in the Priest's house at Scawsby, Stephen
Merkle sat slumped on a stool staring down at his hands.
The floor around him was littered with his drawings; pieces
of vellum and parchment, screwed up and tossed in a corner.
Merkle put his face in his hands. He couldn't lie, not to
himself. He'd come to Scawsby to build that church but,
always at the back of his mind, were the legends of the
Templar treasure. When he had heard about his friend's
appointment to this benefice, Stephen could hardly believe
his good fortune. And, when Philip had begun to talk about
building a new church, Stephen saw it as a sign from God.
He had done his studies carefully. He had heard about
Romanel and, when he had worked as a master mason at
St Bartholomew's, he'd taken time off to study the end of
that ill-fated priest more closely.

Stephen truly believed that he could find the treasure,
enrich himself and his friends, perhaps even pour some of the
money into a new church. It looked to be so easy. Stephen
had really believed the treasure was out at High Mount.
Now he conceded he'd been chasing will-o'-the-wisps, like
the tendrils of that damn fog which seeped in, curling
round the village, cloaking the church in a sea of grey.
Stephen took his hands away. But if it wasn't at High
Mount?

'It must be in the church!' he exclaimed. 'Or the cemetery.'

Stephen had listened very carefully to Philip's discussion with the exorcist. Oh, he accepted there was a curse but he felt he was in no danger. What intrigued Stephen were Philip's references to the old coffin woman. If she wasn't Romanel's daughter, who was she? Did she know something? Could she help?

Stephen went to the window and opened the shutters. Night was falling. He breathed a sigh of relief, the sky looked clear: for the first time ever he heard the chatter of birds in the cemetery. Perhaps the exorcist had lifted the curse? Perhaps it was safe? He would have liked to have talked to the old stone-cutter. Had Father Anthony also reached the conclusion that the treasure was buried in the church? He stared across the cemetery. From where he stood he could glimpse the faint glow of candlelight through one of the narrow sanctuary windows: the coffin woman was keeping her vigil.

Stephen closed the shutters and stood listening. The house was empty. Edmund had gone visiting, ever eager to stay away from the house whilst his brother was absent, as well as use the occasion to get to know his parishioners more closely. Stephen gnawed at his lip. He'd made promises to Edmund but what happened if he could prove them all wrong? He picked up his cloak, swung it about him, left his chamber and went downstairs and out across the graveyard.

A soft, balmy evening full of the promise of spring. Stephen breathed in deeply. Surely Edmund would have no objection to him asking the old woman a few questions? The side door was unlocked. He opened it and went inside. Even the church seemed a little brighter. The old woman was in the sanctuary, hands clasped, staring at the crucifix above the high altar. Stephen knelt beside her. She took no notice so he coughed and she turned, eyes watchful.

'What do you want, friend of the priest?'

'My name is Stephen.'

'I know your name and I know your heart,' she retorted. 'You search for the treasure of the Temple. You break your promise to your friend and trample where even angels would fear to tread.'

Stephen got to his feet. 'What do you mean?'

'Your friend the priest. He's a good man. He and his brother are people of God: their hearts are clean but you are different.' She tapped the side of her head. 'They have made me think. They have brought back memories. I was there, you know.' She continued in a rush as if wanting to confess, 'I was there that dreadful night. Out on the marshes when the Templars were attacked. Oh yes.' She brushed the hair away from her face. 'Good men, strong soldiers.'

'You were there?' Stephen took a step forward. 'You were there!'

The woman backed away. 'I shouldn't have said that!' she babbled.

'No, no, please!'

Stephen went to grip her by the shoulder but the old woman, now frightened, struggled: her body was so thin and frail, Stephen's hand slipped and her ragged cloak ripped. She staggered and fell back. Stephen went to catch her but her body hit a small plinth, the base of a statue long gone. Stephen watched in horror as the back of the old woman's head hit the jagged stone with a crack like that of an axe hitting wood. She opened her eyes, almost smiling up at him. She then gave a small cough and her head slumped sideways.

'Oh no! Oh my God, no!'

Stephen crouched beside her and felt vainly for the pulse in her neck. The skin was dry, even cold, as if her spirit, only too eager to be gone, had sprung from the corpse. He laid her down carefully, resting her head against the floor. When he took his hand away, he noticed the streaks of blood. Stephen got to his feet, wiping his fingers on his jerkin, and stared up at the cross.

'I did not mean to kill her,' he whispered.

The carved face of his Crucified Saviour stared impassively back. Stephen's mouth went dry. He had killed a woman in the sanctuary of a church, her blood was on his hands. He ran through the rood screen but stopped in horror. The eyes painted on the pillars down the church now seemed to be glowing with a life of their own whilst, in the transepts on either side, he heard the shuffling of mailed feet and the clink of harness. Stephen recalled the words of the exorcist, about how the sanctuary was safe, yet, try as he might, he couldn't go back. Something evil, something loathsome was crawling through the darkness towards him. Stephen drew his dagger.

'I didn't mean to!' he shouted. 'I didn't mean to kill her!'

'Spectamus te, semper spectamus te!' The words came in a whisper. 'We are watching you, we are always watching you!'

Stephen turned.

'Spectamus te, semper spectamus te!'

Now the words were chanted, deep-throated as if some invisible choir was watching him. Suddenly the corpse door slammed shut. Stephen whirled round. He could see the Montalts' tomb and the door into the sanctuary where the corpse woman lay. He should go back but a plume of black smoke was coming up out of the floor. The phantasm took shape. Romanel was standing there, head lowered, those malevolent eyes watching him.

'Spectamus te! Semper spectamus te!'

The words were now being roared at him. Stephen dropped his dagger and ran. If he could only reach the main door of the church, lift the bar and escape into the night. He fled, those awful sepulchral voices still chanting; behind him, a slithering, malevolent evil. Stephen lifted the bar and tugged at the door but it was locked. He turned. Romanel was gliding down the church towards him. The small door to the tower was open. Stephen rushed through, sweat pouring, heart pounding like a drum. He climbed the spiral staircase. Halfway up he paused, the chanting in the church had stopped but then he heard it: the tap, tap of booted feet. Someone was following him up the steps. Stephen ran on and reached the top; pushing back the trap door, he climbed onto the roof of the tower, sucking in the cold night air, staring wildly up at the stars. He pushed the trap door down and ran to the crenellated wall.

'Help me! Help me!' he screamed into the night.

The breeze caught his words and whirled them away like dry leaves in autumn. Stephen kept on shouting. Perhaps someone would hear. Perhaps Edmund would return. He heard the jingle of harness and looked down. A group of knights sat on their horses in the cemetery below. They were mailed and coifed. The great, white cloaks over their shoulders bore the six-sided Templar cross. Stephen sobbed in terror. Behind him the trap door fell back with a crash. Romanel climbed out and stood staring at Stephen. He then walked towards him, hands extended, as if desirous of exchanging the kiss of peace. Stephen moved sideways. He felt the gap in the wall. Romanel lunged. Stephen fell back. He missed his footing. Slowly his body went over and, hands clawing at the air, Stephen Merkle, master mason, fell like a stone from the tower of St Oswald's church.

Philip left London early the following morning, certain that he had the key to the mystery to his haunted church and the curse which lay on Scawsby. He rode hard, stopping just after noon at a tavern on the old Roman road where his horse was rested, watered and fed. Philip then rode on. The weather was good, the breezes brisk, the sky free of clouds so the trackways and roads were hard underfoot and the streams and brooks easy to ford. He stopped at a priory and, after he had celebrated Mass the following morning, rode on. He breathed a sigh of relief when High Mount came into view. So immersed was he in what he had learnt, Philip let his horse amble as he made his way along the trackway through the woods to Scawsby.

At first Philip thought he was by himself. After all, it was mid-morning, the men would be out in the fields, the women busy at the loom or tending children. Philip heard a creak and, looking up, reined in. The forest trackway narrowed just as it reached the centre, now a cart blocked the way. Philip raised his hand in the sign of peace.

'Good morrow, sir. I am Philip, priest of Scawsby.'

The carter made no friendly sign back. Philip felt a touch of cold at the back of his neck. He looked more closely. The horse was black and the man sitting in a seat had the reins wrapped round his hands. He was cloaked and muffled, a black, broad-brimmed hat pulled over his eyes. Philip moved his horse sideways. The cart stood still on the path. Philip glimpsed the coffin, covered with a purple burial pall, which lay across it. His horse, though tired, became restless and skittish.

'If you want to pass on,' Philip called, 'then I'll stand aside.' He urged his horse off the road onto the grassy verge. 'In the name of God!' he called. 'The way is free. Come forward!'

The cart still stood silently. Philip was now fighting hard to keep his horse from bolting.

'Then damn you!' Philip shouted.

He urged his horse forward along the grassy verge. He was almost up to it when the cart abruptly sprang into life, the man flicking the reins. The cart rumbled forward, faster than Philip thought: so quick he was frightened that the coffin jutting out would catch him a glancing blow. He pulled the horse aside, further away from the road. As the cart passed, his horse, ears flat, eyes rolling, reared up, his hooves scything the air. Philip shouted and turned and, even as he did, he glimpsed Romanel's face leering at him from under the broad-brimmed hat. Philip, however, now had to cope with his horse and, by the time he had it soothed, the cart had vanished. Philip dismounted and, hobbling his horse, just knelt, his chest sobbing with the exertion. He did not know whether he had seen a vision or was it some devilish trick playing upon his tired mind? Or a warning that he had come back and must still face the horrors? When he recovered his composure, Philip loosened his horse and rode on into the village. He'd hardly entered the high street when he knew something was wrong. The houses were closed and shuttered and, as he passed the tavern, the old stone-cutter shouted out, pointing up towards the church.

Philip found the cemetery thronged with people: women, children, men from the fields, all gathered round the two corpses which lay on sheets stretched out on the grass. In the far corner of the cemetery, Philip glimpsed the carpenter nailing together two makeshift coffins. At first he thought one of the corpses was his brother.

'Edmund!' he shouted, hurriedly dismounting.

One of the villagers grasped his hand.

'It's the coffin woman,' the man gruffly informed him. 'She was found dead in the sanctuary and your friend the mason, he fell from the tower.'

As Philip reached the corpses, Edmund and Lord Richard came out of the church. Philip stared down at the bodies. Both looked as if they were asleep, though the right side of Stephen's face was all bruised, whilst his head hung slightly askew. Philip crossed himself and knelt down between the two. Edmund came over and patted him on the shoulder.

'Last night,' his brother declared, 'I came home. I found the doors of the church open. The old woman was lying in the sanctuary, Stephen at the foot of the tower.'

Philip crossed himself and got to his feet.

'Do you know what happened?'

Lord Richard shook his head. 'As Lord of the Manor, Father, I am also coroner and justiciar. I had the bodies laid out here and declared their deaths by misadventure.' His voice dropped to a whisper. 'But we both know . . .'

'Yes, yes, we do,' Philip replied. He was stricken by both deaths, still fearful of what he had glimpsed in the woods but now ruthlessly determined to implement his plan. He had warned Stephen: what more could he have done? 'Lord Richard,' he declared, 'I'd be grateful if both bodies could be coffined and taken to your private chapel. Let them be buried quickly in the manor grounds and, when this business is over, I will sing a requiem. Edmund, clear the cemetery! It is not safe for people to be here!'

Philip knelt once more. He finished his prayers, then gently sketched the sign of the cross on each forehead, and although Edmund murmured that he had done the same, whispered the words of absolution. He gently stroked the old lady's worn hands.

'Be at peace,' he prayed. 'Go and join those who went before you. Tell them I have kept faith. I will continue to do so and bring peace to this benighted spot.' He turned and stared at the white face of his dead friend. 'Whatever sins you have committed,' he murmured, 'may the Lord Jesus forgive you and see them as weakness rather than malice.'

Philip stood up. He brushed the grass from his knees and, ignoring the curious looks of his parishioners, walked back into the Priest's house. Roheisia would have fussed around him, like a clucking hen, but Philip, trying to be as genial as possible, told her to put the food on the table and leave as soon as possible. Once she had, Philip brought out some wine and filled three cups. He then cut the meat pie Roheisia had baked and shared that, with a small dish of vegetables, on to three trauncher. Edmund and Lord Richard arrived. Philip ushered them into the kitchen. He closed the doors and windows, took some holy water from a small phial and blessed the kitchen. He said grace and invited his two companions to eat with him. They did so. No one spoke. Edmund kept glancing at his brother who just shook his head. Lord Richard looked tired, dejected, as if the two recent deaths had proved too much. He sat toying with his food, lips moving soundlessly. Finally, he drained his cup and slammed it down on the table.

'Will this business never end?'

'Very soon,' Philip replied. 'At least, I think it will. But what happened last night?'

Lord Richard rubbed his face. 'From the little I know, I think Stephen went into the sanctuary and tried to talk to the coffin woman. I don't think he meant violence but he tried to grab her. She fell away. We know this because shreds of cloth were found in Stephen's hand, his boot marks were in the sanctuary.' Lord Richard paused. 'Heaven knows what happened then!' he continued. 'Stephen apparently fled down the nave. Something frightened him. He drew his knife, we found that halfway down the church. He tried to open the front door but the lock was turned and the key wasn't there. So, terrified, Stephen fled up into the tower: whatever was pursuing him, followed.'

'He must have slipped,' Edmund spoke up. 'Lost his footing and fell between the crenellations.'

'Romanel pursued him!' Philip declared. 'The exorcist said that there was an evil presence in the nave. Stephen would not deliberately intend to harm the poor woman but he had her blood on his hands, that made him vulnerable.' Philip paused and stared into the flickering embers of the fire.

'And your journey to London?' Edmund asked quickly.

'I think I know what happened,' Philip replied. 'Only one last thing remains. Come, follow me.'

He led them out of the house, across the cemetery to the church. Before he unlocked the door, he asked Edmund to bring picks and shovels from an outhouse, whilst he enquired of Lord Richard if there was oil kept at the manor.

'A great quantity,' Montalt replied.

'I am going to ask you a great favour,' Philip declared. 'I want your permission that, when we have finished here, we burn this church to the ground.'

Montalt studied the priest's face, white and drawn, though his eyes were clear and firm.

'Is that the only way, Father?'

'Believe me, sir, it is the only way. I will remove the host from the pyx and consume it. Everything else, including the tomb of your ancestor Lord George, must be consigned to the flames.' Philip tugged at Lord Richard's sleeve. 'When you return to the manor, ask Piers to bring down the oil and other combustibles. Do you have any gunpowder?' he added.

'A little,' Lord Richard replied. 'I took a bombarde from the French. I have a small keg.'

'Bring that as well,' Philip declared. 'But, now, let's begin.'

They went into the church, Philip locking and bolting the doors behind them. He ignored the sense of threatening menace, the icy cold, the musty smell. He knew he was safe. His heart was clean of any wickedness, his will pure in motive.

'Lord Richard,' he began. 'As I rode back from London I reflected deeply about this church. Have you studied the eyes painted on the pillars? Please, go and see in which direction these eyes are staring.'

He and Edmund sat on the sanctuary steps whilst Lord Richard walked slowly round the church. Eventually the manor lord came and stood by his ancestor's tomb.

'They are watching this.'

'Yes, yes, they are. And the inscription on the tomb,' Philip observed, 'reads: "Under the high place lies the treasure of the son of David." Now, everyone, including Stephen, believed Alto Monte referred to High Mount. It doesn't. If you change the words around, it becomes Monte Alto, a pun on your name. I first noticed this when I saw the motto on your banner.'

'And the treasure of the son of David?'

'Ah, I, like many, believed that was a reference to Solomon, David's son. Solomon, of course, built the temple in Jerusalem. Those who searched for the treasure believed it was a cryptic reference to the treasure plundered from the

Templars by Romanel and Lord George.' Philip paused to collect his thoughts. 'I now think differently. The phrase "Son of David" can also refer to Christ. To put it bluntly, Lord Richard, whatever the treasure is, and I have firm suspicions on that, is buried in your ancestor's tomb. Before the church is fired, we must break in and retrieve it.'

'But that would be desecration!'

'No, sir, the real desecration took place many years ago. I want that tomb broken into. When we have finished, you must promise me that your son and future daughter-in-law will take the treasure to wherever I direct.'

Lord Richard hitched his sword belt round his waist.

'Father Anthony believed the same.' Philip walked over to the tomb. 'That's why he talked to the mason. He had some madcap idea that he could burrow into the tomb from the crypt below. I don't think that is now necessary. Do you, Lord Richard?'

The manor lord picked up one of the picks resting against the wall and, coming back, brought it down with a great crash smashing into the side of the tomb. The sound echoed round the church like the tolling of a funeral bell. Lord Richard grinned up at Philip.

'Well, sir, you have your answer. Are you going to stand and watch or are you going to help me?'

Philip and Edmund joined in. Instead of concentrating on the sides, they brought the picks and mallets down on to the top of the tomb. The stone became chipped and cracked but, eventually, a hole was created and, using the shovels and a metal bar Philip found beneath the belfry steps, they were able to prise the top of the tomb loose. They paused. Philip sent Edmund back to the house for a small cask of ale, some cups, bread and fruit. They then wiped the dust from their mouths and faces and ate the food.

Despite his age, Lord Richard betrayed little tiredness for all his exertion and he laughed at how Edmund and Philip's hands had become chapped and blistered. He took his cloak and, before they could object, cut portions off, telling them to bandage their hands. They returned to their labours. Philip was so engrossed in the task, he forgot about the church until he heard a sound, a clink, a metallic rustle as if a knight wearing chained mail was walking along the darkened transept. He paused, resting on the pick, wiping the sweat and dust from his face. He stared around. Somehow the church was not so frightening. The eyes on the pillars seemed to have faded, either that or covered by the clouds of dust now wafting down the church. He heard the sound again, the clink and rattle of chain mail.

'Brother?' Edmund asked anxiously.

'I know,' Philip replied. 'The Watchers have come.' He stared into the darkened transept. 'They will not interfere nor will they allow Romanel to intervene. They know we mean good. Do you hear that?' he shouted, his voice echoing. 'And we intend reparation.'

Lord Richard also paused, putting down the pick, one hand going to the dagger in his belt. Then it came, soft as a breeze, a low murmur, nothing more than a whisper.

'Spectamus te, semper spectamus te!'

'Aye!' Philip shouted back. 'And the good Lord watches us all!'

They worked on until the tomb was nothing more than a mass of rubble. In the centre, at the bottom, resting on a small dais was a long, metal casket: Lord George's coffin. It took some time to prise this open. Inside was another wooden casket. They managed to lift this out. At Philip's insistence, they carried it into the sanctuary where Edmund lit every available candle he could find. Lord Richard drew his dagger. He gently prised the lid loose, pushing back the rotting gauze which covered a skeleton, its bony jaw sagging, the legs pulled up.

'It's as if he moved,' Lord Richard whispered. 'It's as if something pushed his body together.'

Philip studied this carefully. Lord Richard was correct. Corpses were usually laid out, legs straight, feet together, hands over the chest. Yet, although there were no marks on the coffin, it looked as if some invisible force had plucked the corpse up, shaken it and thrown it back again. Around the coffin he could see the glint of jewels: rings from Lord George's fingers, the glint of a silver pectoral cross, its cord long rotted.

'What is this?' Philip plucked from the top of the coffin a small leather cushion. Usually for the burial of a manor lord like Lord George, the coffin pillow was fashioned out of samite stuffed with goose feathers but Lord George's was made of leather, its edges stitched closely together. Philip drew his dagger and cut away at the stitches. The pillow now became a small bag. He put his hand carefully inside and drew out the bundle wrapped in samite. He lay this on the floor and unrolled the samite. At first it looked as if the cloth inside was covered in dark, rusty stains. He could tell the fabric was ancient but, because of its thickness, was well preserved.

'Edmund!' he ordered. 'Pick up this cloth! Handle it carefully!'

His brother did so.

'Turn it round, that's right! Lord Richard, bring across the candles!'

When the manor lord did so, he studied the cloth, gasped and fell to his knees beside Philip. They stared in wonderment: the picture on the cloth was vivid and dramatic. A man's face, imprinted in blood, the cloth had even picked up the cuts and bruises to his cheeks, the blood-soaked hair which straggled the face, as well as the crown of thorns thrust deep into the brow. Philip crossed himself. Edmund lay it on the floor and crouched down to study it himself.

'It can't be!' Lord Richard murmured.

'It is.' Philip felt the cloth, which was thick, more like parchment than fabric. 'This is the veil Veronica used to wipe the face of Our Saviour. You are looking on a face which millions adore. This was the treasure of the Temple!'

'How has it been preserved for so long?' Edmund asked.

'The cloth is naturally thick,' Philip replied. 'Undoubtedly, those who've held it before have used special oils to fight off decay. It is miraculous. Hold it up again!'

Edmund did so, bathing it in a pool of candlelight. Philip stared: the imprint was dark red, slightly rusty but a perfect image, picking up even the contours of the cheek and chin. A solemn face: lacerated but majestic, suffering but serene. It was the eyes which held him: large, cavernous, the lids half-closed. They too, must have been soaked in blood, for their imprint was very clear, yet, the more Philip stared at these, the more eerie they became: as if the lids were opening and the eyes were staring out, searching his heart, probing his soul. He felt cold, his mouth went dry. These were the eyes Romanel and Lord George had seen when they had slaughtered the Templars and unpacked their so-called treasure hoard. And how these eyes must have scorched their minds! Judgemental, condemnatory, no wonder Romanel and Montalt had slipped into madness. Philip continued staring: those haunting eyes held him. They were not so forbidding but gentle: his body grew warm, the blood returned to his hands and feet. A sense of well-being, of

229

deep calmness pervaded him, as if he had finished a task well done. He had no difficulty in looking on that face, no fears, no anxieties.

'Put it back,' he murmured. 'Put it back in its cloth.'

Philip got up and, leaving his companions, climbed the sanctuary steps. He took down the silver pyx, opened the casket which contained the sacred host and consumed it. He then extinguished the sanctuary lights and looked round the church.

'Leave everything here!' Lord Richard grated. 'Leave my ancestor's skeleton and its sad remains. Leave the statue, the altar cloths, the sanctuary chair and the lectern.' He got to his feet, his voice was harsh, his face suffused with anger. 'Forgive me, Father. This is the house of God but my ancestor and Romanel turned it into a robbers' den.' He stared around. 'Let it all burn from crypt to tower!' He walked up the altar steps and placed his hand on the crucifix. 'I swear,' he shouted, his voice ringing through the church, 'that no trace of the blasphemy, of the horrible crimes committed by my ancestors should be allowed to remain. This church shall be destroyed. A house of prayer will be built here. Reparation will be done!'

Lord Richard walked down the sanctuary steps and followed Edmund, who now carried the veil in its leather covering, out of the corpse door.

Philip stayed a while. He walked round the church, looking carefully at everything. Lord Montalt was correct. On such occasions, Holy Mother Church decreed drastic action: purification by fire, nothing would remain. He walked to the front door, lifted the bar and placed it carefully on the ground. They would need to open that later when the oil arrived. He walked to the corpse door and didn't even flinch at the whisper: whether it echoed through the church or only through his mind he didn't care.

'We are still watching you! We shall always be watching you!'

Philip paused, his hand on the latch of the corpse door. He knew either that mysterious voice, or his conscience, was correct. He was responsible for resolving the secret mysteries of Scawsby. Now he knew of the terrible sins which lay behind these mysteries, he realised he would have to spend his priestly life atoning for them. He had also brought Stephen here, so, to a certain extent, his hands were not totally clean. He genuflected, crossed himself and left the church to rejoin the others in the Priest's house. Edmund had already placed the sacred relic on a special table in the small parlour. Out of respect, he had placed a lighted candle on either side of it. Philip told Lord Richard to sit. He went to the kitchen, put three cups on the tray, filled them to the brim with the best claret and brought them back. For a while they just sat sipping, reflecting on what had happened.

'Now it is finished,' Lord Richard spoke up, his voice still harsh.

'Not yet,' Philip replied. 'Oh, I know the church and house have to be burnt. I agree, the site should be occupied by some holy order but there's more to be done.' He sighed. 'But we will have to leave here.'

Lord Richard looked up in surprise.

'Philip, no!'

'My brother is correct,' Edmund spoke up. 'We cannot stay here. Scawsby needs a new priest, as well as a new church. Once we are finished, we should leave.'

'And the veil?'

Philip breathed in deeply. 'Let's go back to the beginning,' he said. 'Let us, at least in our own minds, put the pieces in place and accept what has happened. Then I can tell you what should be done with this great treasure of the Templars.'

Chapter 3

'The origins,' Philip began, 'of this great mystery lie in the winter of 1308. The Templar order in England was about to be crushed, its members imprisoned, its land and property seized. The English Templars held this sacred relic, probably on loan from their Mother House in Paris, when the Templar crisis broke. Now they did not wish it to fall into the hands of the English Crown or anyone else. They decided that a party of knights under Sir William Chasny would ride across Kent and take a ship to France where they would hand the relic over to the Chasny family.' He pointed to the veil. 'Now the Templars were fighting men, but also monks. They believed that the relic should be carried, in accordance with its history, by a virgin, a maid. However, Chasny was in a hurry so he took a young girl, a foundling being educated at the local convent. She would carry the veil, escorted and guarded by himself and his companions. Knowing the little I do of the Templar Order, Chasny and his companions also swore the most solemn oaths to carry out their task.'

'And that explains the interest of our young Frenchman?' Lord Richard asked.

'Oh yes. Perhaps the Templars got a message across to France saying the veil was on its way: the legends would spread and perhaps, though I have no evidence of this, the veil was first brought into the Templar order by the Chasny family. Anyway,' Philip continued, 'everything went well until Sir William and his party tried to cross the Vale of Kent. They intended to skirt Scawsby, but what they did not know was that Romanel, with the connivance of Lord George Montalt, led a most villainous gang of smugglers.'

'So, this wasn't the first and only attack?' Edmund asked.

'Oh no,' Philip replied. 'Romanel was a ruthless and wicked man. He had the blood of many innocent people on his hands. Now I know something of the customs of Kent.' He smiled at Lord Richard. 'And how its smugglers work. They always have men to watch the roads. Romanel was no different. His spies discovered there was a party of Templars fleeing from London, that wicked priest thought he was on the verge of seizing a fortune.'

'But a group of armed men?' Lord Richard asked. 'Seasoned warriors, desperate fighters?'

'I thought the same till I went out onto the marshes. True, the Templars were warriors used to charging across sands or attacking a castle. Romanel was cunning. He led them into the marshes and then his coven of outlaws simply struck from afar. The attack,' Philip continued, 'probably occurred at night. Eventually Romanel and his companions would close in. Those Templars who survived were wounded and easily finished off. They then turned to the treasure, only to find it was a piece of painted cloth.'

'And the young girl?' Edmund asked.

'I suspect she hid during the attack. Romanel and his coven would discover her holding the relic.'

'Why didn't they just kill her?' Lord Richard asked.

'God knows, sir, perhaps some spark of pity. Romanel might have done; indeed, he still wants that. However, your ancestor and men from the village with children of their own were present. They'd argue the toss and draw the line at slitting the throat of a child.'

'Aye,' Edmund agreed. 'And their blood would be cooling.'

'Yes it would,' Philip agreed. 'Their victims were not just a party of ordinary travellers but soldier monks. Moreover, there was no treasure or none that they could see. I suppose they'd make some profit. The Templars undoubtedly carried gold and silver for their passage abroad. Romanel later used this to start renovating the church, a pathetic attempt at reparation.'

'And the dead Templars?' Lord Richard asked.

'Well, Edmund was right,' Philip replied. 'Blood would cool. Romanel and his gang would reflect on what they had done. They must have known questions would be asked. After all, it was common knowledge that the Templar Order was condemned. The authorities in London might well send out commissioners to find out what had happened to Chasny and his group.'

'So, that's why they used High Mount?' Edmund intervened.

'Yes, Romanel and his gang had never killed so many, and so important, people. It's easy to dispose of the occasional journeyman or pedlar, even two or three merchants unlucky enough to fall into their power. But Templar knights? The marsh would have been dragged, the corpses pulled out and stripped, then taken to High Mount. The old graves there were plundered and emptied, the Templars' corpses laid beneath the burial slabs. In another part of the ruins the young girl's clothes and the saddlebags of the Templars were hidden. Their arms were a different matter.' Philip paused to drink from his cup. 'Remember, Romanel was an avaricious, violent man. Swords and daggers cost money. Perhaps he intended to use them on a latter occasion, which is why he marked the graves in the ledger, but he couldn't very well leave them strewn about the vicinity of the village. So he brought the arms back and buried them in coffins deep in his cemetery.'

'And the horses and harness?'

'The latter are probably hidden in a pit somewhere. The horses which survived were turned loose. The poor beasts did not know the area. Any horse found wandering without a saddle or bridle could easily be seized by some peasant or farmer and no questions asked.'

'Did Romanel know what he had seized?' Edmund asked.

'I doubt it,' Philip replied. 'Not until he got back to Scawsby. He'd feel disappointed, cheated, perhaps even frightened of what he had done. You can imagine him and Lord George gathering here: the relic being held up. Only then, perhaps, did it begin to dawn on them what they had done. You do not have to be a scripture scholar to look at that veil and recognise the face of Our Saviour. Now Romanel and Lord George were in a terrible trap. People would pay a king's ransom for such a relic but how could they explain how it came into their possession? More importantly, Romanel must have realised the blasphemy he had committed. It was too late to kill the little girl, she'd been noticed, so Romanel passed her off as some by-blow.'

'But why didn't she remember?' Edmund asked.

'She was of tender years. Can you imagine what that night of fear must have done to her mind? It would unhinge anyone but a young girl frightened, terrified, constantly watched by Romanel. Eventually she forgot because she wanted to forget and so began her life here, keeping up the pretence of being the local priest's illegitimate daughter.'

'And the Watchers? The eyes? The demons here in Scawsby?'

'The Mills of God, Lord Richard, grind exceedingly slow but they do grind exceedingly small. Romanel handed the veil to your ancestor, Lord George, so it could be hidden, whilst he began to kill members of his coven who might threaten him. The royal commissioners came and went. Romanel was relieved but the hand of God intervened.' He glanced at his brother. 'Remember, Edmund, what the exorcist told us: the thin line between our visible world and that of the spirits? The Templars returned to haunt Romanel, Lord George and the rest. At the same time the evil which had been done here also made its presence felt. The wives of those men, guilty of the Templars' murder, always died within weeks of being birthed. A chilling reminder from God of what they had done.'

'And the sins of the father are visited upon the son, yes,' Lord Richard quoted from the scriptures. 'Even unto the third generation.'

'Yet there was more to come,' Philip added. 'The Templars exacted their vengeance but so did the veil. Romanel and Lord George had caught the eyes of Christ the Saviour and those eyes began to haunt them.' Philip shrugged. 'The rest of the story you know. Romanel tried to exorcise his fear by painting those eyes in the church, by trying to forget. Lord George slipped into madness, realising what had been done, knowing that he could do nothing about it. All he could do was recall the sixth picture from the Way of the Cross, Veronica wiping the face of Jesus. That's why he constantly scribbled six and fourteen: the name "Veronica" and, above all, the word "REPARATION".'

'But why did my ancestor have the veil buried with him?'

'To save it from other people's hands. Or, perhaps, Lord George saw it as a warrant to escape hell fire; like wicked princes who want to be buried close to the altar. Romanel would agree. Lord George was buried with the relic. Romanel had the inscription written and, in the months following, he, too, slipped into his own private hell.'

'And the later hauntings?'

Philip spread his hands. 'Lord Richard, a terrible crime had been committed, innocent blood cried for vengeance. Evil had to be resolved, reparation to be made. Now, for the ordinary priests who came here, such things were beyond them. For those who tried to discover the treasure, by entertaining such impure motives, they were drawn into Romanel's evil and had to pay the price, as Father Anthony discovered.'

'But why us?' Edmund asked. 'Why were we different?'

Philip shook his head. 'I don't really know. Perhaps that's why God called us to be priests, why we came to serve at Scawsby? God does choose people, whether they like it or not. I am not saying we are any better, or any worse, than those who went before us, but there was a task to be done and we had to do it.'

'And now?' Lord Richard asked.

'We must go. The work of reparation has to continue. St Oswald's must be destroyed, a religious community given the site to occupy, and a new church built at High Mount.'

'And the relic?'

'Lord Richard, Lady Isolda, she is still a maid?'

The nobleman coloured. 'I think so,' he stammered. 'Of course!' he snapped.

'You, she and Henry must make a pilgrimage. You must take this relic back to France to its rightful owners. What happens to it in the future will be up to the good

Lord and the Chasny family. Promise me you will do that?'

Lord Richard held his hand up. 'As God is my witness!'

'Do not tell the Chasnys the full story, in fact the less they know the better. Let Isolda carry the relic. She must finish the task of the Templars.'

'And you?'

'I will leave Scawsby tomorrow morning,' Philip replied. 'Today I will pack my belongings, as will Edmund. I must, in lawful obedience, go and tell my bishop what has happened. I must continue the reparation. Christ came to serve the poor and so will I. I will ask for the poorest village in Kent where a priest has to plough before he can eat his bread. Edmund, if you . . . ?'

'No,' his brother intervened. 'Where you go, Brother, I will follow. I, too, have been party to this. I, like you, invited Stephen here.'

Lord Richard got to his feet. 'Are you sure, Philip?'

'Yes, sir, I am. In fact I will not even wait to sing the requiem Masses. They can be given to someone else. The sooner we are gone the better. But we still have some other business to complete.'

Lord Richard stayed for the rest of the day. He helped the two brothers pack their belongings. He offered them money, fresh robes, swifter horses, but Philip was adamant. They would leave as they came. Deep in his heart, Philip blamed himself for Stephen's death and, although he knew he would leave Scawsby, Scawsby would never leave him. He glanced out of the window, noticing how the buds on the trees were beginning to sprout. He called Edmund over.

'Every year,' he said, 'wherever we go, Edmund, whatever happens, when spring comes, when the April showers have fallen, we will go on pilgrimage. We will never leave

Kent but pay homage to St Thomas of Becket: go on our knees before his shrine in Canterbury Cathedral and pray that he will intercede for us with God, for our souls, for that of Stephen and for all those who have died here.'

They continued with their preparations. They had finished and were seated in the kitchen when Piers and another of Lord Richard's retainers arrived. The verderer asked no questions: he and his companion helped the two priests and their lord unroll the vats of oil from the cart and up a makeshift ramp into the church. Philip ordered the vats to be broken, the oil spilling out, bundles of faggots were also brought in and stacked along the oil-soaked transepts. Philip went down to the crypt and continued the preparations there, telling Edmund to bring anything dry that would burn and pile it high. After that, Edmund took care of their visitors whilst Philip paid a visit to the empty, cold cottage of the coffin woman.

He found the place desolate, the fire long dead. Some of the pots had been broken and Philip suspected that a curious villager, or one of their children, had already paid a visit here. He went through the dead woman's belongings: nothing remarkable, only the pieces of vellum on which she had scrawled her memoirs were now more plentiful. One thing was added: the name of Catherine.

'Was that your name?' he asked the darkness. 'When you were a little girl, warm and comfortable in that London nunnery, was that your real name? Not Priscilla, not the coffin woman but Catherine.'

Outside a bird screeched. Philip sat on a stool and watched the daylight fade in the doorway. He felt at peace, no longer frightened. He had learnt a great deal, in his short stay at Scawsby, about good and evil, about the human will and the need to repair what was broken, for man to answer for what he did. On the evening breeze he heard the faint jingle of harness and heard the murmured words:

'Spectamus te, semper spectabimus te!'

Philip caught the refrain. No longer, 'We are watching you, we are always watching you!' The ghosts of those dead Templars were picking up his future intentions: 'We are watching you, we shall always be watching you!'

Philip got to his feet and, searching round the cottage, found a small cup of oil. He spread this over the makeshift bed, struck a tinder and, as the flames began to lick greedily at the cloth, walked out into the darkness and joined the others in the Priest's house.

They waited late into the night, Philip and Edmund finishing off the details, so that nothing would be remiss when the new priest arrived. They went down to the kitchen where Lord Richard was sitting with Piers, the other retainers having been dismissed.

'It's best if we begin now,' Philip declared.

They went back into the cemetery, the air thick with the smell of wood smoke. Philip went to check on the charred remains of the coffin woman's cottage, then into the church. Lord Richard had brought the small keg of gunpowder and was laying a trail from the sanctuary out through the corpse door.

'Stay well away, Father!' he warned. 'When this is fired, the heat will be terrible.'

'Strike the tinder,' Philip replied.

Lord Richard did; Philip watched fascinated as the small, yellow-blue flame ran along the string covered by gunpowder. They saw it move into the sanctuary. Lord Richard pulled Philip out, slamming the corpse door shut. They went and stood with the others at the far side of the cemetery. From one of the narrow sanctuary windows, Philip saw a flash of light and then from other windows the glow of flames. The fire soon caught and, within minutes, a blaze was roaring throughout the church; all the windows turned a fiery red-orange whilst columns of smoke began to escape through the gaps in the roof. The tiles began to shatter. There was a rumble like that of distant thunder followed by a terrible crash as the roof caved in. The tower, too, was alight, standing like a burning finger pointing up into the night sky. Eventually the noise, the smoke and flames roused some of the villagers, who came running along the high road. Lord Richard went out and told them to go back to their homes.

'Thank God there's little breeze!' the manor lord murmured. 'No sparks will be carried. Father, you should go back. Piers will stand guard.'

'No, no,' Philip replied. 'I wish to see the end of this.' He smiled round at them. 'Please!' he begged. 'I will stay and, if there is any danger, I will come for you.'

Edmund protested but Philip insisted.

'The fire has caught hold,' he declared. 'There is nothing more you can do. The fire cannot spread either to the house or anywhere else.'

Lord Richard and the rest left. Edmund returned with a small jug of ale, some bread, dried meat, cheese and a rather bruised apple. He found Philip sitting beneath one of the old yew trees, eyes fixed on the burning church. Edmund put the food and drink down and left his brother alone.

Philip didn't mind the cold and the dark. He just sat and watched that church burn to its foundations. The walls began to crumble; the one facing him collapsed completely under the burning heat which seemed to race across the cemetery till Philip flinched and had to turn away. When he looked again the church was now a burning shell. Philip wondered if Heaven was giving it assistance; of the tomb, sanctuary, pulpit or lectern there wasn't a trace. He got up and walked towards the fire. It was now losing its intense heat though it still burnt fiercely in the middle of the nave. Philip gasped; as he stared into the fire, he saw shapes forming, as if people, cloaked, cowled and hooded were standing in the heart of the fire. At first he thought it was just one but others, like columns of smoke, also rose up. Philip counted at least fifteen. He stared in disbelief. The foremost figure advanced towards him: like something in a dream, not walking or moving its feet, but gliding like a shadow along a wall. Philip stepped back. The figure kept coming: as it did, it lost its fiery cloak, the hood falling back. Philip made out the ghoulish features of Romanel: eyes blazing with fury, mouth twisted in a sneer, hands outstretched, formed like claws as if he wished to pluck out Philip's heart. The priest stood his ground. He refused to be frightened. Am I dreaming? he wondered. Is this a phantasm of my imagination? He could smell burning cloth. Romanel was no longer moving smoothly. He was beginning to walk, stumble towards him. Philip made the sign of the cross. Romanel drew near. Philip could see his pointed teeth and red-rimmed eyes. Behind him he heard the jingle of harness, the clip-clop of hooves. Romanel looked up at a point behind Philip's head. He was moving back, his mouth open in a soundless scream, into the flames which seemed to roar more angrily, then the shape disappeared. Philip spun round: there was nothing, only the yew trees and long grass bending in the stiff breeze. He looked back at the church. The fire was dying as if the flames, their hunger sated, had lost their intensity, their desire to consume everything. Philip went back and resumed his seat beneath the yew tree.

He was fast asleep when Edmund shook him. He opened

his eyes with a start. It was daylight, birds were singing in the trees above him. The acrid smoke from the church made him cough and gag.

'Brother, did anything happen last night?'

'Yes,' Philip replied, getting to his feet and stretching himself. 'I saw Romanel, or I think I did: him and all those imprisoned here because of their attack upon the Templars. Romanel came towards me, a look of murder in his eyes, but then he went back into the flames. I do not think he will trouble this place any more.'

Ignoring his brother's warning, Philip walked into the charred remains of the church. He could smell the oil as well as the odour of burning wood and cloth. Lord Richard and Piers came out of the house; walking swiftly across the cemetery, they shouted at Philip to be careful.

'If the good Lord saved me from Romanel . . . !' the priest called back, 'he will save me from falling stones!'

Nevertheless, he glimpsed the anxiety in their faces so he came out to join them.

'What you must do,' he informed Lord Richard, 'is now level this place. Leave not a stone standing upon another. Pull down the gravestones. Have some good priest bless and exorcise the place with salt and holy water. The house, too, must be utterly destroyed!'

'Won't you stay, Father?' the manor lord declared. 'You have hardly slept?'

'No. Our panniers are packed, our horses are waiting. We'll stop somewhere on the road. I would like to be in Rochester by nightfall!'

They made their farewells. Philip washed his hands and face. He and Edmund collected their horses from the stables. He kissed Roheisia and gave Crispin a silver piece. He repeated his instructions to Lord Richard and then left, riding quickly through the village, before his parishioners could find out what had happened.

They entered the woods but, instead of skirting High Mount, Philip took the trackway leading up to it.

'Why?' Edmund asked.

Philip shrugged. 'I wished to make my farewells.'

They reached the top, dismounted and led their horses into the ruined sanctuary. Philip knelt before where the high altar had stood. He crossed himself, closed his eyes and said a short prayer. Edmund joined him. Afterwards they unpacked one of the saddlebags. Philip filled two cups from the wineskin they carried. He smiled at his brother.

'Let us toast ourselves, Edmund, as well as Stephen's memory. Look around, Edmund, we shall never return here again.'

They moved into a corner, resting their backs against the wall, reminiscing about what they both agreed was the climax of their priestly lives. Philip threw the dregs of the wine to the ground. He was about to get up when he heard the jingle of harness just out beyond the wall.

'Oh, my God!' he groaned. 'Oh, Lord, save us!'

Edmund rushed to join him. He, too, stood, mouth gaping; at the other end of High Mount, blocking the path down the hill, a group of horsemen had gathered. The bright sunlight reflected on their steel helmets and chain-mail coifs. From where they stood the white surcoats of the Templars, with the great six-pointed crosses, were clearly visible. Philip narrowed his eyes. The Templars were dressed as if ready to participate in some solemn cavalcade: their horses were beautifully groomed, saddles and harness of brown leather, their weapons were of silver whilst their cloaks were as white as virgin snow.

'Do they mean us any harm?' Edmund gasped.

The group came forward; try as he might, Philip could not make out details of their faces. Behind the leading Templar, the rest of the group formed an expanding 'V' like a phalanx ready to charge. A flash of colour caught his eye. Looking down the line of horsemen, he could glimpse a young girl seated on a brown-berry palfrey, she was wrapped in a cloak of sky-blue wool. Again he could make out no details. Abruptly the leading Templar drew his sword and held it up so the sun shimmered brilliantly from it. He lowered his sword before holding it up once more.

'They are saluting us,' Philip whispered. 'They mean us no harm.'

The leading Templar re-sheathed his sword. Philip heard the words again. He didn't know whether the Templar spoke and the breeze carried his words, or whether his soul just caught an echo. He closed his eyes and, when he opened them, the Templars were gone.

The Epilogue

The pilgrims roused themselves just after dawn. They built the fire up and the old ruined church was soon full of the savoury smell of cooking meats. The pilgrims were eager to leave. All exclaimed at what a beautiful day it promised to be. The sky was cloud-free, the sun was already strong with not a wisp of mist in sight. Each went his own way to do his or her toilette whilst the Cook, despite the ulcer on his shin, took a leather bucket down for water from a nearby spring. The horses were checked and saddled and the pilgrims, chattering cheerily amongst themselves, gathered round the fire to break their fast. They laughed off their fears of the previous night when the darkness seemed to close around them and the Poor Priest's tale had filled them with secret dread.

Once the story had finished, the pilgrims had sat quietly reflecting on what he had said. Once again Sir Godfrey had gone out, sword drawn, to discover why they had heard the sound of rustling, of footsteps in the disused cemetery round the church. His search had been fruitless. Nevertheless, all the pilgrims confessed they had felt a shiver up their spines, as if people were outside watching them.

'It was only a ghost story, wasn't it?' the Shipman asked.

'Now, now,' Mine Host intervened. 'We all know better than that.'

247

He winked at Sir Geoffrey Chaucer: he and the little, cheery-faced diplomat from London had often confided how it was strange that so many of the pilgrims knew each other and how these stories told at night were not just fables but, perhaps, based on truth.

'I can't say,' the Cook declared proudly, 'whether it's a story or not. I come from Scawsby. The Montalts do own land there . . .'

'And the old church?' someone asked.

'As I have said,' the Cook replied, 'the old church has gone. A community of friars now occupy the site. Prayerful, holy men,' he added, glancing sly-eyed at their own friar now filling his mouth with bread and meat.

'And at High Mount?' the Lawyer asked.

'A beautiful, greystone church with a spire reaching to Heaven,' the Cook replied. He waggled a dirty finger. 'And, before you ask, Lord Richard lies buried before the high altar. As for the curse.' He shrugged. 'Lord Henry and Lady Isolda are in the best of health and the proud parents of five vigorous children.' He paused, his face screwed up in puzzlement. 'So, I am not too sure, Sir Priest, if your story is true. However, I do remember how Lord Henry and his young wife went on pilgrimage to France. They were gone for months.'

'And the village?' the Ploughman asked.

The Cook looked at this grey-faced labourer and then the ascetic face of his brother the Poor Priest. Were these really the two young priests who had come so many years ago to Scawsby? The cook's memory had dimmed but sometimes he caught a glance, a look which jogged his memory, but he wasn't sure, and he didn't want to embarrass them. He smiled at the Ploughman.

'Scawsby is a pleasant place, happy and prosperous.

Father Melitus has been with us for many a year. A good shepherd who looks after his flock.'

'Do you know something?' The Wife of Bath got to her feet and put her broad-brimmed hat on her head. 'When I was on pilgrimage to Cologne, I did hear about a famous veil which held the image of Christ's own face. But,' she gave her gap-toothed smile, 'they are only stories.'

'Well, come on.' Sir Godfrey brushed the crumbs from his travel-stained doublet. 'It's time we were gone. We have to find the road again and, after such a chilling tale, perhaps the Miller can tell us a funny story?'

'Yes,' the Reeve snapped. 'About a friar, hot and lecherous as a sparrow!'

Another squabble would have broken out but Sir Godfrey clapped his hands and Mine Host intervened. The fire was doused, the church combed to ensure they had left nothing. The pilgrims, chattering noisily, went out to collect their horses, already arguing over who would tell the next tale. The Poor Priest and the Ploughman remained by the fire, staring down at the blackened ash. Sir Geoffrey Chaucer came across.

'You are, aren't you?' he said. 'The priests, Philip and Edmund? Please!' His merry eyes were now clear and solemn. 'I won't tell the rest.'

'We are what you think we are,' the Poor Priest replied. 'More importantly is what we have become. My brother and I now live by digging the soil. We fast, we pray. We serve Christ and our flock. We turn no man away.'

'Reparation?' Chaucer asked.

'Yes.' The Poor Priest smiled, picking up his threadbare cloak. 'A life of reparation for the sins of many.'

Chaucer nodded and, turning on his heel, went out to join the rest.

'They were here last night, weren't they?' the Ploughman murmured.

'Yes, indeed, I know they were.'

'You know!'

The Poor Priest took his brother over to the far wall. The Ploughman looked at the pair of eyes which had been drawn in charcoal on the fading plaster; beneath were scrawled the words: 'Spectamus te, semper spectabimus te! We are watching you, we shall always be watching you!'